Me
and the
Foreign Girl

James McCarthy

PNEUMA SPRINGS PUBLISHING UK

First Published in 2010 by:
Pneuma Springs Publishing

Me and the Foreign Girl
Copyright © 2010   James McCarthy
ISBN: 978-1-905809-98-1

Pneuma Springs Publishing
A Subsidiary of Pneuma Springs Ltd.
7 Groveherst Road, Dartford Kent, DA1 5JD.
E: admin@pneumasprings.co.uk
W: www.pneumasprings.co.uk

A catalogue record for this book is available from the British Library.

Me

and the

Foreign Girl

This book is dedicated to Carmel and Richard

1

An explosion rocked the trawler from stem to stern, and threw Pat O'Malley forward on to the spokes of the steering wheel. His chest took the brunt of it. He couldn't be sure but he thought he heard a scream before he landed on the floor with a thump. He couldn't breathe properly because of the pain in his chest. As this eased he looked around for Tarja; she was sitting on the wheelhouse floor behind him sobbing. Propelled off the bench she must have hit the floor hard.

'Are you all right?' he asked, while checking his ribs for fractures. They were sore to touch but none had broken.

'I'm OK. Did we hit something?' She was now sitting up and rubbing her right shoulder.

'We'll soon find out.' He got painfully to his feet and headed down the companionway to the engine room. Before the explosion he had felt a vibration coming from the stern of the trawler. He had thought that seaweed was caught in the propeller, and had expected the spiral blades to mash it up and throw out the mulch behind them.

His guess now was that he had let the engine overheat, and that it had blown up. Would he ever get it right? He should have stopped the engine ages ago when it first started overheating; but he didn't want to worry Tarja. If anything happened to her, his decision to take her onboard would haunt him for the rest of his life. Water was getting in somewhere; it was a foot deep on the cabin floor. His uncle the skipper and the deckhand Coleman, held securely in their bunks by the guard rail, had their eyes open, but they were out of it - a tribute to alcohol and sleeping tablets. Just as well. He knew what the skipper would call him: 'A bloody eejit!'

When he got to the engine room it was in shambles, full of smoke and steam with water gushing in through a hole in the hull. The propeller drive shaft had snapped and gone through the side of the trawler, and the engine was a write-off. It was an accident waiting to happen. The boards in the hull had been worn paper thin from rubbing against the shark-skins, as the trawler towed them along. That was in the trawler's previous incarnation. Hitting the pier wouldn't have helped either. It had been a bad decision to continue with the fishing trip.

'Oh, we're sinking,' said Tarja with her hands clasped together so tightly that her knuckles were white.

'We'll be ok.' He switched on the pumps. Who was he kidding?

They were in serious trouble, stranded in the Atlantic Ocean miles from anywhere, with a dead engine, and water gushing in through a hole in the hull. With Tarja's help, and lathered in sweat, he nailed planks over the hole. The water was as high as his knees, and despite their best efforts, there was still a lot pouring in. The noise of the incoming water combined with the slopping sound of the pumps was creating a crescendo of sound in the confined space of the engine room. There was nothing more he could do and with Tarja splashing behind him, they made their way back to the wheelhouse.

Half doped, the skipper and Coleman were there before them.

'We need to get ready in case we have to abandon ship,' said Pat. He took off his shoes and emptied the water out of them. His socks would have to do; he didn't have a dry pair to change into. It was no time to shilly-shally. Their situation was grim; and he would need inspiration if he was going to save the trawler from sinking. His beard tasted salty.

'Rubbish...rubbish...rubbish,' growled the skipper, trying to steer the trawler. 'The pumps will hold. This is no place for a yellowed livered good-for-nothing little shit.' The usual insult, thought Pat drying his beard with a towel. 'Gimp makes the best poteen in the country,' yelled the skipper as he gulped from a bottle sitting in front of him on the instrument panel.

Pat was angry. 'Look at the state you're in, you bloody dipso, you're a danger to yourself and everyone else onboard.'

The skipper was a stubborn hellion who made his own rules as he went along.

'I think we shouldn't fight with him,' said Tarja.

He felt that being busy probably helped her to cope, as he watched her start to label specimen jars of fish livers, in preparation for a detailed examination back in the laboratory. The dolphins had thrown these fish out of the ocean and on to the deck of the trawler. Given their present state, it was nearly an impossible task, but she struggled on with it.

'People have gone blind or mad, drinking that stuff,' said Pat, angrily throwing the towel into a drawer reserved for dirty washing.

'He's paralytic,' said Coleman, 'it's criminal to have anything to do with that stuff.'

'What did the cripple say,' roared the skipper, turning around in the swivel seat and letting the trawler steer itself.

'None of your business, you bloody eejit,' snarled Coleman, quickly hiding his withered left hand inside his coat. His usual poker - faced expression changed to rage, hurt by the skipper's insult.

'That man could insult for Ireland, he makes enemies as fast as other people make friends,' said Pat in a low voice, trying to appease Coleman.

Coleman didn't answer but went down the narrow companionway to the cabin. His mood was bad and he could be like that for hours or even days, awkward and uncooperative. Well, that was one constant on this trip.

'Right!' Take the wheel, little shit. I'm going for a kip,' yelled the skipper, letting go of the wheel and staggering across the wheelhouse.

Pat grabbed the steering wheel, steadied the trawler and checked the compass heading to see where they were going.

Pat knew what the skipper and Coleman were thinking; he would get on the radio and call up the other island boats for help. Normally fishing close together they would get alongside in a half hour or so and tow them back to port. It was a regular occurrence for a trawler to get into trouble and call for help. Knowing that other boats were close by gave them a great sense of security. This was different: because of the storm warning they were the only boat to leave port. They were on their own.

'Damn and blast it,' howled the skipper as he stepped from the companionway into the water on the cabin floor. It was leaking from the engine bay through the bulkhead into the cabin. Eventually, the cursing stopped and snoring replaced it. Pat knew that he shouldn't let them take sleeping tablets with alcohol; but for God's sake as grown men it was their choice to do so. Nevertheless he sometimes worried that they wouldn't wake up.

He could see Tarja at the rear of the wheelhouse, trembling with her mouth moving silently, while trying to pack specimen jars into a cardboard box.

'Are you OK?' He adjusted the steering to hold the trawler on course.

'I'm praying. It's a hymn I learnt at Sunday school.' He went over to her, and she came into his arms. She was so slight, and so vulnerable he wanted to look after her. He'd have to tell her a lie about their situation. There was no other way to protect her.

'We'll be okay,' he said, trying to sound positive. It wasn't his style anymore - he had too many misfortunes in his life already; and this looked like another one.

He needed to get away from her for a little while, to think about how to keep the trawler from sinking. He tied down the steering wheel and stepped on to the deck to look at the weather, as he had done hundreds of times before. This time the trawler was dead in the water and the storm was coming in fast. Trapped in a dome of mist and fog, visibility was down to a hundred yards; and torrential rain was turning the decks into a skidpan.

Tarja joined him on deck. He didn't want that - what he needed was space to think about how to keep the trawler from sinking. He couldn't tell her to get back inside and stop bothering him. That wasn't him - gutless as usual, he would opt to say nothing. That was how he was; and there was no sense in beating himself up about it.

'We need to be careful,' he said, rubbing the toe of his boot back and forth on the deck.

'Yes, it's slippery.' She was holding tightly to his arm.

'This will hold us.' He attached them to the rail with safety lines. Something caught her attention and she loosened her grip on his arm.

'What's that all about?' She pointed to the small nameplate L.O.V.E over the wheelhouse door. Women were something else! Even at the height of their life-threatening situation she was thinking of love.

'It's broken love at this stage. It was between the skipper and his wife. Before she returned to England, she renamed the trawler L.O.V.E and re-re-registered it. After she left, he changed the name back again. That's one sign he missed although our call sign is still L.O.V.E. Let's get back inside.' He turned and ushered her into the wheelhouse. Love wouldn't help much in keeping them afloat.

The cooker on the trawler used bottled gas and on cold nights, a gas heater warmed the wheelhouse. They stored the spare cylinders below decks in the engine room. He often worried about a freak gas explosion blowing them to kingdom come, but he had never imagined the tough old trawler, holed and sinking in mid Atlantic. This predicament was real. He would need to spare the battery power to keep the pumps going for as long as possible. The longer they lasted, the longer the boat would stay afloat.

'I'm going to light the lantern, it's time it earned its keep.'

'It's so high up.' Tarja was looking up at the paraffin oil lantern fastened to the wheelhouse roof, swinging back and forth with the motion of the trawler.

'I wonder if it works.' No one had tried to light the lamp during his time on the trawler; but there was no reason why it shouldn't work; it wasn't exactly high-tech. Pity he didn't have a ladder onboard to get up there. If they made it back to port, he would change the way they ran the trawler; he wouldn't take any more nonsense from the skipper or his sidekick, Coleman. Up to now, he had been passive with them and if the truth were told he had little interest in what was going on, punching in the days and nights in a daze and not caring what happened.

Looking around, he spotted an upturned fish box in the corner of the wheelhouse; he could use it to reach the lantern.

'I'll get it.'

She saw what he was looking at, went over, and pushed the fish box with her foot into the centre of the wheelhouse. His teeth were tingling from the screeching noise it made on the floor. He stood on the fish box and with a stretch, managed to reach the lantern. It was difficult to balance on the fish box with the surging of the trawler and Tarja wrapped her arms around his legs to steady him. He released the spring and removed the globe from the lantern. It was black with soot.

'Hand it down and I'll clean it.' She reached up, took the globe from him, blew on the glass, and started cleaning it with a cloth.

Without her steadying him, he lost his balance and tumbled on to the floor. He jumped to his feet.

'Sorry, I shouldn't have let go.'

'No, I'm ok. Give me back the globe.'

She handed it back to him and held him firmly when he got back on the fish box.

It was strange that above all the other smells in the wheelhouse, paraffin was the strongest. He lit the wick with a match, replaced the globe, and stepped down from the fish box.

'Will I turn off the electric light?'

'That'll save some power.'

Coleman, with a hangover, joined them from his bunk.

'Are any of the other trawlers here yet?'

'Not yet.' He would tell Coleman the score later when Tarja wasn't listening. They'd be in the proverbial Davy Jones's locker if they were waiting for the other island trawlers to rescue them.

The light from the lantern was a lot dimmer than the electric light; and rocking with the trawler it cast shadows around the wheelhouse.

'It takes me back, we had paraffin oil lamps when I was young,' said Coleman

It took Pat's eyes a while to see in the dim light and flickering shadows. It was unreal.

'Is there any more paraffin?' asked Coleman.

'No, except what's in the lamp.' Paraffin oil was not on their list of spares. He opened the wheelhouse door and pushed the fish box on to the deck and out of the way.

It was anybody's guess how long the batteries would hold and keep the pumps running to stop them from sinking. Was there anything more he could do, Pat wondered?

2

Pat was sitting with his eyes closed, mulling over their predicament. He'd go through the exercise of sending out a distress call but with no other island trawlers in the vicinity it was a waste of time. It was a long shot, to think that a passing Spanish factory ship might hear it. That would be some luck; the trawler had an old wireless with a short broadcasting range. He couldn't bluff any longer about the seriousness of their predicament, he picked up the handset and tuned into the emergency channel.

'The other trawlers are not coming?' said Coleman quietly.

'No,' whispered Pat.

'Just to be on the safe side,' he said to Tarja sitting at the back of the wheelhouse.

Here he was again, apologising for their predicament, as if he were the cause of it.

'Mayday, mayday, this is the fishing trawler the Annie L, call sign L.O.V.E. We are taking water and drifting without engine or steerage near the Porcupine shelf.'

He waited for a reply and after a few seconds sent the message again. The only sound was the crackle of static. He continued broadcasting the distress call.

'Let me help.' Tarja took the handset from him and repeated the emergency message. Her hands were shaking and her voice was shrill and nervous.

Loaded with ice and offal the trawler was sitting low in the water. When the storm hit they could capsize. But it was a bit soon to abandon ship and take refuge in the life-raft; they had not reached that stage yet. It was just possible that jettisoning the ice and the offal would lift the hole in the hull above water.

'Let's empty her out,' said Pat.

'What? The skipper will throw a fit. There is no need for that, the boat can take it,' said Coleman.

'Fit my backside, the boat is sinking, and if we don't do something about it, we're going to go down as well. Don't you worry about the skipper; he wouldn't have a trawler at all if I hadn't bailed him out money wise,' said Pat. Perhaps, he shouldn't have given away that information about his financial arrangements with the skipper. Macho man wouldn't like people on the Island to know that he had money problems; and Coleman would spread it around. Forget about it, this wasn't the time for niceties.

'I'm not throwing hard-earned money overboard. Without ice, we can't fish,' said pigheaded Coleman. It was near impossible to get Coleman to change his mind when he was in this mood.

'We need to do something,' said Tarja, keeping her voice low as she tied a scarf around her mouth and nose to protect her from the storm on the deck. Pat ignored her and turned to Coleman,

'Will you steer then?' The trawler was in bad shape and this guy was thinking about money. It was no wonder they thought on the island that Coleman was a bit strange; and then there was that business with the teenage girl. The islanders didn't talk about it much.

'There's no need to empty her out, and I'll have nothing to do with it,' said Coleman moving back from the steering wheel. He sat on the bench at the rear of the cabin. It was up to Pat and Tarja. She looked more suitable for a modelling assignment than emptying the forward hold of a smelly trawler, caught in an Atlantic storm. He should leave her behind in the wheelhouse, although he could do with another pair of hands out there. The thought of getting rid of all the tons of ice and rotting fish debris was daunting. He had cleaned out the hold after the last trip, and then the skipper took on the load of offal to dump at sea, a week's waste from the fish processing plant on the island. It was illegal of course to deposit such a cargo at sea, but it didn't worry the skipper. If the authorities caught them dumping this stuff, the penalties were high, probably even prison.

Without a working winch, they would have to manhandle the cargo overboard.

Oh, to hell with it thought Pat, this was the last time he'd go to sea with this bloody lot. He'd sell his share in the trawler - that's if there was a trawler - and the skipper could get some other dogsbody. He lashed the steering wheel in the straight-ahead position to the hooks in the floor. It should be all right until he got back from the forward deck.

'I'll turn on the searchlights.'

'They're a drain on the batteries,' said Coleman. It seemed that he was going to oppose every move.

'We need them,' said Pat.

It would be madness to try to work on the forward deck in the dark, and Coleman knew that better than anyone.

Out on the deck there was a change. The cradle rocking motion of the swell had gone, replaced by fifteen foot waves banging against the bows and sending sheets of spray high into the air. The full force of it hit them when they emerged from the wheelhouse. The plunging trawler, the wind, and the water underfoot made it impossible to stand upright without being blown over.

Bent double, they edged their way along the rail to the front of the wheelhouse and down the ladder to the forward deck. It was awash with spray coming over the bows and clogging the draining slots.

'Crawl!' Pat shouted.

'Ok.'

On all fours, like commandos, they inched their way towards the forward hatch. With his nose close to the wooden deck, the stink coming from the boards of rotting fish mixed with diesel oil was overpowering.

'Watch out for the cleats and nails. They'll take lumps out of you,' he shouted to Tarja.

Steel straps bolted to the deck held down the forward hatch covers. He lay flat on the deck, and started to unscrew the bolts before pushing back the hatch covers. The waves coming over the bows blinded him, and he worked mostly by feel. Tarja crawled up alongside him and copied what he was doing. When he looked across at her, sharp slivers of rust from the bolt heads had hacked her fingers into a bloody mess.

'This is stupid, stupid, we are getting nowhere with it,' she shouted above the noise of the storm. Frustrated and crying, she kept working.

'I should have given you gloves.' Instead of lying in the wheelhouse drawer, the gloves would have protected her hands from damage.

He could throttle those eeigts Coleman and the skipper. They should be up here helping him to keep the trawler from sinking, but instead they were down below drugged out of their minds with alcohol and sleeping tablets. He controlled his anger by clenching his teeth, but he couldn't stop his hands shaking.

In the glare of the searchlight, he could see the cold air from the ice floating up from the hold like steam from a boiler. The inside of the hold resembled an open plan office with walls of marine plywood forming cubicles. In heavy seas, this design prevented the cargo from shifting and capsizing the trawler. He opened the last cover. It was a good time to ask her to go back to the wheelhouse before the heavy work started, throwing blocks of ice and offal overboard. To be fair, she had tried her best to do a good job.

'I'll finish here. Maybe you should go inside?'

'I'll stay, you need help.' She brushed aside her broken fingernails. 'Sorry I made such a fuss, I was being silly.'

'No harm done.'

She was of little further use to him out here. He could see her looking over the edge into the hold. The last thing he wanted was to see her go flying in there head first.

'It's like a box for Dinosaur eggs,' she said, looking at him and trying to smile.

He was being too hard on her. What the hell, he decided to respond in kind.

'The lair of a Tyrannosaurus Rex or the skipper.' He couldn't manage a smile. They were not insured to carry passengers. It would probably cost a small fortune to compensate her for what she was going through.

Pat lowered himself into the hold. He heaved the first box of offal on to the deck. The smell was terrible.

Tarja tried to move it.

'I can't shift it, it's too heavy,' and then she vomited.

He was about to climb back on deck to help her when Coleman came crawling towards them. He had relented. He didn't speak but went to

Tarja's aid. It was a slow assembly line - Pat yanking the boxes out of the hold and Tarja and Coleman pushing them across the waterlogged deck into the sea. Some boxes floated away on the crest of a wave and others disappeared into the deep. They were so far from land but by some mysterious force of nature, seagulls gathered to feast on the offal. He could hear their raucous screeching above the noise of the storm. Hovering was difficult for the gulls, the wind blew some of them away and others flew into the hold. Pat shooed them away. He didn't need bits of half eaten offal rotting below deck.

Pat looked up and saw a towering thirty-foot wave about to break over the trawler. It hit them with a bang like a bomb going off, and the force of it threw him across the hold. He picked himself up and, apart from a few lumps and bumps, he was OK. Good Lord, were Tarja and Coleman swept into the sea. He climbed out of the hold; and thankfully they were still there on deck, clinging to the mast support.

'That was a big bugger,' said Coleman to no one in particular.

The trawler was rearing like a wild stallion all the while they were dumping cargo overboard. They had emptied several cubicles before Tarja collapsed. She was a sorry sight lying on the deck with gallons of water pouring down on her, and her hair matted around her face like wet seaweed clinging to a rock.

'Leave me for a few minutes, and I'll be all right,' she said.

'Let's go inside. We've done enough here for now.'

'Sorry, I couldn't keep going,' she said when they got back to the wheelhouse.

'We need a break or we'll all collapse,' said Pat.

Getting rid of some of the ice and offal made the trawler lighter, and it was sitting higher it the water. They needed to rest for awhile and later, would dump the rest of the cargo overboard. They wouldn't need Tarja on the forward deck again; he and Coleman could do the rest of the work. Given that it would all be in vain if the pumps packed in.

They crawled back to the wheelhouse. Tarja was grey and gaunt from retching all over the deck; and Pat felt sorry for her. He hated vomit, although it would wash away quickly with all that seawater lashing down on the deck. He felt ashamed for thinking about cleaning up vomit while she was so sick.

'It's supposed to settle the stomach.' He handed her a bottle of diet Coke with the cap removed. She sipped it without saying a word. She was no longer the feisty type; the young woman that had come aboard at the start of the trip with an answer for everything.

'Haute Cuisine is not an option on this cruise liner, it's more like a transport café,' he said, trying to lift the feelings of doom and gloom that threatened to overcome them. Without trying, Coleman could be the most depressing person in the world, and now he was trying. For a quick energy boost, Pat decided on chocolate bars. Tarja could only nibble at the chocolate.

'It's madness throwing all that money overboard,' said Coleman, holding the bar of chocolate in his one good hand and tearing the wrapping off with his teeth. "Like a shark with false teeth" was how the skipper described Coleman chewing his food. He'd say anything to annoy Coleman; and he knew how to hurt him.

'It's a small price to pay for staying afloat,' said Pat. He had sympathy for Coleman, although he didn't show it. A man locked into himself, the butt of all the one-armed jokes and the knowing looks. Then there was this business about the fourteen-year-old girl who alleged that he kissed and fondled her when he gave her a lift home in his car. If true, these were serious allegations. He denied any wrongdoing and claimed he only gave her a lift. It wasn't unusual, on the island, to give anyone walking along the road a lift, be they eight or eighty, and the islanders thought nothing of it. Her family didn't pursue the matter and never accused Coleman of wrongdoing.

Pat felt that the girl had made up the story, looking for attention, but in the process she had almost destroyed Coleman. Already vulnerable, he was an easy target for the rumour-mongers; and wild stories about him abounded. He took solace in alcohol and soon started to drink heavily. He became morose and spent time on his own. Through it all, his confidant was the skipper. Pat felt he had a raw deal, while admitting that to work with him would try the patience of a saint.

When drunk one night, he had told Pat why he needed money. He planned to have a prosthetic arm fitted in the USA, if he was a suitable case for the procedure. In order to be assessed, he would need to travel to the Mayo Clinic, in Rochester. The operation would not be pain-free; but to him it was worth any sacrifice. Even for one day, to have two hands like everyone else. He'd tell Tarja about Coleman when he got the chance; it would give her a better understanding of the man.

'The wailing of wind in the stays is terrifying,' said Tarja.

'It might get worse. It's blowing 8 and gusting 9,' said Pat.

It helped her a bit knowing the wind speed. Maybe it was having something tangible to deal with rather than the noise and the ructions of the storm, as when a doctor giving a name to some vague symptoms.

'I'd better turn off the searchlights and save the batteries.'

With the searchlights switched off, the lantern cast a dull glow around the wheelhouse. The rest of the trawler was in darkness, the masthead light had gone out. This had been a visible warning to other crafts of their presence. Without it they were in danger of anything in the vicinity hitting them - another trawler, a factory ship or, God forbid, a nuclear submarine going who knows where.

Over the years, he had read about submarines sinking trawlers. The last big scare was in the Irish Sea, where a submarine pulled a steel-hulled trawler backwards, for over an hour. The submarine had caught in the trawlers keel, and the sub's crew didn't know anything about it. It was a miraculous that they had remained afloat. The speed and power of these nuclear subs is something else. Anyway, he had enough to worry him without thinking about submarines. They had an immediate problem: in the deep wave troughs created by the storm, the masthead light was the only visible part of the trawler and without it, the risk of a collision increased.

There were no two ways about it, even in this storm, the masthead light needed repairing. It was unlikely that two bulbs would blow at the same time. It was probably a broken wire at the masthead; and he would have to climb up there and repair it.

He didn't tell many people that he was an epileptic. Right enough, he hadn't had a seizure for years. He liked to think that he was in remission, if there was such a lessening with epilepsy. He carried no medicine, and if anything brought it on, hanging on to the top of a thirty-five foot mast in a storm was a good bet. It probably wasn't the right time to tell her. He would bluff it out and with luck, he'd be OK.

'I haven't a great head for heights, I get vertigo even standing on a chair,' he said.

'Do you have to go up there?'

'There's no choice, I have to fix it.'

'I'll go up there instead of you.'

Now there was a girl with guts.

'No, No, it's ok, I'll do it myself.'

'Think of something else and don't look down,' she said.

That would help a lot if he was having a seizure at the masthead but that wasn't the way to look at it. She was so caring and helpful; he respected her for that. This was going to be a difficult assignment. His motto, 'Do whatever it takes,' he was now going to test. Coleman said nothing.

3

'I'll need some tools.' Pat took a flash lamp with him to the engine room, where he had the tools stored.

'I'll come with you.' She was holding on to his sleeve. He hated anyone hanging on to him. Let her be - probably holding on to him was helping her to cope with it all.

Down below, passing the cabin door, He looked in on the skipper. He was lying on his back in the bunk with his mouth open, mumbling away in his sleep.

'Probably hammering someone in his dreams,' said Pat moving on down the passageway to the engine room.

'He has demons to fight,' said Tarja splashing about behind him.

'And real people as well, he's not without enemies.'

In the engine room, water was pouring in, but the pumps were more or less managing to force it back out. Tarja looked scared. Floating around their feet were filters, hoses, bulbs, injectors and plastic containers, which were normally stacked on the lower shelves. The inside of the hull, stained by sump oil looked charred.

'There's terrible damage; it's some mess.'

'I'll help to clean it.' She must be intending to remain on the island for a while if she was going to help him clean up this mess when they got back. That wouldn't happen in a day. Although, she probably wouldn't stay long after he told her that he wasn't ready for a relationship with her. His head was full of it. Stop this nonsense and get on with the job. He picked up a screwdriver, pliers, leather belt and a box of light bulbs. The belt would hold him to the masthead if he got that far.

They were leaving the engine room when Tarja spotted it,

'Is that a motor-cycle helmet?'

He hadn't noticed it before. It wasn't a usual piece of equipment on a trawler and how odd it was to see it stacked away on the corner shelf.

'The skipper owned a motorbike at one stage. Having him ride around on a motorbike doesn't bear thinking about. Even dangerous men think he's dangerous.'

He hesitated for a moment; the motorbike helmet gave him an idea.

'I think I'll take it with me for going up the mast.'

'For safety.'

'The visor will keep the wind and rain out of my eyes.'

Safe! She didn't know the half of it, but what else could he do? He knew the mantra for epileptics: don't do heights, but needs must. The only other one onboard who could climb to the top of the mast was the skipper, and that was a maybe, if he were sober. Pat had known that the drunken skipper would land him in deep shit one day and he hadn't been wrong; that day had arrived.

Ah well, think ahead. When the storm blew itself out, if they were still afloat – and they might not be – he would get a tow back to port from one of the other trawlers. He would rebuild the engine first and then repair the hull. The trawler would be as good as new, and of course, Tarja would have a great adventure story to tell her friends back in Finland.

When they got back in the wheelhouse, Coleman was working hard with the steering, trying to keep the trawler running straight before the wind. Pat knew the risks. If they came around broadside to the wind, the trawler could capsize and might not right itself. Now there was a thought he wouldn't share with Tarja; how they might all get trapped upside down in the trawler, somewhere in mid-Atlantic, and far from help. It wasn't the way to go.

With Tarja close behind him, they crawled on all fours to the base of the thirty-five foot mast. Not used to wearing a motorbike helmet it felt claustrophobic, as if he were a diver at depth. To wear it wasn't the best decision he'd ever made. What would she think if he suddenly pulled off the helmet? That he was losing his grip, which might drive her into another wild panic.

'I feel so afraid for you, perhaps we shouldn't do this?'

'I'll be ok, a walk in the park.' That was some lie, and where did the Americanism come from? It was getting more bizarre with the words of an old song buzzing around in his head, "Don't show the white feather wherever you go." Now there was a thought; if he had enough white feathers, he could make a pair of wings and fly to the top of the mast. That was another idea he wouldn't tell her about. It was irritating the rubbish that went through his head, non-stop from morning to night. A switch to turn it off would be great.

He started climbing, and the ladder was narrow. The steps weren't wide enough for his feet to fit side by side, he had to place one foot awkwardly above the other. Half way up the ladder he felt sick and dizzy, he wanted to vomit. That would make some mess inside the visor, and it would go all over his face. He felt faint, with sweat running down his back. He had never felt such fear. The rain hitting the helmet was like the noise of hailstones on a tin roof. He needed to get a grip. Talking to himself was a bad sign: shift your left leg, hold on with both hands, don't look down, you're nearly there.

The mast was shifting and swaying, going away from him, then coming back, dipping backwards and forward, all in one movement. On the crest of a wave, he was looking down at the sea and in a trough; the sea was like a mountain above him.

He wasn't doing well. He tied the leather belt around the mast, closed his eyes, and waited for his head to stop spinning. It seemed like ages until he could start climbing again.

At the masthead, he unscrewed the cover from the lights and exposed the broken wires. He twisted the wires together, and his fingers tingled from the mild electrical shock. With low-level battery power, it was safe enough to touch the wires with his bare hand. A better job would have to wait until they got back to port. The lights came on at the top of the mast and dazzled him. Thank heavens they were working, and he started to climb back down the ladder.

He got a warning it was coming, the unreal feeling and aura of light. He tried to hurry; and he wished he had told Tarja about his epilepsy. That was his final thought before oblivion came.

4

When he came round, Tarja was on her knees on the deck beside him. She had taken off his helmet and was cradling his head in her arms. He'd have drowned in the water on the deck, had she not been there. It was all a bit hazy, but it was coming back to him. He remembered the seizure coming on when he was climbing down the mast, and he must have fallen to the deck. He was lucky to be alive. He didn't know yet if he had any fractures or other injuries.

He must have scared her, shaking and twitching, with froth coming from his mouth and his eyes turned up in his head. He had let himself down big time. He tried to talk but she had put the rubber-handled pliers between his teeth to prevent him biting his tongue. She must have managed to put it there before his teeth locked. Hopefully, he didn't break any teeth. She was talking to him, but she seemed so far away that he couldn't hear it. He was sleepy and drifting.

'I wouldn't have let you go up there if I had known about the epilepsy.' She was shimmering like a mirage before his eyes and then there was nothing.

He didn't know how long he had been comatose, but now he was back in the real world and lying on the deck of the crippled Annie L., caught in an Atlantic storm. The swollen waves breaking over them felt like sitting under a waterfall. The noise of the water rushing out through the draining holes was real.

She took the pliers out of his mouth and kissed his damp forehead.

'You were so brave to do it,' she said.

'I had to do it,' he mumbled.

Brave my ass; it was self-preservation. He tried to sit up, but didn't get far before the pain in his shoulder kicked in, he almost blacked out again.

'It's my shoulder!'

'I think it's dislocated,' she said.

The full effects of the seizure wouldn't wear off for awhile, but now he was in pain. His shoulder seemed broken as well as dislocated, just when he needed all his faculties to get the boat home. He was feeling terrible. The only good luck yet on this trip was the fact he had stocked the first aid box with morphine tablets for emergencies. Normally, all it contained were seasickness tablets, sleeping pills, sticking plasters and Germolene.

With Coleman close behind, she returned from the wheelhouse with the first aid kit.

'Can you move your shoulder?' asked Coleman, crawling up next to him.

'No, I think it's out of the socket.'

'You're lucky to be alive. You got some bang when you hit the deck,' said Coleman. He was a real Job's comforter.

'Take those, Pat,' said Tarja, giving him two morphine tablets. They would dull the pain but make him more confused. He had been there before; disoriented for hours from the effect of a seizure.

'We need to get you inside,' said Tarja, tying her scarf into a sling to support his shoulder. With Coleman pulling his good arm and Tarja pushing his legs, he slid along the water on the deck towards the wheelhouse. The throbbing pain in his shoulder nauseated him. They finally made it to the wheelhouse. He lay down on the bench and closed his eyes. It was a relief to be inside, out of the storm, although feeling secure wasn't a choice with the storm raging around them and the trawler just stopping short of doing back flips.

'Pat, I think it's safe to give you more morphine tablets.'

'Ok.' Safety didn't matter to him anymore, just get rid of this bloody pain. It seemed like ages before the pain eased. Then he knew what he had to ask her to do.

'Tarja, will you put my shoulder back in place?'

'I could make it worse, maybe we should leave it until we get back to port. We have painkillers,' she said, gently stroking his head.

'I need to be on my feet, or we might not get back at all.' He had probably scared the life out of her. His head was a bit fuzzy, and he'd need to watch what he was saying. Keeping his mouth shut was the best choice.

On trawlers, dislocated shoulders are common enough, and he had seen doctors checking for a break before putting the shoulder back in its socket. Unfortunately, he didn't know how they did it, and equally, he had never seen a shoulder put back into its socket at sea.

'I know the theory on how to twist the joint back into place but that's a long way from doing it,' she said.

'Do you know how to check to see if it's broken?' He just wanted to sleep, and it was taking all his will-power to stay engaged with what was going on around him.

'That's something else I don't know,' she said.

'Please give it a try.' He could not feel much worse regardless of whatever, she did to him. The storm seemed louder and the trawler more sluggish, signs that they were sinking deeper into the sea from the water onboard. He needed to attend to it and soon, before they sank beneath the waves. It wouldn't solve the problem to tell them about it and get them more alarmed.

'Ok then. I'll need something to bind your shoulder after I put back in the socket.'

'Get some sheets and foam from the cabin.' He should have said please but his mind had gone into slow motion.

'Please,' he said, the words were drifting away from him.

She kissed his cheek.

'Politeness doesn't matter now; sleep until I get back.'

He had her consent to sleep, that was enough permission for him, to let go of his resolve to stay awake. He couldn't remember if he told her not to wake the skipper, it probably didn't matter. Now there was a man for manipulating a shoulder back into place, though he would probably wrench it clean off.

When he woke up, she had cut sheets into strips for bandages and had made a neck support from a foam mattress using the scissors from the cutlery drawer. His shoulder needed tight bandaging to prevent it popping out of its socket again. Although he knew how the procedure worked, the thought of all that pain scared him. He had seen other people have their shoulder joints manipulated back into place, a hard pull of the arm and a twist and Bob's your uncle. What was scaring him?

With the patient well sedated, it was a simple and quick procedure for a doctor. That said it all - a doctor and sedation. Out here on the ocean, it was like frontier medicine, whiskey for anaesthetic and a penknife for a scalpel.

Although she had courage, he knew he was asking too much of her. She must have found the skipper's stash somehow - a bottle of his best poteen was standing on the draining board next to her. She came over and sat down close to him, and kissed his wet forehead. She started to cry.

'I could cause you pain.'

'It should be Ok.' Now there was a lie if he ever heard one. It wasn't her fault; but her inexperience could cause him irreparable damage.

'We'd better get on with it,' he said.

'Ok, drink some of this stuff, it might help.' She raised the bottle of poteen to his lips, and he took a drink. It was real firewater, burning his throat and down his gullet. Choking, he coughed and like a stab of a knife, a spasm of pain went through his shoulder. He waited a few minutes for the pain to subside. He wouldn't move like that again, if he could help it.

'It tastes like bad gin or burned newspapers', he said.

She laid a reassuring hand on his forehead and pushed his wet hair back out of his eyes.

'Coleman, will you hold Pat steady?

'Ok, for all the good it'll do.'

This was one time he needed support, and he wasn't getting much of it from Coleman, just the usual glum pessimism.

She tried to organise, putting everything she needed down on the deck, wrapped in oilskin. She had even had the foresight to take the parallel ruler from the map drawer for splints.

'If only the noise would stop everything wouldn't be so frantic,' she said, kneeling down beside him. She put the rubber handle of the pliers between his teeth. Exposed to the full force of the storm, water pelted down on them. It was running down his forehead, into his eyes and pooling on the pliers. His mouth was full of saltiness. He kept blinking but couldn't focus fully.

'Come now,' she called out to Coleman.

Coleman moved over slowly, knelt down and placed his arms on Pat's chest pinning him to the waterlogged deck. Pat watched Tarja. She had gone on to automatic pilot, carrying out the procedure step by step. Tarja was a thinking woman; she had rehearsed the procedure in her mind and was methodically following through.

She lifted his arm, pulled it gently and twisted. Nothing happened. Afraid of hurting him, she wasn't decisive enough, and he felt a surge of pain in his shoulder and across his chest. Without the pliers between his teeth, he would have screamed.

The second time around she pulled harder on his arm and twisted it quickly, there was a crunch of bone as the ball-and-socket joint went back together. He moaned and almost fainted, his heart was pounding in his ears; and he was drifting into semi-consciousness from the pain. Determined, he held on until the pain finally lessened. He was relieved in one sense to have it over with, but there was still a lot of pain in his shoulder.

She pulled the sides of the parallel ruler apart and used them as splints, one on each side of his arm. The poteen and the morphine were making him drowsy. This probably masked some of the pain in muscles and sinews and whatever else had been wrenched allowing his shoulder to slide back into place. He didn't know exactly, but it would all probably take a long time to heal. So far so good, and in their circumstances, it had gone reasonably well. She bound his arm to his chest.

'Thanks Tarja, it took a lot to do that,' he said weakly. She gave him a reassuring tap on his good shoulder. Procedure over, she picked up the bottle of poteen and took a long drink. Coughing, she couldn't get a breath for a few seconds.

'I guess it's an acquired taste. The skipper is welcome to it.' She pushed the cork back into the bottle and thumped it home with her fist.

'What's good for the patient is good for the nurse,' said Coleman.

'It's hot like curry and tastes like burned toast,' she said. Pat was feeling weak and tired and Tarja's voice was indistinct, like the reception on the trawler's radio.

'I would like to sleep, but I'll have nightmares after the seizure.'

'Take those sleeping tablets - they'll help,' said Tarja. He wouldn't drift off for some time yet. He was going over in his mind how Tarja came into his life and how she came to be on aboard the Annie L.

5

Pat's first glimpse of Tarja, the foreign girl with the flaming red hair was when she parked her ancient 2CV on the forecourt of the pub across from the forge. He was sitting on a bench outside the pub drinking a pint of Guinness at the time. He had never seen anything like her: the red hair caught his attention first, but what held his gaze was the silhouette of her long legs in jeans that his confessor would surely describe as an occasion of sin. It all but made him spit a mouthful of stout across the table.

Tall and poised, she made her way to the forge. Pat would bet that she had never even smelt the stuff before let alone been nearly up to her ass in it – horse manure. The smithy worked not ten paces from where Pat was sitting, and he could hear her shouting to him over the noise of the bellows. She probably guessed, correctly, that he was nearly deaf.

'I'm looking for the skipper of the Annie L.'

He continued working on a pony's hoof. Pat didn't know the blacksmith's age, but he guessed that he must be past the biblical three score and ten, more like four score and a bit. If he was anywhere near the smithy's age, he'd have retired or died years ago. The blacksmith let the hoof fall to the ground before straightening up and looking at her from under the peak of his cloth cap. He took the horseshoe nails out of his mouth before speaking.

'He's up there in the pub.' He gave the pony a sugar lump.

'Who told you about him?'

'He said his name was Scottie.' She patted the pony on the rump. Pat pictured Scottie wearing his kilt and Tam O'Shanter sitting on a bollard at the end of Purteen pier, repairing fishing nets like he always did at this time of year. Scottie's proud boast was that real Scotsmen wore nothing under their kilts. They called him Bare Bum in the pub. Pat knew that whoever she asked in town would have sent her to the blacksmith. The forge was the island's drop-in centre, where one and all went at some stage, for a chat or to pick up local gossip. Discretion was not among the blacksmith's virtues.

'I told him I wanted a berth on a trawler. He said to talk to you first, and then try the skipper of the Annie L.'

Pat smiled.

'What else did he say?' asked the blacksmith, shaking the stiffness out of his bowlegs.

'That he didn't want the skipper on his tail.'

The blacksmith laughed.

'Don't worry about the skipper. You can tell him I sent you.'

'Scottie quoted Rabbie Burns. Something about men being villains and "little to be trusted."'

'That's Scottie. He's a long time out of Scotland, but he talks like he was just there yesterday.'

'Thanks.' She turned to leave.

Pat knew the blacksmith, good-humoured but nosey, and the old man wasn't going to let her get away that quickly, not without finding out more about her and perhaps a bit of juicy gossip. The islanders were like that anyway, but the blacksmith a bit more than the rest. Every encounter with him was an opportunity for a long conversation.

'We don't see many of those anymore.' He pointed his hammer towards her red 2CV. She hesitated for a second, and then she must have decided to play along.

'I got it in Dublin.' She let the pony smell the back of her hand.

'It's a left-hand drive?' The blacksmith adjusted his cloth cap.

'No one else would buy it. They thought it was unlucky. Seemingly, the first owner, a French girl, died shortly after getting married to a Galway man, and people blamed the car.'

'You never know about the curses that can be on things like that. Did you hear about James Dean's car?'

'I didn't,' she said, still patting the pony.

'Jinxed, the car he died in, and people who took bits of the car for mementos either died or suffered a serious injury. I was a big fan of his, but I wouldn't have touched that car for anything.' The blacksmith seemed thoughtful for a few minutes, and then he pointed his hammer out to sea.

'Be careful out there.'

The islanders thought the blacksmith had second sight, and they were always asking him about the future. He always offered some cryptic response loaded with possibility. Pat wasn't superstitious and considered it rubbish. He overheard the blacksmith say, 'You have worked with horses?'

'Yes,' the girl replied.

'Hold his head while I shoe him then. He's nervous.' The blacksmith walked back to the fire.

'Okay.' She went to the pony's head and stood stroking him between the eyes.

Pat watched her as she took stock of her surroundings. The forge was nothing more than a shack with a tin roof filled with smoke from the smouldering fire. The smoke was perhaps the cause of the blacksmith's hacking cough, sometimes bringing up a lump of green phlegm that he spat on the earthen floor. Pat kept out of the place as much as possible to avoid stepping in the mixture of spit and horse manure. It stuck to everything like fresh concrete and her shoes would need some cleaning after her visit to the forge.

The blacksmith gave the bellows a few pumps and the coke fire reached white heat. He selected a preformed shoe and reddened it in the fire before reshaping it on the anvil. His work had a rhythm, two ringing beats on the anvil followed by a dull thud on the hot metal shoe. He then tested the shoe for size against the pony's hoof. Unprepared for the smell of burning hoof, she put her hand to her nose, and it looked like she might run away.

'It's okay,' said the blacksmith, as if he sensed her unease, even though he wasn't looking at her as far as Pat could tell.

'He doesn't feel any pain.' The blacksmith blew away the smoke to get a better look at what he was doing.

'I'm not used to the smell,' she said, turning her head away, probably hoping for a breath of fresh air.

The old man trimmed the hoof with a bone-handled knife and finished off the job with a rasp.

'That should do it!' He said as he quickly tapped in the final nail and used the clincher on it to shape it to the outside of the hoof.

'We're done here. If you have trouble with the skipper, talk to his nephew Pat over there.' The blacksmith discarded his hammer, as if he was never going to need it again, throwing it with a clang into a box of assorted shoeing tools, before straightening up with some difficulty.

'Thanks.' She gave the pony a final pat and turned to walk towards the pub.

'Anyway, I'll be up there myself a bit later if you have any problems,' he shouted after her.

6

The Cabin pub was a thatched cottage with whitewashed walls and a red half door. A small window let in daylight. Outside the owners had gone for a retro look, a designer's creation of a traditional Irish cottage pub from another age. For Pat it didn't work - it looked gaudy and out of place, more like a stage set gone wrong than a pub.

In contrast to the outside, the interior was an authentic Irish pub, mainly undisturbed since furnished back in the early 1880s. It could be the model for Irish theme pubs from Boston to Bulgaria, down to the sawdust on the floor. It had a long bar, the top stained from many spills and the small snug near the door. The low ceiling was black from the smoke of turf fires. There was an odour of Guinness combined with burning turf in the room. Pat followed her into the pub. The drone of male voices hushed as she came through the door and went up to the bar.

'A Guinness, please.' she ignored the stares. If she felt uncomfortable, Pat couldn't see any evidence of it. In this male enclave to walk up to the bar looking that cool and composed took nerve. Of course it could be the old duck story, cool, on top and paddling like mad underneath. He did that a lot himself; being the strong silent type, don't complain, don't explain although scared shitless at the back of it all.

'The first pint is on the house for strangers,' said Kate, the barmaid, as she polished the bar top with a yellow duster.

'Thanks, strangers are friends we haven't met yet.'

Kate looked to the heavens.

'O, do you not say that in Ireland?'

'Only on postcards. Welcome,' said Kate pushing a glass of Guinness along the counter towards her.

'I want to go out on a trawler. Scotty told me to ask for the skipper of the Annie, L.'

'There's a young woman here asking for you skipper?' said Kate.

'Not too many young women ask for me anymore,' said the skipper, holding on to the pint in front of him on the bar counter.

'They never did,' said Coleman. He was a permanent member of the crew of the Annie L., who'd known the skipper since their school days. '

'A hell of a lot more than asked for you, cripple,' roared the skipper, thumping his pint down on the counter and showering the bar top with froth.

'They must be invisible then,' said Coleman, a child polio victim. At three years old, his left hand had stopped growing. Pat could see the hurt showing in his face from the skipper's jibe.

The skipper was shaped like a beer barrel with limbs attached, and when he shouted his voice came from somewhere deep inside. He was wearing a muscle-man vest. A mermaid was tattooed on one shoulder and on the other, 'I love Mary' with a heart and an arrow going through it. After his outburst, there was silence in the bar for a few minutes, apart for the sound of Kate pulling pints.

'So you want to go out on the shark killer's boat, do you? Sort it out with that useless little shit over there in the snug,' said the skipper, in the same loud voice, turning his back to her. The usual insult, thought Pat - he could have said 'my nephew,' or even 'that fellow over there,' but no, it had to be abusive. Pat had better call her over before any more nonsense developed. He stood up in the snug and raised his hand.

She sauntered over and sat down at the table across from him. The froth from the beer was clinging to his moustache and beard, and he had no tissues to clean it. He could give it a swipe with the back of his hand before she came over, but now it was too late. You didn't do that in polite society. Maybe he should make a joke about it. Better not. Leave it be. He didn't know this woman and anyway, he wasn't ready for chat. He wished she would go away and leave him alone, although in the bereavement sessions they had told him to start talking to women again.

'The skipper is a bit short on the social graces. I'm Pat O'Malley, his nephew,' he said, holding out his hand.

'My name is Tarja Lastinen. I'm a marine biologist and I would like to see what toxins are in the fish taken from the Atlantic,' she said, shaking his hand.

'It's been some dumping ground; we don't know what's out there.'

'Yes, it could be affecting the marine life,' she said, taking a cautious sip from her glass.

'Is that your first pint of Guinness?' She would need a thick skin if she was going to sea with his uncle and Coleman - they weren't exactly choirboys.

'Yes, I think I like it.' She was looking intently at the white head on the glass of Guinness.

'Where are you from?' He guessed from her accent that she was from somewhere in mainland Europe, although it could be anywhere from France to Poland.

'From Helsinki,' she said, taking her attention away from the pint and looking directly at him.

'People think of snow and frost and reindeer when Helsinki comes up.' He was buying time to find a way to let her down gently. She was too glamorous for their untidy trawler, smelling of dead fish and diesel oil. With no doors on the loo and shower, it wasn't suitable for taking a woman on board.

'There's a lot more to it than that,' she said, as she shifted about on the hard wooden bench.

'You're a long way from home. It must be lonely for you in this isolated place?' He stared at the pattern left on the inside of his glass. It reminded him of something, but he couldn't think what it was. She probably had a boyfriend somewhere. Why stop at one, this girl would have a slua in tow.

'I needed to get away for a while,' she said, looking down at the floor and avoiding his gaze.

He decided not to pry further but took a drink from his glass. There probably was a lot more to tell, but he didn't need to know the life dramas of every stranger he met. Why not be sociable and think up a believable excuse for not taking her to sea. Something like not having insurance to carry passengers would do.

'Your English is good,' he said, fidgeting with the mats on the table in front of him.

'We study it at school all the time,' she said. The more they talked the more at ease he felt with her.

'Have you family?' She asked as she emptied her glass.

'That's my last living relative over there.' Pat gestured towards the skipper, who was in full flow.

'What about your family?'

'I have my parents. I am an only child, spoilt brat.'

'I didn't say a word,' said Pat, smiling.

She took her purse out of her bag.

'Put that away. Same again,' he called to Kate.

'Coming right up.'

Kate placed the pints on the counter and Pat collected and paid for them.

'Good health,' he said, as he raised his glass.

'Kippis,' she said as she lifted hers.

As the night wore on, he lost count of the number of times that Kate refilled their glasses, and he sensed Tarja was drinking a lot more than she normally did.

'It's a bit rough on board, but you're welcome to come on the next trip.' He could hardly believe what he had just said. Talk about chickening out of the hard decision. There would be some ructions when the others found out. He'd say nothing to them; she might not join them at all. He blamed it on the drink and letting all that glamour turn his head. Drink made a fool out of many a man.

'When can I come aboard?

'We'll leave the Purteen pier on Sunday evening.'

'I'll be there.'

7

A commotion had started at the back of the pub with two youths squaring up to each other.

That's all Pat needed - a row to start in the pub. It would leave her with some good impression of the island.

'Sorry about this. They're from a tough part of Dublin with that accent.'

Here he went again. Why did he have to start apologising to her? He was so pathetic, pretending the islanders were above all this. Pull the other one. With the skipper in the pub, anything could happen.

He pushed his pint to the centre of the table for safe keeping in case he had to intervene. His role since he came back to the island was trying to keep the skipper out of trouble, being his guardian angel. He was the peacekeeper, although in pub scuffles he could take care of himself. It was then that his weight training was useful. In the past, he felt good about his physical strength, but now he rarely felt good about anything. Nevertheless, he often wished he had a less volatile uncle than the skipper. Tarja was talking to him.

'All Irish accents sound the same to me. I think it would take a long time to know the differences.' She was looking uneasy.

'I'm the best bloody man in here,' shouted one of the youths, thumping his chest like a king gorilla before shoving the other towards the bar.

'Wanker!' he roared in reply.

Locked together in a wrestling tussle, they pushed this way and that, knocking people out of their way. Guinness spilling from broken glasses was running in little streams along the floor.

'We'll soon see who the best bloody man is,' roared the skipper, getting to his feet and pushing his pint away from him into the centre of the bar counter. Tarja looked terrified. It was doubtless her first time near a bar brawl.

'He'll half kill them, if he gets his hands on them,' said Pat, getting up and rushing over to stop the fight.

Here he was again - the peacemaker. He would need to watch that they didn't hit him over the head with a beer bottle or something. That would make some mess, although his big fear was knives. The locals in their brawls did a lot of pushing, shoving and shouting but used no weapons. You couldn't be sure about this Dublin lot. Caught in battle, they didn't see him coming until he grabbed them by the shoulders and pulled them apart.

'Enough of this.'

'Culchie bastard.' They turned on him, their own fight forgotten. He tried to push them back on to their seats, but with their combined strength, he couldn't. If they knocked him to the floor, they would kick the crap out of him, and he wasn't going to let that happen. Conversation had stopped and a group gathered around the brawlers, forming a circle for them to grapple in. They whistled, stamped their feet and shouted encouragement to Pat. Without either side gaining advantage, they pushed backwards and forwards until Pat kneed the taller one in the groin. He roared and let go. He did the same with the smaller youth, and with both doubled up in pain, he propelled them backwards until they toppled on to their seats.

It was a close call – with their combined strength they nearly defeated him. Maybe he should have taken them on one at a time but it was over now and he felt a great weariness. When aggression sprang up in the pub it could hang around all night. It wouldn't surprise him if there were another flare-up of some kind before closing time.

'Thanks Pat. Any more nonsense out of you lot, and you're out of here for good,' Kate declared. She came out from behind the bar with a bucket and mop, to clean up the mess.

'Pay up for the broken glasses,' said Pat, letting go of the youths and returning to his seat. His hands were trembling. Tarja was silent and he hadn't a clue what was going on in her head. She was probably thinking that these people were savages or something like that, not the land of saints and scholars. Then again, who knows what a woman is thinking. Trying to disguise his shaking hands, he took a drink from his glass.

The upheaval quietened the drinkers and Pat could hear the skipper talking to Coleman.

'Soon I won't be fit for that little shit,' He gestured in Pat's direction.

'You never were,' said Coleman.

'Any time you want it out there on the street. I'm fit enough for you, cripple.'

'Now, lads, keep it peaceful. What about a song, skipper?' coaxed Kate.

Pat had seen her use that technique before to divert the skipper from getting involved in a fight.

'Here,' she said, producing a violin and bodhran from behind the bar. She stored them there for safe keeping. The drinkers cleared a space for the bony-fingered fiddler and the bodhran player.

'Is that a local man?' asked Tarja gesturing towards the bodhran player.

'Don't know where he comes from. They call him "Weed warrior" around here. He gets terrible LSD flashbacks.'

He looked the part. A throwback to the Californian flower power era, "Weed warrior" wore a dirty orange robe embroidered with flowers and open-toed sandals. He had his hair tied back in a ponytail, under a red and white polka dot bandana and his eyes looked vacant, in an emaciated face. He was muttering away in a world of his own. The music got underway and the skipper, propped up by the bar, started to sing.

'Irish music is sad – yes.' She turned around in her seat to survey the scene.

'It can be.' It was cringe time. The skipper would murder the song. No more high Cs for him. The years of heavy drinking and roaring had done this to his voice. In fairness, people who had known him in his young days thought his singing voice was good.

'What's the song?' asked Tarja.

'It's "The last rose of summer" from Moore's Melodies.' She was making him nervous and his hands were still trembling. He would have to do something with them. He couldn't hold on to his pint all the time but she might think he was up to something else if he put his hands in his pockets. The complimentary strip of matches was the answer. He started to pull the matches from the pack, one by one leaving the stubs. It was keeping his hands busy, and he liked doing it anyway. He got the same satisfaction from bursting bubbles in bubble wrap. Bet she was thinking he was some head case; it probably wasn't a habit for practicing in public.

'It's a lovely song. Was Moore Irish?'

'O yes, all before the days of radio and TV, it was the first song to sell over a million copies worldwide.' Pat, returning the matches to the centre of the table and humming the tune, moved his hand from side to side in time with the music.

'Had he some tragedy in his life?'

'Don't know.'

'It's so mournful and romantic.'

'I suppose.' He hadn't thought of it like that before.

'We all have tragedies in our lives,' she said.

He studied her face before saying, 'It's set to an old Irish air for the harp, "The Groves of Barley."' He stopped pretending to conduct.

'Moore's Melodies popularised Irish music throughout the world,' he said proudly. The patrons of the pub shouted, jeered, clapped and thumped their feet on the floor as the skipper came to the end of the song. Pat wondered what she was thinking about it all. Probably not the same as Irish people liked to think of themselves; Mediterranean type people living in a cold climate with an interest in music and a great capacity for not taking life too seriously. Dream on. He was second-guessing her and not putting a good spin on it, although it wouldn't surprise him if she saw them as a drunken crowd of nutcases. She was staring at him in silence. He felt she was taking stock of him, and then she said in a low voice,

'Marriage was my misfortune.'

She looked away and went silent again as if it was all coming back to her.

'I'm divorced.'

What was he supposed to say to that?

'I thought there might be something.'

She was looking at the floor preoccupied with her thoughts.

'Where was your husband from?'

'Moscow. Viktor was one of the few Russians studying at the University of Helsinki. He was older than my other classmates; and he singled me out. He sent me flowers everyday to the lecture hall. The lecturer used to make fun of it, by asking the class, "What blooms can we expect today?" I was so embarrassed, but I suppose I felt special by all the attention.'

'He was determined,' said Pat, wondering where all this was going.

'I took him to meet my parents and my mum was far from impressed. "There's something false about that man," she said. My dad said nothing, but I could see it in his eyes that he felt this Viktor wasn't right for me. My wedding took place in a hotel, if you could call it that, in the red light district of Moscow. We had a pastor of some sort, and he spoke nothing but Russian.

I didn't understand a word of it. It was strange, but none of Viktor's family attended. The staff pulled two tables together and covered them with a grubby white tablecloth. The pastor stood at one side of the table, and we stood across from him with the best man and bridesmaid. I was wearing a wedding dress and the others were dressed in scruffy clothes as if the wedding ceremony didn't mean anything to them. In hindsight, it didn't. The best man's jacket bulged from the outline of a gun in the inside breast pocket.

I asked Viktor about that later. "Everyone in Moscow carries a gun for protection," he said. 'I didn't meet the bridesmaid until minutes before the ceremony, and she seemed to know Viktor well. 'Later that evening I saw her standing on her patch outside the hotel soliciting. I asked Viktor about it.

"Are you mad? That's a different woman," he said.

'Call me naïve, but I accepted his explanation. It must have been the shortest wedding service on record. The pastor read from a prayer book for a few minutes and then motioned to us to exchange rings. That was it, after Viktor paid him for his services, the pastor couldn't get out of the hotel fast enough. It was as if the place was on fire.

The wedding guests, all Viktor's friends, were a tough looking bunch and at the wedding breakfast they argued and drank vodka from the bottle. Mum and Dad looked frightened by them. In retrospect, they were a bunch of heavies on Viktor's payroll. He was so drunk that he couldn't drive my parents to the airport, we got a taxi. I'll never forget the worried look on their faces when I said cheerio to them at the airport. They had visibly aged.

"You know where your home is and don't hesitate to come back anytime," Dad said.'

Pat felt troubled by what he was hearing; there was one question he had to ask,

'Did you have any children?'

'No, thank God. Our honeymoon was a rushed affair and when we got back to the university, the accommodation office granted us married quarters on campus. Viktor set about taking control immediately. He changed my bank account into a joint account and large lodgements of money started to appear. He told me they were donations from his wealthy parents.'

'Mm,' said Pat. He didn't want to interrupt and anyway there was no comment he could make on the story.

'I put our communication problems down to language and cultural differences. He often went away for days without explanation and, at times, he would sit in the flat for hours, brooding. We had separate bedrooms but we didn't discuss it. At other times, he would sleep during the day and sit up at night with his pals, talking in Russian, drinking vodka and watching videos. He mostly ignored me. To call him a poor student was an understatement, he didn't study and never went to lectures. While we were dating, I had built up an image of him in my mind, and it wasn't anything like the real Viktor. He had deliberately misled me. In retrospect, I knew little about him, and I shouldn't have married him.' She was still staring at the floor studying the patterns in the sawdust caused by a countless number of feet walking hither and thither over it.

'We all make mistakes,' said Pat, although in her case to have married Viktor was a costly one.

It wasn't the time to talk about his problems. She obviously had more to say so he said mildly, 'It's hard to understand how someone as clever as you, could have been so deceived. Maybe it had something to do with 'love is blind?''

'I led a sheltered life, and I didn't know anything about relationships. I suppose he swept me off my feet. I couldn't accept the way he was living and in a fit of anger, I had it out with him.

'You're a lazy good-for-nothing,' I said. That was the first time he hit me, across the face with his open palm and the force of the blow knocked me over the back of a chair. He left the room without a backward look. It was terrible, just married, and he was abandoning me. I felt so alone and inadequate.'

She looked across at Pat for a response. He didn't know what to say. It was outside his experience - he had never encountered a wife beater. Even the skipper at his most violent never did that. She was expecting him to say something.

'That was awful.' It was a cop out; but what else was there to say?

'Viktor was full of remorse and when he returned, he brought me a present of a Rolex. He was such a Jekyll and Hyde character - he could be so nice one minute and the next a raging lunatic. I was such a fool then. I blamed myself and put it down to cultural differences. Maybe that's the way Russian husbands treated their wives if they answered back. I was ignoring my mother's advice, "If anyone raises their hand to you, get away as fast as you can and don't come back."'

'Wife beaters are in every country,' said Pat, glad of the opportunity to have some input into the conversation.

'I know that now, but I was young. The beatings didn't stop and to disguise my bumps and bruises, I took to wearing dark glasses and plastering my face with makeup. It became a way of life. He was so unpredictable; he would fly into a rage over nothing. He terrified me. In retrospect, I realise no one believed my long repertoire of excuses, they guessed what was happening, but to save my embarrassment, they said nothing. Walking into doors and tripping over the carpet was becoming a less plausible excuse to my family, looking at my bruised face. My visits to them were fewer, and eventually I stopped going to see them altogether. I was under his control at that stage.'

'I can see that, without your family, you were at his mercy.'

'Sport bags full of money were appearing everywhere in the flat, under beds and on top of wardrobes. I dared not ask where it was coming from, but I suspected his role as a student was a cover up for some other activity.

"Pack your belongings, we're going to Moscow in the morning," he said one day and handed me a flight ticket. He left the flat without further discussion.'

'He should at least have talked it over with you,' said Pat.

'Yes, that would have been nice. There were so many unanswered questions. I didn't have time for trips with my exams less than three weeks away. To my horror, the ticket was one-way. Did he expect me to give up everything and live in Moscow? I was afraid to disobey, and I did what he told me, and packed my suitcases. If I didn't obey, I would have got another beating. I was in an impossible situation and I cried so much.'

'I can see why,' said Pat, looking at her with concern.

'I asked him about the one-way ticket and he told me that we were returning on a private flight. I didn't dare question him further although I was suspicious of his intentions. Was it a ploy to get me to Moscow and imprison me there? We flew to Moscow Airport the next day and booked into another backstreet hotel with linoleum on the floors. The springs had long since gone in the bed and the linen was grubby. I didn't know Moscow but this must have been as seedy as it gets. He came and went several times, filling up the wardrobe with large bags tied with duct tape. I was curious to know what was in them, but scared to open them. He ignored me and, his work done, stayed out all night. In the morning he presented me with a flight ticket,

"You are going back today."'

'Just like that,' said Pat.

'It was a command. He dumped all my clothes on to the floor and started to fill my suitcases with little plastic bags of white powder. I knew then, I was the mule and, shaking with fear, I decide to make a stand. I told him I wasn't taking drugs back with me. I didn't see the punch coming, but I heard a crunch of bone as my nose fractured. The force of the blow flung me across the bed. Blood was running into my throat, choking me, and I was trying to cough it up. My eye was swelling up, and I couldn't see him clearly, but I remember the door banging as he left the bedroom.'

'That was horrendous,' said Pat. Almost unaware of it, he took a quick look at her nose. There didn't seem to be any long-term damage. She caught him staring.

'It's not straight, it's twisted,' she said, crying out.

'No, it's ok.' Right enough, the surgeons had done a good job, there wasn't any sign of displacement.

'It spoilt my face?'

'No, no, your face is perfect.'

'That's not true.'

'I wouldn't lie to you, I wouldn't have known.'

She looked at him for a minute, and he wasn't sure if he had convinced her or not.

'I had to get out of there, and I took the backstairs to the hotel foyer. I figured; I was less likely to bump into him than if I took the lift. With a black eye and blood running from my nose, people stared at me. They probably took me for a working girl, battered by a client. My heart was pounding and I was panicking.'

'You did well to get out of there. They were no choirboys. They might have killed you if you hadn't left when you did.'

'I had a bit of luck. There was a taxi parked outside the door. He thought I wanted a hospital and with the language barrier it took a lot of gesturing to get to the airport. With my nose in such a state, it affected my breathing on the flight.'

'Breathing on planes is difficult enough at the best of times,' said Pat. Talk about saying the obvious, but he hadn't been in this situation before.

'The flight attendant gave me oxygen. I thought the problem through during the flight and when we landed, I contacted the police. I was angry but to inform on him was the most fearful thing I ever did.'

'Most people would find it difficult,' said Pat aware that other drinkers were noticing the intensity of their conversation.

'Arrested when their private plane landed, loaded with drugs, at a disused military airstrip outside Helsinki, my husband and his henchmen got long prison sentences.'

'I hope they keep him there. Will you be OK when he gets out?' Pat was thinking that these criminal types have long memories.

'I don't know.'

'If he comes this far, we'll deal with him like we deal with all upstarts. We'll kick his backside off the island.'

He was trying to create the impression that she was safe with them.

'I spent time in hospital recovering from a broken nose, eye socket, cheek and a cracked jawbone. The physical pain was obvious, but the mental pain was more difficult to cope with. It has taken years trying to get over it. I still wake up at night in a cold sweat and some nights I can't sleep at all just tossing and turning.

Kate interrupted by addressing them from behind the bar,

'Come on, Pat, it's time for you to do a turn, and we won't take no for an answer.'

'You'll have to take no. I'm not in form tonight for telling stories,' said Pat.

8

'Who's next up then?' asked Kate. 'What about this new girl giving us a song or a story?'

'No, you would have heard all my stories before,' said Tarja.

'I've heard everyone's stories in here before; but they lose nothing in the telling,' said Kate.

'She hears everything in here. They tell all their secrets to the blacksmith, and he tells her,' said Pat.

'Like a community counsellor,' said Tarja.

'More like the ancient Greeks, they had a man you told all your scandals to, the filth eater, and he went and told everyone else. That's our blacksmith,' said Pat.

'I don't feel the need yet,' said Tarja, laughing.

'Come on Cripple, get up there and do a turn. You can't even tell a yarn. A good-for-nothing useless cripple,' roared the skipper.

Pat glanced at her and she looked as if she was feeling sorry for Coleman. When she got up, walked to the centre of the room and sat down, maybe she was trying to save him from further humiliation.

The room went quiet as she started to tell her story.

'You know that long ago in Persia there lived two brothers, Ali Baba and Cassim, and that Ali Baba discovered the robbers' cave?'

'Tell us again,' yelled the drinkers.

Pat had expected a Finnish story, but no, this was what they were getting. He felt a bit disappointed. The Finns, well what little he knew about them, had some great fables. She continued with the story and regaled them with the tale of gold, thieves, and treachery.

Pat, surprised to see her getting up in the first place, decided that it was out of kindness to Coleman. That took guts; and she looked vulnerable sitting in the middle of a circle of male drinkers.

She kept her eyes on the floor a lot and didn't look up.

Pat felt she was trying to cut the story short, to get out of the hot seat as quickly as possible. It was a shame to have let her get into this fix, but what could he have done to prevent it. Maybe he needed to tell the skipper to shut up now and again.

The fiddler played Arab music softly in the background.

When she came to the 'Open Sesame' part of the story a wild roar of 'Open Sesame' filled the pub.

Her face went a bright red and Pat could hear her voice falter. She looked up and looked around the room quickly and her eyes stayed on him for a few seconds. He had deserted her and she looked as if she was about to cry. Feeling contrite he shouted

'Tarja, don't heed these bog men, carry on with the story.' She recovered enough to continue.

'Close Sesame,' said Tarja and again the drinkers shouted 'Close Sesame.'

Tarja came to the part where Ali Baba loaded his three mules with bags of gold coins and covered them with wood.

'Donkeys not mules,' said a voice from the back of pub.

'Don't spoil the story,' the others shouted. Tarja looked so pained that Pat couldn't stand by any longer; he had to act. He picked up his chair and sat down beside her.

'OK, we'll go with mules,' he said.

Her voice was steadier now, and she continued to where Cassim's wife covered the bottom of the measure with lard before handing it over.

'I haven't seen a lump of lard in a long time,' said the drinker with the largest beer belly in the room.

'You mustn't have a big enough mirror in the house,' said another voice from the back of the pub to more guffaws.

'Let the girl tell the story without interruption, or you're out of here,' said Kate.

'They needed to sew Cassim's remains together for a decent burial. Ali Baba's slave went out, with a handful of gold coins, to find a shoemaker and bring him back blindfolded to sew Cassim's remains together. The shoemaker did his best, but he was no anatomist.

Nevertheless, most bits fitted together all right.

'Could our shoemaker do that?' shouted a heckler.

'I'll sew up your big mouth any time,' said the shoemaker from somewhere in the crowd.

'That would stop him heckling, and he was never that well put together, it would improve his face,' shouted another voice. Bravely Tarja went on with the story.

'Ali Baba then married his brother's widow, as was the custom.'

'I hope it doesn't catch on here,' said the voice from the back of the pub.

'Let's drink to that,' said another, raising his glass amid raucous laughter.

'Now shut up all of you and listen to the story,' said Pat, standing up and glaring around the pub.

'Ali Baba rewarded the slave girl by setting her free, and she married his eldest son and they all lived happily ever after.'

A round of applause greeted the end of the story, and Tarja, sitting beside Pat was shaking and breathing fast. She took a long drink from her glass.

'Thanks for helping me out, I was so scared,' she said.

'It's not easy to get up and talk to these fellows,' said Pat. He was thinking you couldn't help liking her. When he first saw her, he thought she was a red-headed ice lady but in truth, she just seemed more confident than she was.

9

'The standard is high today. Who's next for a turn?' asked Kate.

As Pat expected, even though humiliated by the skipper, Coleman got to his feet to tell a story. It seemed the more the skipper put him down, the stronger he responded. He had that nature. He glanced at Tarja and she looked astonished as Coleman headed for the chair in the centre of the room. She was probably thinking that Coleman was putting himself forward for further embarrassment; after all she had done to prevent it. He felt she didn't know how to read these fellows yet. Now she was looking at Pat with an enquiring frown on her face.

'What's going on here?' was the unstated question. Well, that's what he thought the stare meant. What could he tell her? Say nothing - she would find out for herself.

'I knew you wouldn't let me down, Coleman,' said Kate. He started his tale.

'On the most westerly corner of Ireland, Achill Island is direct across from Cape Cod. It is about 10 miles long by seven miles wide and connected to the mainland by a bridge. It's a holiday island, and the population of one thousand five hundred increases twofold over the summer months.'

'We know that, we live here, get on with the story,' said a voice from the back.

'The new girl doesn't know that. Now, the best of good order for the speaker,' said Kate.

Pat was thinking that if Tarja were here for the next thirty years, she would still be the new girl on the island. That's the way isle communities like this one worked.

Coleman continued. 'The Garda Sergeant was a local man and, after completing training at the Garda headquarters in the Phoenix Park, he returned to the island with his Dublin born wife, Mairead. She was an artist.

Not that daft old story again, thought Pat. If she didn't know it before, she would know now that she was with a pub full of crazies. Could he not have thought of some other half sensible tale to tell her?

"I suppose I miss the Dublin coffee shops but this island has always been a haven for artists," Mairead often said.

'One dark November night, the Sergeant was returning home, following a late emergency call to the old coastguard station in Keem Bay, now owned by a Dublin man, who had converted it into holiday apartments.

'Is this a ghost story?' Tarja whispered, mischievously cupping her hands to her mouth, and leaning across the table towards Pat, as if they were sharing a secret.

'I'm afraid so,' said Pat, moving back a bit from her.

'I love ghost stories,' she said, sitting back in her seat, smiling.

'The islanders had cut into the side of the rocky cliff face, three hundred feet above the Atlantic, to make the Keem Bay road. It was a clear night with a full moon and the breakers were pounding the rocks below. He felt a strange loneliness. He reached the entrance gates to the Corrymore House.'

'Is this a real or imagined place?' whispered Tarja.

'It's real all right and not far from where we are now,' said Pat.

"Beautiful view but I would prefer my bed at this unearthly hour...I'll be home soon," he thought.

'How do you know what he thought?' said a voice from the back of the pub.

'None of that from you,' said Kate pointing her yellow duster towards the heckler.

'I think he's making it up,' said another voice.

'Ghost stories are not real, people make them up,' said Tarja, turning towards the voice. Pat took another eyeful when she was looking away. There was no doubt, she was a beautiful. With that red hair, she could have been a local girl although her complexion was different. Compared to their ruddy features, she looked sallow skinned.

Pat looked away quickly as she turned back towards him.

'Do you agree with me?' she asked in a low voice.

'Of course I do.' He wasn't sure what he had agreed to. Distracted, he had lost the thread of the conversation. If he kept looking at her, he would agree to anything. He was drinking too much.

Coleman continued. 'The Sergeant remembered with a smile his grandfather's tales about the ghostly presences encountered on the Keem Bay road.

"No one should be out there late at night," he would say. Grandmother was more pragmatic. "Watch out for the live ones, they can do you more harm," she would say.'

'Start praying, we're all for it now,' said the heckler with mock fear in his voice.

'Opposite the gates to the Corrymore House the engine cut out. He engaged the starter several times without success.

"Better not to run down the battery, probably dirt in the carburettor – I'll leave it a few minutes and try again," he thought.

'He knew the history of the Corrymore House. The disgraced landlord, Captain Boycott built it in the 17th Century as a refuge. His tenants responded to his harsh measures by "Boycotting" him and in the process gave the English language a new word.'

'You must tell me more about that later,' said Tarja to Pat.

'O sure I will,' said Pat, but there wouldn't be any later if he had anything to do with it. The alcohol, the girl, all of it was clouding his judgement. Once sober in the morning, his grief over the loss of his family would return in full force.

'Still thinking about Captain Boycott, the Sergeant looked towards the Corrymore House and to his surprise the entrance gates started to swing open.

"Caught in the breeze coming down from Slievemore Mountain," he thought. In the background the mountain loomed huge in the night sky. He was cold and shivering.

'That would be a north-westerly coming over the shoulder of Slievemore,' said an old fisherman in a peaked cap sipping away at his pint.

Coleman continued. "I must stop this nonsense...I shouldn't have listened to my grandfather's ghost stories when I was a child," he thought.

'Then he heard the clip-clop of horse's hooves above the sound of the Atlantic breakers.'

'Not a good sound to hear up there late at night,' said the heckler derisively. The drinkers let it pass.

'Slowly through the gates came a black hearse pulled by four horses with their heads elaborately decorated with white and black feathers. Three men, in top hats and long coats, followed carrying a coffin. He could hear his grandfather's words.

"If in the dead of the night you see three men carrying a coffin, then the only way to prevent your own death is to become the fourth pall-bearer," he would say.

'It was all surreal and the Sergeant was shivering although it was not a cold night.

'I'm beginning to feel the chill myself,' said the heckler shivering.

'He is witty,' said Tarja in a low voice to Pat.

'Clogs is too clever at times; he's caused a few rows in here with his cutting remarks,' said Pat, looking towards the heckler.

'There must be some logical explanation to this, low blood sugar or something,' the Sergeant thought.

'That's the way you feel when they come for you,' said an old man sitting at the bar, pretending to know the spirit world.

Coleman went on. 'Is this story true?' whispered Tarja.

'Of course,' Pat whispered back, and winked at her. She seemed perplexed. Here he went again making an idiot of himself. Maybe a wink in Finland meant something different, and maybe he had made an indecent suggestion, as the Redemptionists would say. What could he follow that with? He should keep his mouth shut and head for home. Then her face relaxed and she smiled,

'You are joking, yes.' She gave him another playful kick under the table. The kicks were getting stronger; it was a pity, he wasn't wearing shin guards. If this went on much more he would have black and blue shins in the morning.

Pat nodded his head. That was a close call. He'd probably taken some liberty, but he didn't even know what it was. He'd have to be careful with this one. Women were difficult enough without them being foreign as well. Coleman was getting on with the story.

'Transported by some unknown force to Slievemore cemetery, the scene changed suddenly for the Sergeant. It was a familiar place; he had buried his parents there. The ground underfoot was mucky and his feet were wet. Strangely, his fear had gone, and he now felt comfortable there. He watched as the three men carried the coffin to the open grave. Through the swirling mist, the word Sergeant…was visible on a newly erected headstone.

"A member of the force," he thought.

The priest carried out the burial ceremony and a lone piper at the top of the cemetery played a lament. He could distinctly hear each shovel of earth thump on the coffin, as they filled in the grave.

'We don't have pipers playing at funerals at home. I think it's so nice.' In what seemed like an afterthought, she took a ladylike sip from her pint; there was something about her, even when drinking a pint.

'We don't have many doing it around here either,' said Pat. She listened to the story, but he had the feeling that she would prefer to talk. In truth, he wouldn't have minded that himself. A wiser man would go home at this stage. He could hear Coleman's voice droning on.

'As if woken suddenly from a dream, the Sergeant was back in his car driving past the Corrymore House gates. It took him a few seconds to adjust.

"I must have dozed for a minute or two and had a nightmare, lucky I didn't go off the road," he thought.

'A few people went off that road up there right enough,' said the old man passing his pint up to the bar for a refill. Kate didn't try to stop him interrupting, as he was helping the story along.

'The Sergeant remembered there was another bit to his grandfather's ghost story "They will take with them, anyone who sees anything up there," were his chilling words.

'When he got home, his wife Mairead had prepared an early breakfast of toast and marmalade.'

'Not many of them would do that for you nowadays,' said the old man, settling back in his seat with his pint.

'You're right there, not like the old days,' was the chorus from around the bar.

'They are lucky their wives and girlfriends are not here,' said Tarja. Pat smiled.

'His feet were wet and covered in mud, "probably from walking around Keem," he thought.

"I'm not going out to anymore late calls from strangers, some of the younger lads can do it," he said.

'He told Mairead about his experience and she thought he must have dozed off while driving and his grandfather's ghost stories buried somewhere in his unconscious did the rest. Anyway it sounded silly-like a UFO story. If it ever got out, he would be the laughing stock of the county.'

'Are there any island UFO stories?' asked Tarja, giving Pat another nudge with her toe under the table, as if to get him to concentrate. If only she knew it, his attention was fully on her.

'UFO's haven't taken on here yet.'

'It was strange the emergency call appeared to have come from the old coastguard station. Yet when he got there, it was all shuttered up for the winter.

"We never talked too much about the incident, but it changed him, he became more aware of his own mortality," Mairead used to say.'

'If he had a blessing from a bishop, he'd have been all right,' said the old fisherman.

'Aye that's true,' said another old fellow. They had cornered the market on how to deal with the spirit world.

Coleman continued.

'Eleven months later in the autumn, the silent killer, pancreatic cancer, claimed another victim, the Sergeant. They buried him on a misty day in Slievemore cemetery and a lone piper played a lament. The local undertaker, Michael Moran, had imported a horse drawn hearse from England, which he restored to its original state, black enamel finish embossed with gold leaf decorations and leather upholstery. The horses pulling the hearse had been expensive. They had come from the Curragh and were jet black.

"My little bit of madness," was how the undertaker described his new purchase.'

'Did that happen? Those old hearses are so lovely.'

'No, it's all made up,' said Pat.

'The Sergeant was the first person buried, using the new hearse. The mourners complained about how the wet, mucky ground in the cemetery was destroying their shoes.

'Mairead didn't marry again. She taught art in the local schools to many generations of island children.

She lived well into old age, and her final resting place was beside her husband in the Slievemore Cemetery.'

'I wouldn't like to go up there on my own late at night,' said the old man with a mock shiver.

'A true believer,' said Pat, laughing. The old man believed in ghosts as much as Pat believed in Santa Clause. There was cheering and back clapping for Coleman when he finished the story. He returned to his seat beside the skipper. As usual they ignored each other.

'I want to hear more stories,' said a more cheerful Tarja.

10

The singing continued and Kate disappeared into the small kitchen and returned with sandwiches from the fridge.

'None of you have eaten anything for awhile, these are all at cost price,' she said, leaving a tray stacked with sandwiches on the counter.

'I think she likes to mother people,' said Tarja, unwrapping the plastic from a packet of tuna sandwiches.

'We're her family. She owns the pub, but likes people to think that she is only the barmaid,' said Pat, taking a bite out of a ham sandwich. He hadn't eaten since breakfast, and he needed food.

He wondered what Tarja was thinking about it all, probably bored to tears listening to their stories and songs and being too polite to leave. He should give her an opportunity to go without putting his foot in it. Knowing him, she would probably think he was trying to get off with her. That was an old-fashioned way, to describe it, in the wham bang and thank you generation. If he could read her at all, she would be more direct about that kind of thing. He wasn't going there.

'I don't know how we get up in the morning with stories and songs going on for half the night. Are you tired of it?'

'No, I like it. It's so different and it's helping me get to know the people.'

'What have you got to know about me then?' Typical of him, it was out before he had time to consider what he was saying. If he could take it back, he would. He was somehow giving the wrong signal, that he had a romantic interest in her.

'Not enough, but I feel you are sad. You are the peacemaker and your uncle is lucky to have you on the board? Maybe I'm saying too much?'

'Not sure he sees it that way.' He could feel her waiting for him to say more, but the arrival of the blacksmith gave him a welcome reprieve.

The blacksmith came through the doorway and stopped to look around the bar. The patrons greeted him warmly.

'Hi smithy.'

'Hi there, I'm molokered today,' he said as he went up to the bar, ordered a drink and took out a red handkerchief to wipe some of the grime and sweat from his face.

'What does that mean?' asked Tarja. The moment had passed and Pat felt they were back on an even keel.

'It means that he feels like a renovated old hat. He's joking of course,' said Pat. He had narrowly got out of an awkward situation. The blacksmith returned with his pint to sit with them.

'Have you ever tried to launch the life-raft?' he asked.

'Like many other jobs we never got around to it.'

Pat knew where this was going, the blacksmith's fifteen minutes of fame. All he needed was one or more willing listener. He knew the story well from hearing it many times before. The trick was to pretend that it was new to him. The drink helped; sober it would be hard to listen to it again.

'In the Maritime Inscription we practiced life-raft drill every week,' said the blacksmith.

'What was the Maritime Inscription?' asked Tarja.

'Few people know about it. We guarded the Irish Coast from invasion during the Second World War,' he settled into his seat for a session.

'I don't know anything about Ireland during the War but I'm interested in it,' said Tarja. The blacksmith took a gulp from his pint and went on with his story. At the start of the Second World War, he was an apprentice blacksmith in Dublin and, with a fellow apprentice, joined the Maritime Inscription. He served as an able seaman until the end of the war.

'A blacksmith is a useful man at sea, he could shoe sea horses,' joked Clogs, the heckler amid much laughter. Pat turned to see him leering at them, drunk as usual with his handlebar moustache flecked with froth. Even sober, Clogs had the annoying habit of interrupting stories. The blacksmith glared at Clogs before Tarja distracted him.

'Was it full-time?' she asked, looking at Pat for support. He didn't have to say anything - the blacksmith was back into his stride again.

'We were part-time volunteers, commanded by commissioned Irish army officers.'

'Army?' said Tarja.

'O yes,' said the blacksmith going silent for effect. A gifted storyteller, thought Pat. First time listeners assumed that he had made a mistake.

'It wasn't until the end of emergency that the government transferred the Maritime Inscription from the Army to its rightful home, the Navy,' he said.

'They then renamed it - An Slua Muiri,' he added after a pause while he put his pint on a tablemat. Next, Pat saw the blacksmith take off his cap and put it on the table beside his pint. He did this when he was comfortable with the people around him. He was enjoying being the centre of attention - he used every opportunity to tell his story to any new people he met. His first faltering step into the military was his call-up to the Portobello barracks in Dublin, to receive his navy kit.

'I felt privileged to put it on,' he said, standing up and saluting at the memory. The drinkers stood to attention and saluted as well. It was pure theatre.

He marched in the Easter Parade with the other able seamen of Maritime Inscription. They were the first to wear Irish Naval uniforms.

'The uniform was lovely, proper bell-bottomed trousers and the sailors' hat had Eire written on the front of it,' said the blacksmith.

'What did that mean?' asked Tarja.

'It means Ireland in the Irish language,' said the blacksmith, wiping his forehead and eyes with his handkerchief.

'The stores kitted out each recruit with a pair of trousers, socks, boots, two jackets and an overcoat. The boots came above the ankles and the leather was soft, they fitted like a glove,' he said.

As ordered, at the end of the war, each recruit, returned his kit, minus the overcoat, back to the military.

'The coat lasted for years, it was nearly impossible to wear it out,' said the blacksmith.

'What training did you get?' asked Tarja as a few other drinkers sat down at the table to listen to the blacksmith's story for the umpteenth time.

'A good question,' said the blacksmith, you're the first to ask me that, and it's what turned us into fighting men.'

'Dad's Army, feather-bed soldiers,' shouted Clogs from the back of the group.

'Best of good order for the speaker or you're barred,' said Kate, putting the empty sandwich plates into the dishwasher.

Ignoring Clogs, the blacksmith continued to describe the training.

'The weekly sessions held in the Atlantic Hotel, Alexander Basin in the Dublin's Dockland, provided our main tuition. The Atlantic Hotel in its glory days, accommodated passengers ferried in from Atlantic liners anchored in Dublin bay, for a sightseeing tour of the city. Training in PE and rifle drill was the responsibility of the Petty Officer; and two civilian yachtsmen instructed the recruits in seamanship. Up to a hundred of us attended these weekly sessions.'

'For me and the other naval recruits, our field training was a week's camping in a field in Skerries. The first field exercise was digging a latrine. The recruits dug a long trench, about half a metre deep at the bottom of the field, well away from the sleeping tents. The loo seats were butter boxes with holes cut in the top, and spaced a metre apart on the trench. They added lime to the trench at the end of each day. Tarpaulin held up on poles provided some privacy, but not much. I suppose we didn't expect it; we were fighting men,' said the blacksmith, straightening up in his seat to dramatise the point.

'During our week at field training, the US dropped the atomic bomb on Hiroshima. We didn't know the horror of it then.'

Tarja shivered, 'I feel like someone is walking over my grave,' she said.

'It's like the Twin Towers or the shooting of JFK. Life is never the same again,' said Pat.

'Well that's true,' said the blacksmith,

'I'll tell you about the connection with JFK. Fill them up again,' he called to Kate.

Pat would have preferred to buy his own drinks, but the blacksmith wanted to pay for this round. Pat would return the favour later.

'We trained on the same type of torpedo boat, USA PT 109, as captained by Lieutenant (Junior Grade) John F. Kennedy when the

Japanese destroyer Amagiri rammed them,' said the blacksmith with great self-importance.

'Imagine that,' said someone in the crowd.

The torpedo boat training trips in Dublin bay were the high point of his naval service.

'It was great, a torpedo boat like in the films,' said the blacksmith. Then he went into his well-rehearsed technical pitch.

'Armed for fighting men, our motor torpedo boat (MTB) built by Vospers UK and made from wood, mostly plywood had two torpedo tubes, four depth charges, and a Bofore gun in the bows. We made our own depth charges from barrels packed with explosives.'

'Did anyone ever fire the gun?' asked the heckler moving forward to the front of the group.

This was a challenge to the blacksmith's authority and with impeccable timing; he took a sip from his pint before answering.

'In wartime ammunition is scarce and every round must count,' he answered.

'I suppose you could have thrown rotten eggs at them,' shouted Clogs, grinning and looking around for support from the group. There was laughter and some guffaws.

'Right, I'm going to bar you,' said Kate, lifting the flap of the counter and coming into the main bar to escort the heckler Clogs from the building.

'Leave him to me. I'll kick his backside down the street,' raged the skipper, sliding off his bar stool.

'No, no sit down,' said Pat, 'let him be, we need people with different ways of seeing life.'

'A boot up his backside would soon open his eyes,' snarled the skipper. Nevertheless, he sat down for Pat.

'You're on notice, a troublemaker,' said Kate to Clogs.

Here I go again, the peacemaker in any hassle involving the skipper thought Pat. Order restored, the blacksmith continued with the story. 'The officer in charge taught each recruit how to handle the torpedo boat. The main exercise was to steer the boat in a straight line towards a landmark on the shore. The blacksmith brought his hand down in a chopping movement for emphasis before saying, 'Straight ahead.' Keeping a straight line proved difficult for many of the recruits, and they practiced the manoeuvre time and again until the officer declared their progress satisfactory.

'We had an anniversary dance for years afterwards, togged out in full naval dress. It was something else,' said the blacksmith.

'Tripping the light fantastic,' said a joking voice from the back of the group.

'We stood up like men when needed,' snorted the blacksmith.

'Yea, sure you did,' someone quipped.

'Young people today have no respect,' announced the blacksmith putting his cap back on his head and sinking into a grumpy silence. The fiddler started to play in the background.

'It's called *An Cualuain*,' said Pat to Tarja.

'I haven't heard it before,' said Tarja, turning around in her seat to look at the fiddler.

Pat could see the drunken skipper, silent and morose, leaning his elbows on the bar counter. Coleman left him and came over to sit with Pat.

'What about the German paratroopers landing on Achill?' asked Pat, looking directly at the blacksmith? It was an attempt to bring him out of his sulk.

'Let someone else tell her about it,' said the blacksmith not yet over the putdown he had suffered.

'You were probably in the service at the time,' said Pat to the blacksmith, trying to get him involved.

'I would have liked to have been here for it, but the country needed me at the time,' said the blacksmith, stirred a little out of his huff.

'Do you want to hear it then?' asked Pat, pushing his pint away from the edge of the table in case it spilled.

'Yes, I definitely do,' said Tarja. 'I have a special interest in the Second World War. They shot my grandfather dead.' Her eyes clouded over with tears.

'Sorry to hear that,' said Pat. 'How did it happen?' He handed her his handkerchief.

'It's not clear. He was crossing the street, and the only shot fired killed him. It could have been either side. He was a well-respected banker,' sobbed Tarja, drying her eyes with the handkerchief. She explained the crisis in Finland during the Second World War.

'At its closest point Russia is only thirty-five kilometres away, and they claim that this region of Finland is rightfully theirs. That's why Chernobyl worried us so much; it's fairly near. We Finns didn't have a large army to defend us and Russia took the opportunity of the Second World War to invade. We retaliated by inviting the Germans to dislodge the Russians. We made a terrible mistake.' Tarja gave back the handkerchief.

'The Germans commandeered the factories and used the output to further their war effort against the rest of Europe. It's a long story and we suffered a lot during the war.'

'Good people die in all wars,' sighed Pat.

They were silent for a few minutes before Pat started his story.

11

Pat was talking more than he had ever talked in a pub; he normally he preferred to stay in the background. It was the heady mix of alcohol and the presence of a beautiful woman, the age-old trap. What was it someone said to him? Real men don't mind making fools of themselves. The way he was going, he couldn't avoid it. A wise man would shut up at this stage, but it was too late. He started telling the well-known island story for her benefit.

'It's a strange tale,' said Pat as he straightened up in his seat.

'The tales in here are always strange,' said Clogs at the next table.

'Not half as strange as some of the people in here,' said Kate, collecting empty glasses from Clogs' table.

Pat was aware that Tarja was staring at him, and he pretended not to notice. He didn't think he looked strange, although people jokingly called him Black Beard or Bluebeard or whatever. She was easy on the eye, but he didn't look directly at her, better not to show too much of a drunken interest by gawking at her. Focus on the story, although he could probably tell it on automatic pilot.

'It was a moonlit night in November near the end of the Second World War and an islander cycling home heard the drone of aircraft engines overhead. He dismounted to walk up a hill and saw a plane coming in from the Atlantic direction. It was flying almost as low as the rooftops. Four parachutes dropped from the plane and landed near the Atlantic drive. The plane flew around in a half circle, passed above his head and went back out over the Atlantic. He thought there was some kind of a cross on the fuselage. Frightened, he lay in a ditch for hours in case it circled back.'

'Your nights are so bright,' said Tarja. She seemed to be talking directly to him. With alcohol onboard he could get ridiculous. Next he'd be imagining that she had a romantic interest in him. Sober he wouldn't even go there.

'A drunken mirage, the villagers claimed,' said Pat.

'That same man could take a good drop,' said Coleman, raising his glass to his mouth and taking a drink as if to reinforce his opinion.

'Later that night, a woman living alone in the centre of the island was woken by a noise outside her house.'

'She lived next to your aunt,' stated the blacksmith, getting back into the story.

'That's right,' said Pat.

'She thought the fox had come for her chickens. There wasn't time to light the oil-lamp, she rushed out of the house and grabbed a walking stick as she went.'

'Who needs a lamp on a bright moonlit night?' said Clogs with more than a hint of mockery in his voice. Pat didn't need to respond; Kate retaliated.

'She was an old woman with poor sight, you idiot.'

'The woman moved silently so not to disturb the fox, hoping to kill him with a blow from the stick and save her chickens.'

'It's so sweet that she had chickens. It's my dream to live in the country surrounded by livestock,' said Tarja as she placed her hand on Pat's on the tabletop. This was getting ridiculous. He pulled his hand away. Near drunk, she was unaware of it. He wouldn't buy any more drinks for her. She was a powerful distraction, and he would need to concentrate on the tale he was trying to tell.

'The old woman passed the derelict family house, her father's birthplace, on the way to the chicken run. She heard the murmur of voices from inside the building.

Moving cautiously forward, she looked through a gap in the stonework and saw two German paratroopers, with swastikas stitched to their sleeves, sitting against the wall facing the doorway.'

'I didn't know the Germans had come to Ireland?' said Tarja looking at Pat. She had her hands stretched out on the tabletop, and he could see her long fingers with perfect nails, glittering in the light. They must be artificial; he couldn't take his eyes of them.

'Only in ones and twos, but the blacksmith knows more about the last world war than anyone here if he cares to tell us,' said Pat.

'Aha maybe later,' said the blacksmith, taking a drink from his pint.

He looked like a black-and-white minstrel. His mouth highlighted in froth, against the grime on his face.

'Tell me more, Pat,' said Tarja, shifting about on the hard wooden bench but keeping her hands outstretched on the tabletop.

'Right,' said Pat. He'd be talking all-night if this one got her way. It was impressive that she could understand their accents.

'The German paratroopers had their pistols placed on a stone beside them. They had taken off their caps and the perspiration was running down their faces. Two kitbags lay at their feet, and they were drinking from bottles while consulting a map opened across their knees.'

'They wore leather jackets and long boots up to their knees,' she said afterwards.

'She saw an awful lot and the Germans must have had bad sight as well, if they didn't see the light from the lamp,' said Clogs.

'Be quiet and let him finish the story,' said a voice from the back of the room.

'Shut up,' came the chorus.

'She thought the sound of her heart beating and her laboured breathing would alert them to her presence. Terrified, she got back indoors as quickly as she could and locked all the doors and windows. She kept a vigil behind the lace curtains.'

'The valley of the squinting windows,' said Clogs with a jeer. Tired of his interruptions, no one responded.

'With kitbags across their shoulders, she saw them leave, and take a straight route across the bog to Bullsmouth.

'Bent double under the weight of the kitbags, they, nonetheless trotted like ponies across the bog,' she confided to me years later with fear in her voice.

'She watched until they disappeared like ghosts into the mist.'

'The Celtic mist, all we need now is the weird music,' said Clogs.

'Celtic mist, it sounds interesting,' said Tarja resting her elbows on the table.

'It's myth and legend,' said Pat, taking a sip from his drink. She looked so vulnerable surrounded by all the male drinkers. Pat's instinct was to take her out of this place. Focus on the story and stop being daft, he told himself.

'For a while the old woman wondered if she had imagined it, but then there were empty bottles to prove that it was real. At first light she ran to my aunt's house for protection and slept there every night from then on. Her neighbours visited the old house and found empty schnapps bottles, smashed into smithereens. Asked later why she didn't tell the authority, she said, 'It wouldn't do any good'.

'A Bullsmouth man up early that morning, saw a submarine surface in the bay and a dinghy, with two onboard, rowing out to it.

'Never heard of a Bullsmouth man being up early,' said Clogs stretching up and placing his pint on the ledge running along the back wall.

'How would you know? You have never got out of your bed before midday,' said Kate, loading up the dishwasher.

'The haze on the water prevented him from seeing more of the action. After taking the passengers onboard, the submarine submerged, leaving a few ripples on the surface.'

'Is this true or a tall story?' asked Tarja.

'It's true,' said Pat.

'What were they doing there?'

'We never found out. Hitler had to have Achill after he conquered Paris,' joked Pat.

'It seems Hitler did consider invading Ireland and Achill would have given him the deep-water ports and the access he needed, to control the Atlantic. It probably was a reconnaissance mission. The Germans must have considered it important to warrant an aircraft, a submarine, and two highly trained paratroopers.'

'What about the kitbags, attached to the other two parachutes?' asked the blacksmith? He had another view.

'For the Third Reich, the paratroopers were hiding something of value in the bog for collecting later when the war was over. The man in Bullsmouth had said nothing about kitbags, and he couldn't have missed seeing them in the dinghy. Somewhere in the bog they had buried the kitbags probably with sealed containers of something valuable. I bet they're booby-trapped,' declared the blacksmith, looking smug and drinking slowly from his pint, having raised himself back to his rightful standing in the pub as the man who knew a thing or two. Tarja winked at Pat and smiled, they both laughed.

12

The monastery bell, ringing out six o'clock silenced the pub for a moment; and some of the patrons crossed themselves.

It got Pat thinking about the Catholic faith, all bells and the smell of burning incense. In the Middle Ages, it blocked out BO in chapels throughout Europe. Well, that's what the teachers told him at school. After a few days on the boat with the skipper and Coleman, the smell of incense wouldn't go amiss. The bells were something else. He wondered what Tarja was thinking about it all.

She was keeping her opinions to herself, maybe in case she offended them. Perhaps he was being too sensitive. It would be great to get inside her head and see what was going on there. He'd drive himself mad trying to predict what this foreign girl was thinking. He had enough trouble trying to work out the women he knew, let alone a woman who wasn't from these parts.

The blacksmith took off his cap, and, holding it in his hand, crossed himself and mumbled a prayer. Pat took no action apart from taking a slug from his pint. Out of the corner of his eye, he could see that she was watching him. It probably was his imagination, but he felt she was waiting for a response from him.

'Imagine the job of ringing the bell that many times a day. The first time at six in the morning, again at six in the evening, at midday for the angelus, and yet again at twelve at night,' said the blacksmith, putting his cap back on his head.

'It would drive you mental.' Coleman grimaced and looked in Pat's direction for a reply.

'I bet there's an electronic gismo doing it now, though the Franciscans stick to the old ways,' said Pat, making an effort to stay engaged in the conversation. This was his longest stay in a pub for some time.

'How do the monks, shut up in the monastery spend their time?' asked Tarja.

'No wine making, unfortunately. They follow the rule of St. Francis in prayer and meditation,' said Pat with a grin.

'If they made wine, we'd all have joined,' said the blacksmith, glancing around the pub looking for likely candidates.

'The skipper would have been first in line.' Pat said, gesturing towards his uncle slumped over the bar. Kate had made a pillow from crisp new dishtowels and had pushed them under his forehead.

'She has a soft spot for the skipper. I don't know why they don't get it together,' said the blacksmith, drying perspiration from his face with the red hankie.

'Behind every successful man is a good woman,' said Coleman, as if he was the first to have thought up the phrase.

'An amazed woman,' said Tarja, laughing. Pat could see she was getting merry and gradually loosing her inhibitions. Hope she didn't go all giggly and silly.

'Ah, by what I see, you could be right enough,' said the blacksmith.

'Tell me about the monks,' said Tarja, giving Pat a playful kick under the table.

'We all went to school up there for all the good it did us. Do you remember the toilets?' said Coleman. He rested his good hand on the table in front of him, and kept his other hand hidden inside the front of his anorak.

'I remember well,' said Pat. He had a few tales about the toilets - one he could tell her and the others he could not. The toilets were five brick cubicles built over a stream which flushed them out effectively in the winter, but not so well in the summer when you could smell them a mile away. The top and bottom of the doors cut away ensured that pupils didn't stay long in there on a cold day. They reminded us of the Victorian beach huts used by the ladies of the day to undress before bathing. Infested with rat families; the toilets had baby rats, parent rats and grandparent rats.'

'Tell her about the shotgun,' said the blacksmith.

'I'll never forget it. I think it was summertime because all the windows were open,' said Pat. 'Brother Ambrose, our primary teacher, came back from lunch in the Monastery with a shotgun under his arm, and he put it down on the table in front of him. Shotguns – or indeed, any guns - were rare on the island, and the pupils, enthralled by it at first, gradually over the course of the afternoon, lost interest in it. Brother Ambrose was waiting for the rats to congregate outside the toilets as they did every day, during the school term, to eat the remains of the pupil's lunches. He didn't tell us what he intended to do.'

The blacksmith looked drowsy.

'When he was ready, he picked up the shotgun, and from where he was sitting at the table, fired both barrels out through the open window.'

'That was so irresponsible,' said Tarja, shaking her head in disbelief.

'We didn't think of it like that - it was the noise in the small classroom that got to us. I was deaf for the rest of the day.' Pat covered his ears with his hands.

'He had killed six rats and he invited all of us out to see them. My stomach was sick from all the splattered blood and guts on the ground. I still jump when a gun goes off.'

'The Franciscans educated Pope Julius II,' said the Blacksmith, pausing to see if anyone else could add further information. 'He didn't join the order of St Francis, but remained a member of the secular clergy, until he became Pope. His nephew, also a Pope, employed Michelangelo to paint the ceiling of the Sistine Chapel.'

'I've seen the ceiling and it's so wonderful,' said Tarja

'It's strange the type of people that monasteries attracted,' said Coleman looking questioningly at Pat for some input.

'OK then. It's another World War II tale, as well as Brother Ambrose's story,' said Pat, glancing in Tarja's direction.

'Oh, I want to hear it. I'm a collector of Second World War stories, and I hope to get them on radio in Finland,' said Tarja.

As always, Pat was second-guessing; these stories probably helped her to cope with the loss of her grandfather, reminding her that others suffered as well, or maybe she was just collecting material for her programme.

'Brother Ambrose was an unlikely war hero. It was difficult to picture the paunchy elderly monk, in his brown habit and open-toed sandals, as a nineteen-year-old Gunner on a warship. He came from Belfast, joined the Navy during the war. They decorated him for bravery.

'How do you know all this?' asked Tarja.

'Good question. His wartime activities became known somehow although he had nothing to do with the publicity,' said Pat, nodding his head in her direction, before continuing with the story.

'Joining the Franciscans was like joining the French Foreign Legion. They gave you a different name, you became Brother somebody or other, and they discouraged you from using your birth or family name again. Your past disappeared, unless you decided to reveal something about it, and for that you needed permission from the monastery superior.'

'When I'm low, I've often thought it would be great to get away from it all and join something like the foreign legion,' said Tarja.

'You're not alone there,' said Pat.

Coleman and the Blacksmith dozed off. Tarja cupped her hands under her chin and moved her face nearer to him. It was closer than he would have liked. It was distracting him.

Pat continued with the story.

'When it became common knowledge, Brother Ambrose decided to use his experience to tell his pupils of the awfulness of war. He used to say,

'When you've been away, the greatest sight in the world is the port of Dublin on your way back.'

'He was antiwar before his time,' said Tarja. She seemed to be studying his face, and this close, she probably could count the individual hairs in his beard.

'The destroyer Brother Ambrose served on during the war was protecting the Atlantic convoys from attack by the German submarines and aircraft. The accommodation was basic. There was no privacy for the enlisted men.'

'I would hate that, at times I need to get away on my own,' said Tarja.

Bunks were steel with no mattress or covering. He slept in a sleeping bag with a kitbag for a pillow, without taking off his clothes. The sea got in everywhere and there wasn't a dry space on the destroyer.

'It was no fun getting into a damp sleeping bag in wet clothes and lying on a cold slab of steel,' he would say.

'With all kinds of skin sores from the salt water, it must have been unbearable,' said Tarja, now so close to Pat that he could smell the Guinness on her breath.

'Brother Ambrose didn't say that, but now that you mention it, they must have had all kinds of raw sores on their skin. Working or sleeping was the gruelling rota. At times, the call to battle stations would blare out across the ship as he was about to doze off; and then for days, they would play cat and mouse with a submarine. In our minds, we were there with him,' said Pat.

Tarja was too close to him, and he shut his eyes, making it look like he was concentrating on the story, to get some distance from her. She gently cupped her hands around his face.

'Keep your eyes open or I'll think you have fallen asleep like the others,' she said with some amusement. He would have to think of another way to get some space.

He went on with the story.

'There was always that strange smell on the boat, the smell of fear, Brother Ambrose would tell us.'

'I heard of that before; it was the same on fighter planes,' said Tarja.

Pat's gaze rested on the blue translucent light of the insect catcher over the entrance door. It emitted a low hiss. Fly-paper, brown and blackened with age was hanging from the roof above the insect catcher. Dead bodies of flies rotting away into spots of gunk, almost covered the fly-paper. It started him off, thinking of the decomposing bodies of soldiers on the battlefield, turning into putrefying flesh. He could feel himself getting nauseated at the thought of the flies, from the fly-paper, falling into someone's pint. It must happen with pints left on the ledge under the fly-paper, between sups. He didn't tell her his thoughts but continued with his recollections of what Brother Ambrose said about war.

"Sometimes in my sleep, I can still hear the screams of men burned alive during an attack," Brother Ambrose told the class as he talked about the horrors of war. He forgot he was talking to schoolchildren as he recalled these terrible memories of horrific death.

'Our glasses are nearly empty, I'll get a refill,' said Pat, getting up with the glasses in his hand and going up to the bar. Kate filled up two fresh glasses.

'You're getting on well with that one?' He thought he detected cattiness in her voice.

'No, it's just that she's a stranger in here.' Sounded rich coming from a grown man; he was apologising for his behaviour, as if he were a schoolboy caught stealing apples. He returned with the pints and Tarja had to move back to make room for the full glasses. He had some of his space back.

Pat stopped in mid sentence, mortified with embarrassment. It sounded like an explosion. The blacksmith had farted in his sleep. The noise was one thing and the smell was something else, like rotten eggs mixed with dead animals. He couldn't look at her. Should he let it go or say something that was his dilemma. If only he could think of a witty remark, or one that wasn't crude. He wasn't with the lads now.

'The Guinness causes that,' he said, pretending to glance at the blacksmith sitting beside him, but focussing on her out of the corner of his eye.

'It's methane gas and the body produces half a litre of it every day,' she said, obviously adopting a scientific approach. The smell seemed to hang around like a cloud in the small snug. Pat pointed to a can of air freshener on the corner of the bar. Tarja stretched out, got it and sprayed its fragrance around the snug. The blacksmith snored.

'He's so tired, he's much too old to be working,' said Tarja.

'Work is his life, he'd be dead without it, but you'll need to follow him around for the rest of the night with the air freshener.'

'There's more?'

'That's only the first tonight.'

'I see why Kate keeps this air freshener handy, and I hope she has more in stock.'

'We'd be in a right state if she runs out.' They both laughed.

Then he remembered something else Brother Ambrose had told the class. He could tell her now.

'The curious thing about allied submarines, was their need to surface a mile or so from port, and open the hatches for up to a day, to allow the smells that had built up to escape. The German subs were probably the same.'

71

The Blacksmith woke up. Pat was thinking how difficult it was to take anyone seriously who had just farted.

'Sorry I was asleep, carry on with the story.'

'You're tired after a day's work,' said Tarja.

'Ah, I must have been, it's old age,' said the blacksmith.

'I hope they need boys like me in heaven, although it seems they have hoofs to take care of down in the other place.' They all laughed.

'Brother Ambrose told us that three deckhands and a Messerschmitt pilot died in one particular battle. The gunners on the destroyers hit the plane, and it left a trail of black smoke across the sky. They could hear the wail of the engine as it crashed into the stern of the destroyer, hitting the depth charges. They exploded in a fireball. The fire-fighters were quickly on to it, but many suffered serious burns. Tremendous heat generated inside the asbestos suits worn by fire-fighters, and they were on a special drinking regime to prevent dehydration,' said Pat.

'I could see the terror in the pilot's eyes as he came in level with us. I will never forget it', Brother Ambrose told us. He would stop abruptly and start to pray for the repose of the soul of the pilot and all others who died in wars.'

They were silent for a few minutes and Coleman, who had woken up, started a conversation about football. Tarja seemed surprised at how quickly they changed the topic. They were always at that, changing the conversation suddenly from one subject to another. She was probably curious to know what thinking led Brother Ambrose, a gunner on the deck of a wartime destroyer, to a monastery on an isolated island.

'Was Brother Ambrose happy with his life?' She was frowning when she asked the question. Coleman and the blacksmith, involved in a football discussion, looked at her blankly. It was almost as if their minds couldn't make the transition. They didn't respond and Pat felt an urgency to say something.

'We never thought of that as children. He was cranky sometimes.' That might satisfy her and the conversation could get back to the football. The two self-styled football experts at the table were discussing the relative merits of various teams. It would be difficult to steer the conversation back to monks and the Second World War, although it seemed she was going to try.

'Were monks running away from their past?'

The blacksmith grimaced, annoyed at the intrusion into his theories on football.

'Or unrequited love,' smiled Pat. 'We know little about them, and it's hard to find a common thread apart from religion.'

'Come here smithy and referee.' Two youngish men with tattoos and skinhead haircuts were calling the blacksmith over to referee an arm-wrestling match. He finished his pint and went with Coleman to the back of the room to take control of the match.

13

Pat stayed with her - it would be the height of bad manners to leave her alone in a strange pub surrounded by a crowd of hellions. He was drinking too much. She was naturally polite; and he thought she was showing a romantic interest him. Maybe she fancied him. Dangerous thinking this for a drunk, it was definitely the alcohol talking.

As the evening wore on, she removed the band tying back her ponytail and let her red hair fall down around her face. From time to time, she flicked it back out of her eyes.

'Closing time,' shouted Kate, 'Time to go home for anyone with a home to go to.'

When she stood up, Tarja was shaky on her feet.

'My head is light. I can't feel the floor,' she said as she struggled for balance.

'Oops, you're not used to drinking Guinness; it has that effect on people.' Pat placed his hands on her shoulder to steady her.

'I am a little drunk, yes.'

She put her arms around Pat and started kissing him, much to his embarrassment and to the amusement of the onlookers. She hung on to him as he helped her into the taxi. She wouldn't let go until he agreed to take her back to the hotel. She'd be waking up with one hell of a hangover, he thought.

'How long have you been a fisherman?' Tarja asked in the taxi.

'Not long. I was in Dublin before that.'

'Why did you come back to the island?'

'It's a long story.'

He was silent for a time.

'I can't forget the morning that my wife Hazel found our baby Mark, dead in his cot. His face the colour of parchment and his little hands were clasping the blanket. She tried to revive him, and I called for an ambulance. I couldn't take it. I passed out and the ambulance crew revived me. I went to the   hospital in the same ambulance as my dead son, Mark.

Hazel blamed herself for Mark's death and she never got over the guilt.

Then she got sick; the doctors thought it was a breast cyst, and in someone so young they didn't expect that it was anything serious. They were optimistic the biopsy would confirm it was a benign lump but, unfortunately, it was an aggressive breast cancer. It ravaged her body until she was bedridden and needed constant attention. She lost so much weight the bones were sticking through her skin and she hadn't enough energy to even talk. I used to read to her, and I was with her at the end, holding her hand when she died.' In the back of the taxi, he was crying silently and holding his head in his hands,

'I didn't mean to upset you.' Tarja put her arm around his shoulders.

'No, no it's not your fault.' He straightened up and brushed her hand away.

'After I lost Hazel and Mark, I came back to the island to work on the trawler.'

He didn't intend to say any more; it was too painful.

'I'm so sorry, it's so sad,' she said. 'I don't know why bad things happen.'

'I keep thinking why me?'

'Life isn't fair. We pray that nothing bad will happen to us or to our loved ones,' she said and her voice trailed off.

'My mother's always wanted me to return to the island to take care of the skipper. I suppose she got her wish but not the way she would have liked it.'

They were silent for a time.

'The skipper is a wild man, and I wouldn't go near the trawler, unless you were onboard.'

'You'll be OK.'

They stopped outside the Atlantic Hotel.

'We're there,' said the taxi-driver.

'Come up for a night cap?'

'It's late.'

'It won't take long.'

The alcohol had kicked in, and he was more open to persuasion.

'OK then, but not for long.'

He paid the taxi-driver and followed her to the hotel door.

The hotel staff had closed up for the night and the place was as deserted as a midweek confessional.

'Follow me,' Tarja said as she headed for the lift.

The bedroom was big with an en suite bathroom and a view out over the Atlantic. From the back window, the mountains loomed large in the dawn light.

'Make yourself at home.'

He sat down on the settee.

Tarja produced a bottle of Vodka and 2 glasses from the dressing table drawer.

"From Finland with love," she said, smiling, 'Do you take a mixer?'

'I do and we need all the love we can get on this island.'

Her laugh was light, full of good humour.

Pat got up to admire the picture on the bedroom wall.

'This is a print of a local painting.'

It was a print from Robert Henri's Achill painting, titled *Himself 1928*. A brass plate on the frame stated that it had won the prestigious Carol Beck Gold Medal award.

'Was he an American?' said Tarja.

'Yes, but he did his best work over there,' said Pat gesturing towards the Corrymore House.

It was visible through the back window, looking dark and sinister.

'I thought it was a castle; it looks deserted.'

'I could tell you some spooky tales about that place.'

Tarja shivered. 'Not tonight.'

She disappeared into the bathroom and emerged later in a dressing gown. She caught her reflection in the dressing table mirror.

'My hair's a mess.'

She sat down at the dressing table and started to comb it. Maybe it was the static from her hair, or maybe it was the alcohol in his system, that caused Pat to see flashes of gold flaring up around Tarja's head as she ran the comb through her hair. Finished, she stood up and, with a smile let her dressing gown fall to the floor. A Grecian goddess carved from marble with long legs and perfectly formed breasts.

'You're beautiful.'

He had never seen red pubic hair before, and although it looked real enough, he wondered if she had dyed it. Real or dyed it was sensuous, and he couldn't take his eyes of it and all he wanted to do was make love to this girl. She walked slowly towards him, still smiling, and he saw the gold ring in her navel. He hated body piercing. She stopped, sensing something was wrong.

'You have your body pierced?'

'Only one, I can take it out.'

'No it's ok.'

Tarja removed the ring.

He found a packet of condoms in his pocket. They had been there for a long time and the latex ring had worn through the cover. He could see that they were past their sell-by date with the number of holes in them.

'If you have to sin, sin safely, it's the new mantra for Catholic sinners,' said Pat, although there was little choice this time except take heed of the priest's message from the Alter, "don't give in to temptation and commit the sin of impurity."

'Lutherans are big on sin as well,' said Tarja.

She sat on his knees, and it surprised him how light she was. He could smell her toothpaste. Slowly, she opened the buttons of his shirt, one by one. He had a powerful body, big chest, shoulders and arms. When he smiled, she liked the contrast of his white teeth against his black beard. Tattooed on his shoulder was the word "Hazel" with cupid's arrow going through it. She kissed him passionately and he responded. They made love, lost in a world of passion.

Afterwards he lay there with Tarja in his arms and suddenly his wife filled his consciousness. Her presence was strong and real. It was as if she were lying beside him. He had never been unfaithful to her before. He had sullied the love they had and thrown it aside as if it didn't matter. Drunk or sober, there was no excuse for making love to this girl. For him there was only one woman, his wife Hazel. He was almost overcome with guilt and grief. Tarja felt his body stiffen.

'What's wrong?'

'I've got to go.' He grabbed his shirt and rushed from the room. He would have cried like a baby had he stayed any longer. He wasn't ready yet, if he ever would be, to move on.

14

It was the usual Sunday evening symphony for Pat: the rhythmic sound of the trawler chafing against the tyres on the pier wall, the noise of the idling diesel engine, and the squawks of the gulls overhead.

At Purteen harbour, reputed to have some of the longest daylight hours in Europe, it didn't seem like evening as he prepared the Annie L. for departure. Anything not tied down on deck would end in the heaving Atlantic. He looked up and saw Tarja parking the red 2CV at the top of the pier next to the stack of fish boxes. After the fiasco in the hotel, he hadn't expected to see her again. He felt embarrassed and wished she had stayed away.

'A red haired woman is bad luck,' snapped a glum Coleman as he checked that the hatches were secure on the forward deck.

'That's only superstition, old wives' tales, they can change the colour of their hair nowadays.' Pat was cleaning down the teak deck with a hose and brush. It surprised him how quickly Coleman had spotted Tarja's car.

'I'm just the hired help,' grumbled Coleman, straightening up.

'Come on, you have equal rights on everything, and you didn't say anything about her before this,' protested Pat as he wound the hose back on to its reel.

'There's no luck in going out before midnight on Sunday or in changing the name of the boat,' said Coleman, inspecting the draining slots on the forward deck. Superstition was rife among west coast fishermen.

'We're doomed,' jested Pat, doing nothing for Coleman's mood. In this frame of mind, trying to humour Coleman just made him worse.

'With that forecast, we shouldn't be out here. He's trying to prove that he is a macho man,' said Coleman, who was checking the anchor hanging from the bows. Pat didn't have time to respond before the engine, opened to full throttle, roared. The noise was deafening.

'You'll blow it up,' shouted Pat as he put his head around the wheelhouse door. Every Sunday the skipper and Coleman went to the pub and stayed there until it was time to board the trawler. Drunk, and with the added aid of sleeping tablets, they usually slept all the way to the fishing grounds. Sometimes they didn't recover for days.

Pat expected an angry reply, but the Skipper merely throttled back the engine. It was going to be a fun trip with those two, though in truth nothing had changed, they were always like this. In some ways, he was looking forward to having another person onboard the trawler. It could be a welcome change from those crusty characters, although there was some truth in Coleman's last remark. They would need to cut and run if the storm hit them direct.

Pat looked over the pointed rear end of the trawler to check the propeller. It was running true and effortless without judder. The surface of the sea between the trawler and the pier was a black soup of crude oil, and diesel flecked with froth. Floating on top were empty beer bottles, food tins, bits of rope, wood, dead birds and fish. It had that nauseating smell of rotting offal. Trawlers, refuelling at the pier were responsible for the spilled diesel, and the crude oil came from oil tankers flushing out their tanks illegally into the Atlantic.

What would Tarja think of this debris? It needed cleaning up; not a good reflection on us, he thought. They wouldn't allow such pollution to happen in Finland. How did he know that? Finland was a foreign country that he knew little about, apart from Santa and his reindeer and a population that by all accounts had no sense of humour. Nowadays that wouldn't bother him, as he didn't have much of a sense of humour left.

A cheerful 'Hi' from Tarja standing above the trawler on the pier wall, cut short his introspection. She had a holdall in one hand and on her back, she was carrying twin oxygen tanks for scuba-diving. The shoulder straps held them securely.

'Get that doll down here, she must be going on a picnic or something,' shouted the skipper, revving the engine again.

Pat shouted 'Hello' and went up the ladder to take the holdall and oxygen tanks from her. She gingerly climbed down before him to the deck. Coleman, his back turned to her, gave a muffled greeting and Pat could hear him muttering to himself, 'If ever I saw trouble, that's trouble.' He went forward in readiness to cast off the ropes holding the trawler, tied fore-and-aft to bollards on the pier.

The skipper roared, 'Failte to the shark killer's boat,' without turning around. Pat led Tarja through the wheelhouse and down the companionway to the cabin. He wished he had put a curtain around her bunk, but it was too late for that. Anyway, privacy was not a high priority on a fishing trawler.

'Sorry about the mess.' He stowed her holdall in the only locker that didn't contain clothes, gear or foodstuff. The place looked like an untidy bachelor flat with shoes, socks, books and papers scattered all over the bunks and floor. The papers were open at the racing pages and the skipper had X'd possible winners. His obsessions were drinking, backing horses and football.

'It's a working boat. I didn't expect any frills.' Tarja, slipping off her dockside shoes and holding them in her hand, walked around barefoot. He showed her how to operate the loo and shower, but it was unnecessary; she seemed to know all about the workings of a boat.

'Right, I'll leave you to it, we'll be underway shortly.'

'I'll be up in a few minutes,' she said, starting to collect rubbish from the cabin floor and deposit it into a black bin liner.

He went back on deck, to his post in the stern of the trawler, ready to untie the line holding them attached to the pier.

He hadn't been long on deck when Tarja joined him, dressed in jeans and a sweater.

'Cast off, cripple,' shouted the skipper to Coleman, who was in the bow of the trawler, and having difficulty, with his one hand, removing the knotted rope from the deck fitting.

'Useless bloody cripple,' said the skipper, as Coleman finally released the tying line. The bow came away from the harbour wall and pointed out to sea.

'Oh, I should have gone to help him, I wasn't thinking,' said Tarja, looking around to see if there was anything else she could do.

'He wouldn't thank you for that. He likes to pretend that he doesn't have a handicap and can manage as well as any man.' Pat bent over the line, waiting for the signal to release the stern from the harbour wall. The skipper opened the throttle and the trawler surged forward, still tied to the pier wall. He had forgotten to give the signal to release the stern line. The rope went taut and the trawler came to an abrupt halt, and then spun around smashing into the pier wall.

Those on deck took the brunt of the crash. The impact knocked them off their feet and only the rail saved them from going overboard. The skipper, thrown from his seat, hit the wheelhouse floor hard. Pat rushed forward to switch off the engine.

'Flaming idiot, I don't know why I'm out here.' Coleman was rubbing the back of his hand against his sweater, leaving a bloodstain.

'Who else would take on a cripple,' jeered the skipper as he levered himself up from the cabin floor using the chair for support.

'I'd be safer anywhere else,' snapped Coleman, making a detailed examination of the cut on the back of his hand.

'If you lose the other one you'll be fit for a circus - a handless wonder,' jibed the skipper rubbing his elbow but not giving in.

'You bloody madman, there's better in the asylum.' Coleman was searching for the first aid kit to dress his injured hand.

Tarja produced Aloe Vera cream from her rucksack and applied it to Pat's burned palms. Her hands were soft and it was nice to have a woman tending to him again.

He checked for damage and leaks to the trawler. It looked OK, apart from superficial scratches on the paint. It was difficult to know if the blow had weakened the planking and a more detailed examination would mean an abandoned fishing trip. He thought about it for a few minutes, and decided on balance, it was OK to carry on. With Tarja's help, he cast off the stern line and took over steering the trawler.

'Take no notice of their bickering - they'll soon go to their bunks,' Pat whispered to Tarja, as he gradually increased speed and headed away from Purteen harbour.

'There's bitterness between them?' said Tarja. She sat down in the second seat beside Pat at the steering wheel.

'Yes, but they're good mates.'

Pat cleared the harbour and brought the boat around to point west into the Atlantic. Had he made the right decision, taking the trawler to sea after the bang it had. The timbers were old and they had just taken a heavy pounding. They might be weak under the water line. In a difficulty like this, he knew that he always took the easy way out. He should have refused ages ago to sail with them, unless they were sober coming on-board.

Anyway, the skipper probably wouldn't abandon the trip, although he couldn't have gone without Pat. Without him, they didn't have enough manpower to handle the boat. The proper approach was to haul the trawler into dry dock and examine the hull for damage. Then there was this girl he had taken onboard. He wasn't half regretting his drunken decision!

The antagonists went to their bunks and peace descended on the trawler.

'With the sleeping tablets and the alcohol, that's the last we will see of them for the next twelve hours or so.' Pat settled into the long trip to the fishing grounds. On Sunday nights, unless bad weather prevented them from leaving the harbour, while the others slept, he piloted the boat in solitude. It gave him time to himself, to think about his life, and mourn his terrible loss in private. This Sunday night with Tarja on board, was going to be different, though it was unlikely that she would stay awake for long.

Their heading was directly into the sun, setting in a ball of fiery red on a hazy blue backdrop. It would be impossible to see ahead without sunglasses.

'Do you have a rhyme to help you know where you are?' Tarja was examining the chart in front of her on the dash.

'No, maybe some old fellows had one, but it's lost.' He lashed the steering to the hooks in the floor and sat back into the high swivel chair. 'I hear the Waterford fishermen have rhymes to keep them from getting lost, but I don't know any of them.'

'The Samoan islanders on the sea and the Aborigines on land use mnemonics to find their way,' she said.

'I heard the Vikings used something like that to get around too,' said Pat.

'They most likely did, and while they wrote nothing, the rhymes probably passed down orally from one generation to the next.'

'Talking about Waterford, there's an interesting story about the origins of, 'by Hook or by Crook.' In the days when sailing boats left Cork Harbour, the skippers went by Hook Head if they turned left for the European countries of England, Spain, France or the lowlands of Holland. They turned right by Crookhaven into the Atlantic heading for America. Those curious about the origins of a sailing ship arriving at the port of Cork would get their answer from the question, 'Did you come by Hook or by Crook?'

'That's a new one on me, I must remember it,' said Tarja, pointing to Hook and Crook on the chart.

'Rhymes for getting around wouldn't suit the skipper, he wouldn't remember them. He doesn't read charts or GPS or anything else, just trusts his own judgement.' Pat was smiling, thinking of where they would land if he relied on the skipper's sense of direction.

'By the way, where are we going?' Tarja was poring over the admiralty chart covered in yellow highlighter marks.

'Our heading is west to the Porcupine Shelf. See it's marked in yellow on the chart.' He bent over to his left and pointed out the direction they were travelling in. He wasn't sure about having her onboard, but he was enjoying her company.

Tarja took his hand in hers and turned it over. She kissed the rope burn on his palm. She remained holding his hand until he pulled it away more roughly than he intended. He didn't want such a close relationship with her. Drunk, he had given her the wrong message by having sex with her in the hotel. It was his sin.

He dreaded having to tell her that he wasn't ready for all this. There was enough conflict onboard without any further tensions. He was taking the coward's way out by not telling her straight; perhaps it would be easier to deal with on dry land.

'I'll make tea,' he volunteered, trying to change the mood.

'I'll do it.' Tarja hopped from her seat and went towards the gas cooker. She was such a willing worker - he couldn't take that away from her.

A few minutes later, she came back and Pat held both mugs of tea until she got back on her seat. Still inside the bay, they were motoring along in a lazy swell, like waves in a bathtub. Later, once past Achill Head, the Atlantic breakers would be a different matter. It was always a rude awakening for day sailors when they hit the real Atlantic; and Pat wondered how Tarja would cope with it. The usual response was less talk, 'a fearful silence' someone had called it, although a Marine Biologist might have sailed in heavy seas.

'Where are we now?' Tarja was examining the chart between sips of tea. Pat pointed out some of the headlands and places of interest. Behind them were the Menaun cliffs and at their base the sea carved Cathedral Rocks, honeycombed with caverns and passages. They had passed Inishgallon Island and were level with Gubalenaun More Point.

'You don't want me to name them all?' Pat checked the compass heading. He felt that she wouldn't want to hear the sound of obscure Irish place names, that she couldn't possibly remember.

'Yes I do, I like the new sounds.' Tarja turned to look into his face.

'OK, here we go. You'll see the places on the chart as I call them out.' To get a clearer view of the map, he pushed up his sunglasses on to his forehead. 'They're the Dysaghy Rocks and they're treacherous.' He pointed to the rocks barely visible sticking out of the water. Pat had marked them on the admiralty chart with a red marker, and local fishermen gave them a wide berth.

'A trawler, The Pride of Cratlagh caught in its whirlpool, and sank during the making of the film Shark Island.'

'Did any of them drown?' Tarja was resting on her elbows on the chart table and staring at the rocks. They looked benign enough in the gathering dusk; however he untied the steering wheel, determined to keep the trawler well away from them.

'I was only a boy, but I think her skipper and two others died.' He turned around to look back at the Dysaghy Rocks as they navigated past them.

'The story goes that the locals told the skipper of Pride of Cratlagh to stay from the Dysaghy Rocks; but he took no notice of them.'

'That was tragic,' said Tarja.

It could be a tale from the pubs. Like seafaring communities the world over, the Islanders liked to think that they knew the seas around their shores better than anyone else did.

'One man managed to swim ashore and the locals saved him. Unfortunately, his wife drowned.'

'I'd like to see Shark Island. Is the film available?' Tarja was clearing mist from the inside of the windscreen.

'Gathering dust somewhere, I haven't seen it, since I was a boy.' Pat tied down the steering wheel when the Rocks were in their wake. He pointed out Croaghaun Mountain, where an eight-man crew of an RAF weather plane died, when they hit it in heavy fog. It was before his time. He told her about the skipper and Coleman climbing to the top of the mountain with the Irish army recovery team, to help them bring down the bodies and later on bits of the aircraft.

'It was a terrible crash with remains scattered all over the mountainside.' He grimaced at the thought of it. The recovery team gathered the body parts of the flight crew and, in body bags, returned them to their families in England for burial.

'Victor Hugo said it right, "Nature is unforgiving, she will not agree".' He could imagine the body bags, bits of flesh and bone sloshing around inside them as they travelled to Dublin in the back of an army ambulance. A shivering sensation started at the back of his neck and went all the way down his spine. How did their relatives cope?

It brought it all back to him - the picture of his dead wife and son. They were more important to him than life itself. His eyes were tight under the lids and there were tears starting to gather. He swallowed hard to calm himself. In his head, it was always as real as the day it happened. Better not to think about it. Life must go on, or so they said in the bereavement class, but that was not easy. What they didn't say is that life would never be the same again.

15

Next in sight came the postcard view of Keem Bay with its white sandy beach in a bowl shaped cove. Pat was seeing it with tears in his eyes, but he couldn't deny that it was beautiful. He didn't think she knew anything about how he was feeling, although she had stopped asking questions. It might be a natural lull in the conversation. He decided to keep it going.

'That's where the basking sharks came in.' He adjusted course slightly for Achill Head and tied the wheel back down again.

'I'm a member of 'Save the Shark's organisation'. It's worldwide and we discuss Achill shark fishing as well as shark fishing in other regions,' said Tarja as she took the empty mugs back to the sink for washing.

'I did a project for school about it, mostly facts,' said Pat as he took a long look at the echo sounder to check what they were passing over. Submerged rocks were a constant danger in the relative shallows near the island.

'The basking shark is the world's second largest fish and is a plankton feeder,' she said, now pompous and schoolmarmish. This was not good; he was obviously going to get a lecture on one of the topics, he knew something about. Tarja continued,

'Basking sharks are the world's largest mammal. They can grow to twelve metres long and weigh about four thousand kilograms.'

An old fellow in the pub used to advise anyone getting a bit pompous, to get off their high horse in case they fell off and hurt themselves. She was on her high horse now. Her information was old hat on the island and he tried not to smile in the middle of her speech.

'They cruise the seas at two knots while filtering water through their bodies for plankton at four hundred times their body weight, every hour.' Deep concentration lines appeared on her forehead as she rattled off facts and figures.

'The shark's liver, the heaviest organ in its body, is about twenty-five per cent of its total weight and is rich in oil – the reason man has hunted them for centuries.'

Tarja was still talking, but Pat's mind had drifted away. He was thinking about when the shark fishing had started on the island, away back in the 1940s, before his time. Fifty men and seven boats worked around the clock at the height of the shark fishing season, from spring to early summer each year. They over-fished and caught an estimated three quarters of the world population of basking sharks. From such depletion the basking shark population never recovered. He became aware of her talking.

'That slaughter was so primitive and unforgivable,' she declared, outrage in her voice. Now he was seeing the real woman. He got angry. She was talking about the islanders, his people. Who did she think she was? What right had she to pass judgement on them? She didn't know anything about the difficulties the islanders had to endure to survive. He would need to keep his cool. What was it, they recommended in the bereavement class for strong emotions? Breathe in for seven and let out for eleven. They called it the seven eleven technique in the class.

'It was fishing in another way; they needed the work,' he said. He thought Tarja was judging the islanders harshly and he felt a need to defend them. It seems she had strong views on everything and not necessarily the right ones.

'Sounds to me like pure greed, there were other fish they could have caught,' she said. It was getting worse - so sweet one minute and then such a mouth. Breathe. Breathe.

'You weren't there. They had wives and families to feed. You know nothing about hard times.' The breathing hadn't helped much - that came out stronger than he had intended. Perhaps Coleman was right, she was trouble.

The awkward silence between them seemed to go on forever, and he did not try to break it. To heck with her. If this is the way she wanted it for the rest of the trip, then so be it. He could slip into his own little world as he always did on these fishing trips. Suddenly, she seemed to have become aware of her surroundings. She dropped the schoolmarm role.

'Sorry, I'm carried away with it all,' she said, looking at him with an apologetic smile. She felt she had let her guard down and was trying to make up for her judgemental outburst but Pat didn't feel like talking; they had said too much already.

'Forgive me. I always jump right in. I was the same about clubbing seals,' soothed Tarja as she shifted about uncomfortably in her chair. It wasn't in his nature not to respond positively to people talking to him. He didn't know why she had the power to annoy him so much. To anybody else he would have probably said 'do you think so' and left it at that, but here he was trying to explain things to her, to justify actions that troubled him.

'It was the times - we didn't understand what we were at,' he mumbled. He untied the steering wheel and made an unnecessary adjustment. This gave him something to do.

'No amount of talking will alter anything that happened in the past,' he said.

'You're right, that's the way it was, and we cannot rewrite history,' she said. They needed to get away from this topic, and he had learnt something: she had the power to annoy him. She was obviously a girl with time on her hands who took up causes she didn't understand much about, like shark fishing on the island.

On the other hand, at least she had a brain in her, even if it was a stubborn one, and an interest in the sea. She couldn't be all bad. He could do without this see-sawing of emotions though - no good for him at all.

'It's a great pity, there wasn't another way, rather than killing those gentle giants of the sea,' she said.

'Yea,' he agreed, in a calmer frame of mind.

He should have been more rational and used better judgement rather than arguing with this one. Moreover, he was an advocate, in principle, of people speaking out against what they considered wrong and often quoted Edmund Burke, "The only condition needed for evil to triumph is for good men to do nothing." When someone annoyed him this much, his freedom of speech principles went out the window, and the naked ape appeared. It's a great pity; he couldn't get her off the boat. She cut into his thinking.

'How and when were the sharks caught?' she asked. She was looking at him intensely, and spoke in a hesitant voice.

He was not going to give anything away. He had a feeling that she already knew the answer and was trying to get their relationship back on an even keel, or else setting him up for further argument. He was ready for her this time, his normal cool had returned - on the surface anyway - and he went on to talk about the methods used by the Islanders to catch sharks.

'In spring and early summer, they came in shoals into Keem Bay where a lookout on the top of Croghan Mountain spotted them.'

'What then?'

'One blast on the whistle to tell the trawlers, standing off, and the hunt was on. A net stretched across the bay imprisoned the sharks.'

Alcohol had got him into this fix. She shouldn't be with them at all. What did that old fellow sing in the pub?

'Its drink and folly that make young men marry, and now I'm off to Amer -a- K.'

It was total abstinence for him from this day forwards - the full nine yards, a pioneer pin if they were still around. Better to get on with it.

'The sharks swam close to the surface and the spotter counted the number of dark shadows in the water.'

'How did he let the trawlers know?'

'He blew a blast on the whistle for each shark in the bay.'

'Did they take the young ones as well?' Tarja asked, cautiously.

'They took everything.' It was a loaded question. Taking the young was a sure way to run down the stock to extinction. It was impossible to defend it. This time he wasn't going to try; he just let it hang in the air. Of course she was right, a quota would have been the way to handle it; and that would have left some in reserve for breeding and renewing the stock.

'It wasn't your fault. It's so sweet how you defend the islanders.' She touched his arm.

'It wasn't theirs either.' She was being so patronising. On the other hand, he would have to remember that English was not her first language. He should try to think of that, he supposed. He'd stick to the shark fishing and steer her away from the 'sweet' stuff.

He went on to tell her how they processed the carcasses.

'They towed them into either Purteen or Keem, and cut out the livers and melted them down into oil. They shredded what they left of the carcasses, and used it in the manufacture of bone meal. The skipper was the foreman, and he took mad chances, even jumping on to a shark's back once.'

Pat had a wry smile on his face.

'He's a risk taker,' said Tarja, tracing their route along the yellow marker line on the chart with her finger.

'Did they ever see any man eaters?'

'Rumours, but none appeared.' Pat pushed the throttle lever forward slightly in preparation for the heavier seas.

'Sharkskin is more abrasive than any type of sandpaper, and when they towed the carcases alongside; it eventually wore away the trawler timbers. Our timbers could be paper-thin, we didn't replace them.'

Out it came and Pat wished he hadn't said it. Thinking the trawler wasn't sound wouldn't help her much. He'd try to take the sting out of it.

'This boat didn't haul many carcases.'

Even to him, it didn't sound convincing. What was the saying? 'If you're in a hole - stop digging.'

Tarja went silent.

16

They moved away from the shelter of the island at Saddle Head and hit the full force of the Atlantic swell. With the tide running against the wind, the sea was churned into a frenzy of white-topped waves. They were beating out a rhythm: three big waves smashing into the bows of Annie L. followed by three smaller ones, a lull and the pattern was repeated over and over again. Clouds of spray shot into the air and landed on the windscreen. It was like going through a car wash. Pat switched on the wipers. The noise of creaking timbers would be with them until they returned to the relative calm of the Purteen pier.

'That's an awesome sea,' said Tarja as she fought for balance on the way back to her seat. The waves were crashing into the bottom of the cliffs, forced back, and churned into froth.

'Nature here is so raw, so powerful, so terrifying and yet it's so romantic.' She was looking up at the skyscraper cliffs on the northwest face of Croughan.

'They are supposed to be the highest sea cliffs in Europe but who knows?' said Pat. She grasped his hand and held it tightly. He eased his hand away. Would she ever get the message that he wasn't ready for that type of closeness? Hazel was the only woman for him.

'What's wrong?'

'I must stay alert, I have work to do here,' he murmured as he released the ropes from the spokes of the steering wheel and started to steer manually. It wasn't necessary; but he wanted to gain some physical distance from her. Tarja seemed to accept as a genuine explanation, that he needed to keep his attention on steering the trawler.

He felt tense but she kept talking, ignoring his tension, or maybe she wasn't even aware of it. It was an admirable trait of not letting long silences develops between them. He hated those long silences that women seemed to keep up forever, over nothing. She went on to tell him about the Atlantic. Her knowledge of the seas and marine life was vast but then again, he shouldn't be surprised at that; it was her subject. She continued talking.

'The worst seas ever recorded anywhere were during Atlantic storms. Even in good conditions an average of fifteen-foot waves could be expected, increasing to fifty feet or more in a storm. Theory is one thing, but the reality is scary,' she said, looking out to sea and gripping the edge of the chart table for support. He expected that in a few days, she would either get used to the Atlantic or else want to turn her back on it forever. She went on explaining.

'The moon, of all things, and the winds blowing over the sea makes the waves. The more water the wind travels over the bigger the waves.' She was treating him like a schoolboy. He was waiting for her to tell him the old guff about the Atlantic having no equal, and that the waves thumping into the island's jagged coastline probably originated in Cape Horn about ten thousand miles away.

'Those waves would have gone through loads of weather systems, getting bigger all the time before hitting the island.' She seemed captivated by the waves. Put that way, he wondered how the islanders survived down the generations, with no particular fear of the terrible forces that nature was unleashing against them. Apart from a few Hail Marys, said by older women during a storm, there was nothing else. They had learned to cope with it. They didn't have a choice. Since his childhood, the storms were there and some years were worse than others. He hadn't thought about it before, but it was an example of how the human mind can adjust.

Tarja went silent and he wanted to know what was going on inside that head of hers. Why was he so interested in what she was thinking? Normally, he didn't give a damn about what was going on in other people's heads, but this girl was getting to him, driving him mental. Since they left port, he had a feeling that somehow this trip wasn't right. Maybe it was this girl? If he carried on like this, he'd soon be as superstitious as Coleman. He had often heard it said that you need to know somebody well before you go to sea with them, or they'd drive you mad. In future, he wouldn't take any strangers on the trawler. Their job was fishing and that was it. Then again, the skipper and Coleman wouldn't be everyone's first choice of companions on the sea, although he didn't have many options - needs must.

The spray blowing from the top of the waves was creating a misty hue in the settling twilight. You could see it, but not through it. He'd keep the conversation light; maybe that was the best approach.

'A square rigger is due anytime,' said Pat with a smile - a forced smile maybe - and he turned on the masthead light. The rocks and the cliffs disappeared behind them and the next solid ground was three thousand miles ahead on the rocky shores of Newfoundland.

'Have any islanders seen a ghost ship?' Tarja was trying to see through the mist with the binoculars she'd picked up from the dash.

'No one sane and sober,' laughed Pat making a slight adjustment to speed and direction. He had read about the *Mary Celeste* and the *Flying Dutchman* coming out of the mist under full sail and disappearing again in an instant, before the sailors' eyes.

'The mind can be a great trickster when you are upset or lacking sleep,' he said thoughtfully, checking the time on his watch. He expected Tarja would have gone to her bunk by now, the sooner the better.

'So many people see things at sea that are not there, I suppose,' she said, unrolling the larger marine map of the Atlantic.

'In this light it would be easy to imagine anything.' Pat was listening to the note of the engine, and he thought it faltered. Talking like this could get to you.

'It's so surreal; I don't want to miss a minute of it,' she said. There went his quiet night alone.

'Newfoundland is straight ahead.' Tarja was using the parallel ruler to chart a course to the other side of the Atlantic.

'That's a long way.' Pat said, glancing sideways over her shoulder at the course she was plotting. If they continued for long enough on their present course, they would pass over the Grand Banks, the best fishing grounds in the world.

'I have never been to Newfoundland,' she said, still engrossed in the chart.

'Not on this trip either hopefully. It would take a factory ship to make the trip worthwhile.'

'The factory ships are not very eco-friendly.'

He didn't like factory ships himself, but he decided to pass on the subject, no sense in getting involved in another verbal battle with this lady. Stay on an even keel.

'Newfoundland was a regular sailing route for generations of fishermen from Waterford and from Cornwall.'

'It was some trip in a small fishing boat,' said Tarja.

'Lots of them stayed on and married Eskimo women.'

'That's what happens,' said Tarja.

'We had a few young people from Newfoundland with us on the island last year.' Feeling more relaxed; he sat back in the swivel chair and let the trawler engine do the work. He was beginning to understand her a bit more; he would keep away from controversial topics and tell her plenty of stories. She seemed interested in that sort of thing.

'From listening to them, it seems that wherever you go, you bring yourself with you.'

'Yes, you bring your baggage along with you.'

'They brought all their religious prejudices between the Orange and the Green with them to the new land.' Pat was again checking the temperature gauge, which had risen sharply. It could be the gauge gone faulty, or it could be a problem with the engine.

'Their accents were a mixture of Irish and Cornish, and they said that up the southern shore, they spoke Irish well into the 1960s.'

He was hoping that the needle, sitting there in the red, was a false alarm and that the engine wouldn't come to any harm. A seized engine in mid Atlantic wasn't the type of emergency he wanted.

'Religious divisions cause a lot of trouble everywhere.'

She was unaware of the drama going on in Pat's head about the high engine temperature reading.

'They told us,' said Pat, trying to sound normal, 'that from November to May the place is covered with snow and ice, if you fall into the sea the water is so cold that you're dead within a few minutes.'

'The icebergs must be a terrible problem when you think of the Titanic. Of course the first wireless signal from across the Atlantic was from St. Johns,' said Tarja.

'Every time they go out in the wintertime they bring a loaf of bread and water with them in case they are caught in a snowdrift. They could be there for up to a week.' He was keeping a discrete eye on the temperature gauge. The wise thing might be to shut down the engine altogether but he decided to leave it for another while.

'We have loads of snow in Finland and our ice hotel is famous for honeymoon couples.'

'I've seen it on TV, and it's awesome.'

He'd let it pass, but it seemed like a strange place for a honeymoon. It might be better under the circumstances to steer away from romance.

'They told one amazing tale about a family of two sons and a father living in a remote part of Newfoundland,'

'Did they kill him?'

'No, he died of natural causes but their only experience of death was slaughtering and salting animals for food.'

'Oh no - they didn't eat him?' Tarja covered her face with her hands at the thought of it.

'No, they gutted and salted the body and stored it until spring.'

'Oh there's something terrible about that.'

'In the days before bulldozers, coffins were stacked above ground in the graveyards and when the thaw came, they buried them.'

'We get lots of snow and ice at home. Nowadays, with big machines they can cut through it without any difficulty.' She rolled up the chart of the far side of the Atlantic and put an elastic band around it.

'It sounds tougher than Finland. What about your island.'

'Our island, as far as the weather forecasters are concerned, is a frost free zone but that's not fully true, we get a bit.'

'You are lucky, though people learn to deal with it,' she said, turning her attention to the chart of the west of Ireland's coastline.

'Loads of boats must have got into trouble in these waters.'

It would have been nice to know more about how they coped with extreme weather conditions in Finland.

'Yes, Westport Quay drowning had a big effect on the island.'

'How did that happen?'

It happened a long time ago, but it was still an emotional topic. A relative of his had died in the disaster. He might as well tell her all about it - fate had arranged it. They had to spend the night together in the narrow confines of the trawler; and talking would shorten the time.

'A yawl left the island with a full load of young people for Westport Quay, scheduled to transfer to a larger boat en route to Scotland for seasonal work in the potato fields. I've heard many versions of what happened as they rounded the headland, on close haul into Westport quay. One account is that a squall from the Atlantic hit the yawl and capsized it, with a loss of twelve lives. It was within the proverbial stone's throw of Westport Quay at the time.'

'They weren't swimmers?'

'No, swimming wasn't a tradition on the island in those days.'

'Horrified, the sailors watched from the bigger boat as the yawl disappeared under the waves. Another version of the story suggested that the yawl was overloaded; the young people rushed to the weather rail to see the larger boat that was to take them to Scotland, and capsized the yawl. Though I think myself, it was the squall that did it. Sometimes I wonder why the disaster has remained in the emotional consciousness of island people for so long. I suppose island communities have long memories, with families connected by a linkage of intermarriage.'

'New input from the gene pool required,' said Tarja seriously.

'Not anymore, times have changed; we have people from all over the world living on the island now.'

'It's strange, but the first train to travel on the Westport to Achill railway line, carried home the coffins of those young people and the last train on the route carried back the coffins of island people who died in a bothy fire in Kirkintillough in Scotland.'

'That's weird.' She was looking at him for a response. What was there to say? He went on with the story.

'The bothy fire may have been started deliberately by local youths in Kirkintillough. They were anti-Irish, anti-Catholic, or both. Before starting the fire they barred the doors of the bothy from outside, to prevent anyone from escaping. I'd prefer to think that it was an accident.'

He looked at Tarja. Maybe he had said too much, he didn't normally stray into these areas. His motto, if he could call it that, was to keep away from religion and politics.

'What kind of people would do that?'

'I think those kinds of people are everywhere.'

Pat was checking the compass heading and making minor adjustments. The high reading on the temperature gauge was becoming more of a worry but he still kept it to himself.

17

Pat broke the silence. He wished to get away from something that caused him pain every time he thought about it. The terror those young people must have felt, trapped and with no escape from being burned alive. He moved to tell Tarja another story about the North Mayo coast, the wreck of the Spanish Armada.

'Invaded by the English and not feeling too happy about it, the Irish were looking for allies to provide fighting men.'

Later he might get around to telling her about the famous warrior woman of the west coast Grace O'Malley, but for now it was the Spanish Armada saga.

'The Spanish and the British were at war, and it made strategic sense for the Spanish to harass them on all fronts, so they sent an Armada to attack the British fort in Kinsale.'

'Where is Kinsale?' She had the map of the North Atlantic spread out in front of her on the chart table, and she was searching for Kinsale.

'You'll find it in the south of Ireland.' Again, Pat checked the engine temperature gauge in front of him on the dash. No change, the needle remained in the red, overheating position. The engine had loads of power, and if there was anything seriously wrong it wouldn't have that; probably, the temperature gauge was malfunctioning. Gauges were always a bit suspect.

'When an Atlantic storm blew up, the ships of the Armada, caught off guard, couldn't hold formation, and separated from each other. The storm drove them up to the west coast.'

'Did they have sea charts?'

'They were inaccurate and depicted the west coast as having a straight shore line from Kerry to Donegal.'

'There's little of it straight.' Tarja was following the contour on the chart of the rugged west coastline with her finger.

'A terrible carnage occurred, with ships wrecked on the rocks all over the place. The British forces killed many of the Spaniards that got ashore, but local people managed to save, and hide a number of them.'

'In the pub it was almost like being in Spain, with so many people looking like Spaniards,' laughed Tarja jokingly. She looked sharply at Pat, and he felt she was checking him for signs of Spanish ancestry.

'A few shipwrecked sailors couldn't have made that much difference,' joked Pat, mulling over the possible causes of the rising engine temperature. Gauge readings fluctuated a bit; but this one was at the top of the danger range for some time. He eased back on the throttle; that might cause a change. He continued with the tale of the Spanish Armada.

'Lying on the rocks at the upper end of the island are the remains of one Spanish ship with its brass cannon and brass fitting long gone. Salvaged and sold for scrap.'

'They must have been exotic looking,' said Tarja,

'Yes, imagine seeing them for the first time in their blue and white Spanish soldiers uniforms as they hauled them up the cliffs on ropes.'

'They wouldn't have a clue what the Spaniards were saying.'

'No and the Spaniards couldn't speak Irish.'

'Is it a difficult language to learn?'

'It's not easy but somehow they managed. Enough rum and wine came from the wreck to supply the island for years.'

'It also extended the gene pool.'

'I suppose. Right, let me tell you about Grace O'Malley or *Granuaille*, the most exotic woman warrior of them all.'

Pat throttled back a little to see if the engine temperature would drop.

He went on to tell her about the myths and legends associated with this pirate Queen of the sixteenth Century. Maybe this one beside him was her incarnation; she also had red hair and a feisty temperament.

'Born on Clare Island, she became the head of the O'Malley clan, an achievement that few women of her day would consider possible.'

'I have Clare Island on the Chart, it is close.' Tarja was using her index and middle fingers like a compass to measure the distance on the chart.

'Achill, Clare Island, Inishturk and Inishbofin are about the same distance apart. The story goes that a giant needed to cross the bay from Mayo to Connemara. He threw fistfuls of rock and clay ahead of him to step on and in this way he formed these Atlantic Islands.'

'He must have been some size to step that far,' laughed Tarja, finding all the islands on the chart that Pat had mentioned.

'And then there was the pirate Queen.' Pat eased back the throttle a further two notches.

'The English were in control of Galway port, the hub of industry and commerce on the west coast until the pirate Queen came along. From then on they couldn't guarantee a safe passage to any merchant ship, either in or out of Galway. Grace and her pirate crew had the fighting ability to pillage any of the merchant ships they fancied. The British proclaimed her an outlaw and put £500 ransom on her head.'

'That was some money in those days,' said Tarja.

'In today's currency, it's probably worth hundreds of thousands of pounds. The situation called for desperate measures, and she went to London to meet Queen Elizabeth I. After a dangerous sea journey, as there were many who would like to collect the ransom on her head, she sailed up the Thames. The courtiers' were waiting, and they smuggled her by a back door into the palace. Rumour from the palace suggested that Grace impressed Queen Elizabeth, although there is no record of what Grace thought of Her Majesty. The Royal pomp and ceremony did not impress Grace enough to change her ways; she returned to Clare Island to continue her pillage of the English and Spanish merchant ships using Galway bay.'

'Is this myth or is it a true history?' Tarja straightened up from the chart table, with a smile and looking directly into his eyes.

'Both, and there's more.'

Pat continued with the story of Grace O'Malley, the pirate of the Elizabethan Merchant ships, and the wine carrying Spanish Galleons.

'Grace gave birth to her son Tibbot-na-long onboard her ship, near the entrance to Galway bay, the day before a Turkish pirate attacked the vessel.'

'O, did Grace marry?' Tarja was concentrating on the chart in front of her.

'Don't know about that but she had many lovers, and she didn't have any qualms about it.'

'She was before her time.' Tarja laughed.

'It was a savage attack and without Grace on deck her crew were losing the battle. She called for a blunderbuss and her male nurse to carry her up on deck, to join in the battle.'

'A male Nurse, you are having me on?'

'No, that's true. Don't forget she wouldn't allow another woman on board. Spurring her crew on, they defeated the Turks and looted their ship, and Grace returned to her bed to recuperate. Her feminine side came to fore when on a pilgrimage to a holy well on her native Clare Island, she heard that a Spanish Galleon was on the rocks off Achill Island. She abandoned the pilgrimage and set sail for Achill, to help the stricken sailors. The Spanish crew hadn't survived and Grace directed her crew to salvaging the cargo of wine and other precious goods. An incentive to the crew was permission to take the dead sailors' uniforms and personal belongings for their own use.'

'With bits of uniforms from all over the place they must have been a colourful lot,' said Tarja with the Achill and Clare island section of the charts spread out in front of her.

'Now there's an image that's not a good fit with the conservative dress of the West of Ireland,' said Pat.

'They were about to leave the Spanish ship when they heard a young sailor groaning, he had somehow survived and was barely alive. One of the pirates had drawn his sabre to run him through, but Grace shouted to let him live. Her men carried the Spanish sailor aboard, and she nursed him back to health. He became her lover.'

'A toy boy, modern women could learn a lot from this girl,' said Tarja.

'The McMahon clan murdered the Spanish sailor, when they captured him while he was out hunting. Grace's revenge on the McMahon's was swift and awful; she routed the clan, burned their castles to the ground, stole their cattle and took them back with her to Clare Island.'

'How did she die?' Tarja was staring ahead into the Atlantic night.

'Well past three score and ten, in her bed on Clare Island.' Pat was wondering if he should switch off the engine to allow it to cool down. There was always the chance that he wouldn't manage to get it started again.

'Isn't that something - I expected a violent death surrounded by lovers.' Tarja was folding up the charts and putting them away.

'You never can tell what life will bring.' Pat was testing the temperature gauge by tapping it with his fingers. It remained steady.

'Will I make some more tea?' Tarja asked, sliding off her seat.

'Good idea.' He couldn't help admiring her litheness and sense of movement, as she waited for the roll of the trawler and then sprang to the sink. Later in the voyage when she found her sea legs, she would walk around as normal.

Waiting for the tea, Pat pulled back the throttle further, and he continued to mull over the reasons for a rise in engine temperature. Usually it turned out to be something simple like an external cooling pipe clogged with seaweed, although they could have a serious problem to deal with, like an oil pump failure.

'Here comes the tricky bit.' Tarja stumbled across the floor of the rolling trawler, juggling two cups of tea in her hands. Apart from spillage, she managed to get to her seat and placed half a cup of tea on the console in front of him.

'Half a cup is better than no tea.' She took a sip from her cup.

Pat hadn't time to respond before the temperature gauge shot off the scale. He switched off the engine.

'We're overheating, probably seaweed in the cooling inlet. I'll go down below and get ready to go over the side to remove it.'

'I'll do it; I need to practice diving in this sea.' She put her hand on his shoulder and gently pushed him back towards his seat at the steering wheel.

'Are you sure?' Pat was holding on to the back of the high seat to steady himself against the trawler pitching.

'Sure I'm sure.' Tarja went below to put on her wetsuit. On her return he watched her striding across the deck to the stern, the tight neoprene wetsuit emphasising her figure.

'Use the ladder, the inlet is near the keel.'

Seeing her in a wetsuit was distracting him. Enough of this mind wandering. Focus on getting them back on track again.

She gave an OK in sign language, switched on her headlight and went over the stern. Without engine power, the trawler was head to wind and facing back to Purteen harbour where they had come from. He could see the glow of Tarja's lamp moving under water as she checked the inlet pipes. Minutes later, she climbed up the stern ladder waving a length of seaweed. That was the problem sorted.

The sudden thump on the side of the trawler caught them unaware. Tarja fell from the stern ladder back into the ocean. Knocked over on the deck, Pat jumped back to his feet. The waves carried Tarja away from the trawler, and he could see her light flashing in the distance. In a panic, he rushed around the deck, until his rational mind took over. To check if they were sinking, he leaned over the side and saw, swimming close to the surface, the unmistakable shapes of large fish - dolphins. That's what hit them. He switched on the searchlight and swivelled it around in an arc, looking for Tarja, but there was no sign of her. He tried to start the engine without success. It probably needed more time to cool. He went to the life-raft and started to unload the clutter deposited in it. They used it to stack bits of gear and rubbish. It would be empty if they had carried out periodic life-raft drill. Directly behind, Tarja's headlight cut through the darkness. He swivelled the searchlight around and saw two dolphins propelling Tarja along towards the trawler.

They took her up to the stern ladder. Before climbing back on deck, she patted their long snouts. They threw dozens of fish over the stern, and jumping into the air, rolled over and swam away.

'What an experience, it was awesome! They were so protective and all my worries vanished. I could have stayed with them forever, just cruising around. They know all about me, even to providing fish for my research,' said Tarja before going below to change out of her wetsuit and take a shower. She was smiling and happy after her ordeal. Pat had heard of the dolphin effect, but this was the first time he had witnessed it.

He managed to start the engine again and was underway when she came back on deck.

'Have they gone?' She went from one porthole to the next in hope of getting a glimpse of the dolphins. There was no sign of them.

'They're away.'

Pat knew that, back home in Finland, this would be one of her favourite stories. Before settling on the wheelhouse bench, she gave him a kiss on the cheek. Delayed reaction had set in and he was trembling, but he did his best to disguise it. Tarja was in another reality, euphoric about her contact with the dolphins.

There were tales about the empathy between dolphins and humans, where dolphins surrounded lone swimmers to prevent a shark attacking. People with mental health problems get relief by swimming with dolphins. He'd heard that Ireland's resident dolphin, Fungi, in Dingle bay, attracted visitors to the region each year, either to see him or swim with him. They left with an abundance of happiness from their brief encounter with Fungi.

He tied down the steering wheel and brewed some more tea to steady his nerves. Tarja was smiling and happy. She seemed unaware that she was drinking tea or anything else. When Pat looked at her again, she had curled up on the bench, fast asleep with a cushion under her head. He covered her with a duvet. For sure, there was something strange about this trip. It seemed as if, everything that could go wrong over a season's fishing had telescoped into this trip. Was there worse to come?

Pat tried to resist the morphine haze, while memories of his time with Tarja, was it days or weeks, came and went disjointedly. He remembered his earlier relationship with her, first in the pub and then in the Atlantic Hotel before she came onboard the trawler. Their first night at sea; her sleeping on the bench of the Annie L., and dreaming of dolphins. It was all a bit hazy; he couldn't remember any more of it. The sleeping tablets and the morphine were taking effect, and he would gladly go with the flow into the void. He fell into a heavy drug induced sleep.

18

As he slowly woke out of the heavy sleep, Pat was trying to work out where he was. He might still be in the nightmare caused by the sleeping tablets, the morphine and the seizure. The pain in his shoulder seemed real enough as did the trawler, ploughing through the storm. The rhythm was constant; the stern rose on the crest of a wave and crashed down into the trough with a thump. For a period in each cycle, they were in total darkness, submerged under tonnes of muddied water whipped into frenzy from the floor of the ocean. The light coloured hues of white, blue and green were near the surface and the darker colours near the bottom. A gushing sound heralded the water draining from the deck through the scuppers and back into the sea.

It was a miracle that they were still afloat after the pounding they were taking so there might be a chance that they would ride out the storm.

'Tarja is that you and are we still alive?'

'Are you in pain?'

'Some, I'm confused.'

Coleman, steering the trawler, turned around briefly in his seat to look back at him.

'What's happening?'

'You didn't sleep for long, the pumps are still working.'

He was steering hard against the storm to keep the trawler on track.

'Do you want to eat or drink?' asked Tarja.

'Give me morphine and a drink.'

She didn't try to walk upright, but inched along the wet floor on her bottom to the drawer, to get the morphine tablets. When she pulled the handle, with the side-to-side rolling of the trawler, the drawer came crashing out on top of her. She scrabbled around gathering bits and pieces from the floor with one hand, holding the morphine tablets with the other. She was stuffing what she could back into the drawer and against the roll of the trawler, she managed to wedge it back into place.

With the same gentle concern as before, she handed him the tablets. He took them with his good hand and washed them down with water. He was lucky to have her onboard, or he would have got some rough treatment from the other two hellions. They didn't have it in them to behave in any other way, and he couldn't see them in a caring role.

'What about this confusion?' she asked.

It seemed trivial to start talking about his bewilderment in a trawler sinking in a severe Atlantic storm. After every seizure, he felt this way, talked about weird things for hours and, in the past, it was always in the safety of his bedroom. He never had an audience before to witness his bizarre behaviour, he knew it wasn't rational, but there was no way he could stop it happening. The surplus electricity generated by the seizure was overloading the wiring in his head, and he wouldn't feel right until he got rid of it. Well, that's how he thought about it. The groaning of the timbers was cutting through him like a knife. Certain sounds did that after a seizure. He hoped the timbers would hold out against the strain they were under and wouldn't suddenly snap like matchwood.

What should he tell her about his muddled feelings; maybe just an edited version of his nightmares.

'I heard thunder first, and then out of the clouds came a dragon attacking the trawler with fire blasting out of its mouth.'

'Strong medicine will do that to you!'

That might be true but he knew it wasn't the tablets that were causing his problem.

'One minute it was like some gargoyle from the dark side and next it changed into a human being.'

'It sounds biblical,' she said, drying the sweat and seawater from his face and neck. It was strange that he was sweating when he felt so cold, lying on the deck in water and more of it bombarding him from all sides.

'I had only a sword to defend the trawler as this monster came in for attack after attack.'

'Thought it might have been a crucifix instead of a sword,' she said. In another setting, they would have laughed at the joke, but he felt a long way from laughing. He was battling dragons as well as the natural elements, the storm. It was a fight to the death with the dragons; and it was real to him.

'The skipper was throwing poteen at it and cursing and Coleman was swearing.'

'That would be about right,' said Coleman, working hard at the steering wheel to keep the trawler running straight before the wind.

'I would hate to miss out. Was I not there at all?' said Tarja.

'Everyone is there for a short time, but I had a lot of fighting to do.'

For a moment, he was logical and figured out that one large wave followed three smaller ones. When the big wave hit, they were vulnerable, but Coleman was handling it well, taking the large ones square on the stern and holding the bows pointing straight ahead. That was the way to do it. If a huge wave hit the side of the trawler and not the stern, there was a good chance that they would turn turtle. He was quietly counting one two three and then waiting for the next big one to blast the trawler. His confusion returned.

'How big is a dragon?' It was his main concern and he couldn't get it out of his mind.

'He's off his head and rambling again,' muttered Coleman.

'There's one in Indonesia called the Komodo dragon. It's a large lizard,' she said. He knew she was playing along with him, but he felt it was important to know about dragons, especially if they were going to attack the trawler again.

'You are not telling me. How big are they?' He felt irritated that she didn't answer the specific question he asked. He needed to know. Did she not understand that the information was vital to him, even more important than the storm? Maybe the dragons were responsible for the storm, and if he killed them, the storm would stop.

'Ten metres long and over, it has such horrendous bacteria in its mouth that one bite, and you're dead.'

'Nice lad to meet on a dark night,' said Coleman, counting aloud to three and preparing himself for the next big strike. When it hit, there was a boom and bang as the wave split over the stern, washed over the wheelhouse, and showered a deluge on to the bow, burying it down with the weight of water. Coleman had just about time to talk between each wave rush and Pat knew he was treating him like a lunatic.

'I think I'd chance that lad before the skipper in one of his moods,' said Coleman.

'*Varanus komodoensis*,' said Tarja. Pat knew it was Latin. He had been a Mass server and anyway Catholics love Latin. It was the technical name for the dragon.

'It's Latin,' he said.

'I think he's much better,' she said, trying to make him more comfortable.

The next big wave hit, and they remained upright with the bow buried deep in the wave trough. If anything was going to turn them over, one of these big buggers would.

He had to hand it to this girl - she knew her stuff. He didn't know the technical name for the study of dragons. She probably wouldn't mind, but he might be letting himself down by asking her. Maybe he didn't always have to pretend that he knew everything, and that he was fearless. He carried that cross for being a man. He was anything but fearless, waiting for the next attack from the dragons. They nearly defeated him the last time.

Now he needed to ask himself a question, should he tell her about the dragon and the drowning? It might be too near the bone but what the hell, they were on a knife-edge with the storm and the dragons. People needed to know about dragons, and if he had to tell anyone, he would prefer to tell her.

'The dragon had me by the throat, and I was going down and down, holding my breath for as long as I could.'

'That won't happen to me,' said Coleman, 'After a few bottles of the skipper's poteen; I'll be dead before I hit the water,'

'What happened next?' she asked.

'I needed to say goodbye to everyone I knew, before I drowned.'

How could he say goodbye to anyone when he was at the bottom of the sea with a dragon trying to throttle him?

'I was denying that I was drowning, and I felt guilty about dying in such a foolish way,' he said, holding on to her.

'It's OK, Pat, I won't let the dragon get you again,' she said soothingly as she placed a towel on his forehead.

It felt good. Did he have a high temperature and was there something else she wasn't telling him? What did it all mean? He'd leave it, might be better not to know, he had enough on his plate with the dragons.

The next big pounding wave hit the trawler and shook it from bows to stern. They survived.

'I was coughing and spluttering, like a drink going down the wrong way and choking me.'

'That was terrible,' She had her arms around him to prevent him from getting thrown about by the violent rocking of the trawler. 'It went dark then and I stopped struggling with the dragon.'

The scene changed and it was peace and euphoria. He was with Hazel again, and she was watching her favourite film, 'The Sound of Music,' with Maria gliding along on a summer's day through lush vegetation with a background of mountains and music. It was restful after all the excitement, and then he was rushing down a tunnel towards a bright light at the end. Hazel and Mark were waiting for him with open arms at the end of the tunnel.

'Pat, stay with me and don't slip into another coma.'

He heard Tarja's voice coming from afar, and he didn't want to disappoint her, although he would prefer to stay in the mist in his head.

'I will,' he said as he forced himself to stay awake.

'Keep talking to me. What happened next?'

Seawater was dripping from her hair on to his beard.

'I think I died.'

'You are alive now.'

He was silent for a time and his head cleared a bit, he became aware of what was happening around him. Over the agonising drone of the storm, he could hear another rhythmic sound coming from somewhere. Something was loose, and it was coming from above them on the wheelhouse roof. Maybe it was the rattle of a slack bolt coming either from the searchlights, the aerial or heaven forbid the roof itself. The waves were trying to overwhelm them, and he would do his best to ignore it. He wasn't in a fit state to investigate what was happening

He had never seen Coleman like this, happy and carefree and in such a crisis. It was crazy, but he seemed elated at the thought of his imminent death.

Hundreds of fish were raining down on the deck and into the open forward hold as another gigantic wave roared over the trawler. The fish were flipping around helplessly on the deck, until they were washed overboard through the draining holes. He had never seen anything like that before.

'Are the fish on deck real?' he asked.

'They are real enough.' She was still holding his head cradled in her arms. It was terrifyingly violent out there. The drumming on the wheelhouse roof continued; and if the roof blew away, there was little hope of any of them surviving the storm.

'That's a net full of fish gone back into the sea,' muttered Coleman winding the steering wheel to bring the trawler back on course.

Pat drifted back into the nightmare. 'We were laying side-by-side on hospital trolleys covered in sheets.'

'Is this where I come in?' She pushed her wet hair back out of her eyes with her hand.

'It was a clinic with florescent lights and stainless steel fittings throughout.'

'A morgue and an autopsy I'll bet. I attended a few of those in my training,' She was supporting him to keep him upright.

'Yes that was it.' To stay upright, he didn't need her propping him up any more. He should go out and repair the aerial or whatever was loose on the wheelhouse roof, though he knew that he was a long way from being able to do anything like that but the clatter overhead was worrying the hell out of him.

He slipped back into confusion and nightmares again. The blond female pathologist burst through the swing doors, followed by an entourage of students. There was no doubt about it, she was in command. Except for her, they wore olive green theatre gowns, and surgical masks. She had her face uncovered, and her mask was hanging down around her neck.

'A drowning,' she said in an authoritative voice.

'She was admiring your red hair Tarja.' He could see her running her gloved hand through it.

'You like my hair Pat? What you see in a dream is what you wish for,' she said. He was conscious enough to know that he was giving himself, away rambling on about her red hair. It was always like this after a seizure, this strangeness in his head. Her red hair wouldn't matter much at the bottom of the sea, although it was so striking that you couldn't miss it.

The next big wave hit and Pat saw water leaking between the glass and the windscreen frame. The last thing they needed was the windows to blow in and leave them exposed to the elements. It was a lack of maintenance. If they had packed silicone into joints, they would have remained watertight in the storm. Life in different ways had failed the crew - the skipper, Coleman, and himself - and they hadn't given a damn about maintaining the trawler, or whether they lived or died. With the trawler in such poor condition, they should never have left port.

Maybe they had a death wish. He made a crazy mistake to take this girl with them. He now had the responsibility of getting her back alive and that wouldn't be easy. He'd keep an eye on the windscreen and when he felt a bit better, he'd prop it up from the inside. It would be impossible for anyone to steer the trawler without the protection of the windscreen. The next wave hit the trawler, and it shuddered. In his head, he was back in the morgue again.

'Totally paralysed on the trolley, I was trying to jump off and stop them cutting you up.'

'It not real, Pat,' she said, gently rocking him from side to side. The pathologist had a Sony recorder in her pocket connected to a microphone in her coat lapel. She switched it on.

'It was awful watching them.' Two other people came into the morgue dressed in hospital theatre clothes carrying white boxes. They were the transplant team to salvage your organs.

'They had their back to me, and I couldn't see what was going on.' She seemed nonplussed by the content of the nightmare and more worried about the storm.

'I hope it never happens,' she said, holding her hand on his forehead as if trying to banish the evil thoughts from his head. The pathologist slipped into her teaching role and went on to explain the post mortem procedure.

The wipers weren't coping that well with the torrents of water raining down on them. Condensation had formed on the inside of the windscreen, obscuring Coleman's view, and he was trying to clean it with a cloth. He was holding the steering wheel in his teeth and trying to rub the glass with his one good hand.

'Tarja, help Coleman,' he said, back again with them in the trawler.

'I will.' She went sliding along the floor on her bottom and grabbed on to the back of Coleman's seat to steady herself. She held on and managed to clean the mist from the windscreen. The next large wave hit and threw her back to the end of the wheelhouse.

'I'm OK, I'm OK, I shouldn't have let go.' She looked frightened. That last wave had been a strong one right enough; but Pat didn't feel concerned. He had other troubles on his mind. The pathologist pulled up her mask over her mouth and nose.

'Pat you must calm down or you'll have another seizure.' Tarja was shouting and lying on top of him to stop his violent shaking. The morgue assistant rolled back the sheer covering and exposed Tarja's naked body to the gawking students. She looked beautiful but he was so annoyed. They didn't have to let everyone see Tarja naked. Still talking, the pathologist held up the scalpel, explaining something about its knife handle. Light glinted off the polished steel blade while a soft Strauss waltz played in the background. It was terrifying seeing blood coming from Tarja's head as the pathologist cut through her scalp with a power saw and removed the top of her skull. It was a smaller saw than the one they had on the trawler. She prized open Tarja's skull with a chisel and mallet, cut the brain stem and carefully removed the brain. She weighed it and put it on a tray for dissection. With a bacon slicer, she cut the brain into thin broad strips like bacon rashers. White bits ran through the brown material of the slices. He wondered what they were. The pathologist examined the slices of brain tissue under a microscope and said something into her microphone.

'They're slicing your brain,' he shouted as loud as he could.

'Pat, it's OK. I still have my brain,' she said.

His sharpness had gone and he didn't understand all Tarja was saying. He'd be OK later. The storm was causing his teeth to chatter. He hoped she understood that he wasn't fully himself, but he didn't know how to tell her that, and anyway he was watching the pathologist. She was drawing what looked like a red pencil line across Tarja's shoulder and down both sides to her navel.

He was trying to think of the name of that particular triangle, it was either equilateral or isosceles. It would annoy his Franciscan teachers if they knew that he was having difficulty with triangles, although they would feel more disturbed by the occasion of sin Tarja's naked body presented.

'Talk to me, Pat.' It was faint coming from afar, but he could just about hear Tarja's voice. He couldn't give it his attention as another noise intruded – like the sound of tearing duct tape. He liked pulling duct tape from cardboard boxes, new TV, washing machines or whatever but this time he didn't like what he saw. The pathologist was peeling back the skin from Tarja's chest and stomach. Her ribs were white and evenly spaced with lumps of red flesh underneath in the chest cavity. It was terrible seeing all these students bending over to get a better look at Tarja's inside. If only he could turn away or close his eyes. Her assistant handed her another shiny instrument like a bolt cutter and seconds later, he heard a sound like chicken bones snapping. She was cutting through Tarja's sternum and ribs and putting corrugated cardboard over the ends of the bones. That would protect her from getting stabbed on the jagged edges of Tarja's ribs. She took something out of the chest cavity and held it up for her students see,

'An almost perfect specimen, this is the engine of the body - the heart.' It was about the size of a closed fist, and she passed it over to the transplant team. Tarja needed it and they would have to put it back where it came from. He was screaming at them but no sound came. The pathologist went on talking as she removed all of Tarja's internal organs. It was like playing a part in a horror movie, and he was crying but no tears came.

'This is the chemical factory of the body,' she said, as she removed Tarja's stomach, liver, pancreas and held each organ aloft for inspection.

'Now we have the large and small intestine at approximately 1.5 metres and 7 metres long.' She removed them from the body.

'We're done here. Put everything back and close up,' she said to the morgue assistant and, turning around, she removed her mask and protective gloves. It was good the medical team were replacing all Tarja's bits. She would need them to get going again. The pathologist donned a fresh mask and gloves. He could hear the clunk of her theatre clogs as she walked towards him.

'Right let's do this one next,' she said to the entourage of students. She removed the white sheet covering his body and with the scalpel poised, was ready to make the first cut. His terror was indescribable. Since locked accidentally in the cupboard under the stairs, as a child, he had not felt such fear, and panic. Tarja shouting at him woke him out of his trance. He was screaming and she and Coleman were holding him down. His head was clearing, what a fiasco he had caused.

'Sorry, you can let me up now.' They helped him sit up and Coleman rushed back to steer the trawler. The next wave hit and the trawler trembled along its length like a wounded animal. It was as if to remind him of the reality of their situation, the next wave could sink them.

'You were hysterical; we had to hold you down.'

'I know.' That was the worst reaction he ever had after a seizure. They had been getting worse over the years. He dreaded the thought of all of them trapped in one of those nightmares forever. It was his definitions of madness, living in a terrifying make believe world for the rest of his life. Could it happen? He didn't know but thank goodness that one was about over. He was weary and he couldn't hold up his head for much longer. It got so heavy that he had to let it fall on to Tarja's shoulder. He was drifting away again. She gently lowered his head on to her lap. He felt her thighs against his neck and head and other thoughts came to him. Damn it, he shouldn't be thinking of such things in this situation. The next wave hit and he could feel the vibrations coming through Tarja's thighs up from the floor. That was the last he remembered.

19

Pat woke with a start. It was dark and the waves were still pounding the trawler sending sheets of black sea tipped with white foam over the top of the wheelhouse. The next wave hit with force and he held his breath; but everything settled down and they were still afloat.

He didn't know how long he had been unconscious, but this time he was in the real world and his head was clear. How bad would his shoulder ache without morphine? With his head cradled in her lap, Tarja was holding his neck steady with her hands. The juddering of the trawler as it crashed into the wave crests was shaking his whole body. Tarja was mothering him. Cosseted in her arms, he felt protected from what was happening around him. It was an illusion of safety and comfort with the storm threatening to destroy them. Coleman was slumped forward, looking exhausted. He had tied the steering wheel down to the floor. Tarja had her eyes closed. Pat realised that he had misread this girl; she was such a decent human being who had offered nothing but help and kindness since she came onboard. He tried to sit up without waking her but when he moved she opened her eyes.

'How are you feeling?' She laid her hand on his forehead to check his temperature.

'Weak and in pain. Is everything holding?'

'Yes. What's our next move?' asked Coleman, straightening up

Pat got to his feet and took a cautious step, supporting himself against the wheelhouse wall. With everything moving around him, it was like trying to walk inside a rolling barrel. He stumbled and it took a few minutes to get his sea legs. Tarja was hovering over him, ready to catch him if he tumbled over. A wave hit and she caught him in time, otherwise he'd have ended on the wheelhouse floor. He grabbed on to a trawler rib which was vibrating from the force of the wave. How long would the trawler stand up to this battering?

'We're rocking badly.'

He stopped to catch his breath. The next powerful wave hit, and it tore the cross-shaped aerial from its mountings on the wheelhouse roof. On its way down it hit the windscreen in front of Coleman and split it from top to bottom. The bang startled Coleman and he jumped up in his seat. If the aerial had come through the windscreen, it would have decapitated him. It was hanging there, swinging backwards and forwards, held to the roof by guy wires. One of the securing bolts must have broken and caused the rattle that had disturbed him so much. If the guy wires snapped, the aerial would come in on top of them.

He knew what he had to do - go on to the deck and climb up the ladder to the wheelhouse roof, cut the guy wires, and push the aerial overboard. In this storm and with one immobile hand, it wasn't going to be easy.

'Tarja, get me the wire cutters, it's under the dash.'

'Pat, you can't go out there. I'll do it.'

'No give me the wire cutters.'

'I'm coming with you.'

'One of us out there is enough.'

'No matter what, I'm going with you.'

'Then watch out for every fourth wave, it's a big one.'

He didn't waste energy arguing, but started to crawl towards the wheelhouse door to get on deck. His timing was bad and the next wave hit him as he crawled on to the deck. The sheer volume of water pushed him backwards along the deck. It got inside his oilskins and ran down his back. He shivered. It was a big effort to crawl forward, but finally he reached the bottom of the ladder. Using his one good hand, and holding the wire cutters in his teeth, he started to climb to the top of the wheelhouse. He couldn't see much with water lashing his face. He felt Tarja climbing up behind him and, at the top; she put both arms around his legs and held him tightly against the ladder. The waves were threatening to tear him off the ladder and without her holding him, he wouldn't have been able to reach out and cut the guy wires. He severed them, one, two, three and the aerial fell to the deck and bounced into the sea. It floated on top of a wave for a while before sinking. He tried to hold on to the wire cutters but it slipped from his hand, hit the deck and went overboard. It was too heavy to float and disappeared into the deep. He hadn't meant that to happen as he might have further use for it.

They crawled back to the wheelhouse, where he sat down on the bench seat, and Tarja sat beside him.

'Good God, I'm exhausted.'

'That's the radio gone, no more distress or any other calls,' said Coleman, working the steering wheel.

'We still have a windscreen.'

If there was a negative aspect in a situation Coleman would find it but apart from that, he was doing good work in steering the trawler. It was demanding without engine power, spinning the wheel this way and that to keep them from broad siding.

Pat peered through the windscreen. How was Coleman missing what was happening?

'There's tons of water blowing into the hold out there.' He was holding on to the back of Coleman's seat to steady himself.

'The water in there now is about the same weight as the offal and ice we threw overboard,' said Coleman.

'What the hell is wrong with your head? You saw the bloody hold flooding, and you said nothing.'

Pat was livid and he couldn't control the anger in his voice. Coleman didn't answer.

'Right, we'll close down the hatch covers and use the pumps to empty the hold,' he said, aware of the extra drain that would put on the batteries.

'I'll crawl out there and close them,' said Tarja, standing behind him.

'No I'll do it myself.'

Apart from her, the others were bloody useless to him - dumb and dumber - and if he were able to walk on water, he'd get the hell away from them now. There was no sense in getting hyper, and as his anger cooled, he wondered how he would manage out there with a defunct shoulder. Getting to the forward deck was the first part of the problem, although he probably could crawl along on his good shoulder. Once there, however he'd still have difficulty closing the hatch covers.

'Pat, you need a break, let me and Coleman do this job.'

What she said made sense – drained, and in his present condition, he probably didn't have enough strength to haul himself from one hatch cover to the next. He could stay behind in the wheelhouse and keep the trawler running straight before the wind.

'If I see anything coming, I'll give a blast of the foghorn to let them know we're here.'

To avoid a collision, if there wasn't time to give a blast of the foghorn, he would have to broadside the trawler. Without a fully functioning engine, it was a dicey manoeuvre. There was a risk of getting blown over, and settling upside down in the sea, with no chance of survival. An impact with whatever was out there was another choice, although the likelihood of getting smashed to smithereens in the collision was real. He didn't mention any of that to them, it was more than they needed to know, and anyway it was all conjecture, the ramblings of someone getting over an epileptic seizure, or was it?

Coleman grunted and that was as much as he was going to get out of him.

'You need to be careful out there,' Pat said to both of them.

He hoisted himself on to the seat vacated by Coleman and tied the seat belt tightly around him. If he blacked out again, it would stop him from falling to the floor.

He started to spin the steering wheel to keep the gale blowing straight astern of the trawler. If he could keep the blue triangular flag on the forward mast blowing away from him, the trawler was on the right heading. He would have preferred to use the compass; but it was shimmering before his eyes each time he looked at it – another after effect of his seizure that in truth hadn't fully gone away. He wouldn't mention that to them either, they had more than enough to contend with out there.

The storm was propelling them along inside a dense grey bubble of Atlantic fog. It reflected the glare of the searchlight back into the wheelhouse, and he had to shade his eyes to see the forward deck. They were making good progress. Working as a team, they were pushing the hold covers into place without bolting them down. They would have needed spanners to tighten the bolts, and it would be difficult work for the one-handed Coleman and an inexperienced Tarja. It would have taken much longer; and they didn't have the time to spare.

The skipper, still drunk, and doped from the sleeping tablets, staggered up from his bunk into the wheelhouse. It took him a few minutes to realise the cargo hold was empty except for seawater.

'What's going on? Have you lost your bloody mind? Let me out there.' He stumbled out of the wheelhouse. He would soon sober up out there.

Without warning, it came straight at them out of the fog, the lifeless hulk of a factory ship. It was like a skyscraper towering over them.

In desperation Pat spun the steering wheel hard to port, but it didn't prevent the trawler from taking a hit as the ship went past, probably unaware that they had hit anything. A judder went through the trawler and the steering cable snapped with a sharp resonating twang. The wheel went slack in Pat's hands as he tried to right the trawler from its forty-degree list. They were going over, and tied tightly into the steering seat wasn't the best place to be. Underwater and one-handed, he would find it impossible to free himself. They seemed to hang there forever, before the trawler started to right itself, a tribute to its Clyde side designers. The pumps were still labouring, but the masthead light had gone out.

Pat had heard another sound - the crunch of bone on wood as the skipper, stumbling outside the wheelhouse, lost his balance and fell headlong on to the lower deck. He lay there motionless. The violent coming about had thrown the others around the deck as well. Tarja had hit against the outer wheelhouse wall; she looked dazed and blood was running from a cut in her forehead. Coleman had been hurled against the mast step and was barely conscious with blood streaming from cuts to his face and head.

Pat crawled forward on all fours, along the side of the wheelhouse and made his way painfully down on to the lower deck to the skipper. The rain driven by the storm was pouring down on him. He could just about see the skipper lying there with his face covered in blood. He was unconscious and looked dead, apart from the rise and fall of his chest. Most of the blood was coming from a nasty gash in his forehead and the rain was spreading it all over his face.

Tarja and Coleman were also crawling along the deck to the skipper, and she started to clean the blood from his face and head. Pat felt a surge of emotion; that was his uncle lying there, probably dying, and he couldn't do anything about it. Against his best efforts, he was crying. He needed to control himself. He swallowed hard, shook his head and let the rain wash away his tears. That was it, no more of this nonsense.

Coleman, also bloodied but conscious was lying on the deck with his eyes closed, with rain lashing into his face.

'How…are you?' asked Pat.

'I feel strange. I am seeing two of everything and I can't remember much.' said Coleman.

'It's double vision, you must try to stay awake,' said Tarja, bracing herself as the next wave washed over them. Down low on the deck, they had shelter from the worst of the storm, but the rain was bucketing down in a constant deluge.

Pat had read somewhere that it was important to keep a head injury case awake until medical help arrived. If Coleman went to sleep, he might not wake up. It sounded dramatic and maybe he had misunderstood the article, but he would try to keep him awake. They didn't have that same option with the skipper and medical help was a long way off.

'We'll move the skipper back to the wheelhouse,' shouted Pat.

'We shouldn't move him but he'll die of the exposure if we leave him out here,' shouted Tarja.

In their situation, it would be impossible to pull the unconscious skipper up the ladder to the wheelhouse. Maybe a better route would be to drop into the forward hold, swim almost the length of the trawler to the companionway. This lead to the wheelhouse and they could haul the skipper behind them.

'I'll go and get some kind of stretcher,' yelled Tarja. He could hear the water sloshing as she crawled back along the deck and away from them.

'Are you still awake, Coleman?'

'I'm sleepy.' His eyes remained closed as he talked.

Tarja returned and gently wrapped foam around the skipper's neck and tied it with the strips cut from a dishcloth. She had found a plywood board to act as a stretcher. They pushed it under the skipper and tied him to it ready for the move to the wheelhouse.

With Pat pulling and the others pushing, they moved the skipper towards a forward hatch. The storm was all but wrenching the stretcher away from them.

'Coleman, open the hatch!' Pat shouted. It was like watching a slow motion scene as Coleman painstakingly opened the hatch. Tarja switched on her headband light and jumped feet first into the hold. Pat heard the splash as she hit the water. With a wetsuit on, she was the most suitably dressed person on the trawler.

'Stand well back, the stretcher is next,' Pat shouted, leaning over the edge of the hold. He couldn't be sure that she had heard him, and he should have warned her before she jumped. If the stretcher hit her, falling from that height, it would kill her. He would have to change his plans.

'Push the stretcher in after me and close the hatch?' he shouted into Coleman's ear. Coleman nodded his head. Pat felt he understood. He didn't relish the thought of swimming one - handed the length of the trawler, while pulling the stretcher behind him. Tarja was a Godsend - without her it would be impossible to do any of this. He could become claustrophobic; easily, and then there was the additional problem of the watertight door separating the forward hold from the rest of the trawler.

He would deal with that one when they came to it. He sat on the edge of the hatch and the storm would have blown him in, if Coleman weren't holding him. He motioned to Coleman to let go, and dropping into the hold he went under. He surfaced, coughing and spluttering, next to Tarja. He motioned to her to move away to a safe distance. The stretcher, with the skipper attached, splashed into the water alongside them. Immersed in seawater, Pat's injured arm felt frozen. The hatch closed over them.

The water inside the hold sloshed from side to side as the trawler rolled from port to starboard and in the same movement, either mounted the crest of a wave, or descended into a trough. The noise inside the hull was ear splitting, like the drum of a steel mill. Without Tarja's light, he would have found it impossible to continue. She swam over to the stretcher and set about examining the skipper.

'No change,' she shouted.

Pat waited for the bows to lift again and shouted,

'Push!'

The stretcher shot forward and they reached the waterproof door. He waited for the trawler to descend into a trough and shouted,

'Turn anti clockwise!' Together they tried to turn the wheel to release the lock; but it wouldn't budge. It was stiff and rusted. He had never seen it opened during his time on the trawler. Imprisoned in the forward hold, there was no way he could get to the hatch cover above their heads, and even if he could, it would not open from the inside. That's the way the designers planned it.

Trapped, Pat panicked. The hold was half-full with water and the frenzied movements of the trawler were tossing him about like a rag doll. He was claustrophobic and a slow death in a sealed wooden box, filling with water wasn't the end he wanted but there was nothing he could do, it would soon be over.

Banging coming from the other side of the bulkhead interrupted his thoughts. Was it his imagination or could it be Coleman? He answered by thumping the bulkhead door with his fist. The reply was one hard knock with something heavy – maybe a lump of wood or iron. For Coleman to get there, in his condition, was an extraordinary achievement. Pat waited for the trawler's bows to rise, before trying to rotate the wheel to release the door lock. It wouldn't budge; rusted solid from lack of maintenance, and all it needed was a squirt of grease, so that they wouldn't be in this predicament. They tried repeatedly to unlock the door without success. He hoped Coleman, on the other side of the bulkhead, was also trying to free the door.

Without warning, the door burst open and the force of water funnelling through from the stern propelled Coleman, head first into the bows. They all surfed forward and, thankfully, the stretcher remained upright. The next change in the wave cycle lifted the bows, and washed them backwards, through the bulkhead door to the bottom of the companionway. Pat grabbed the handrail and crawled up the steps, pulling the stretcher behind him. The others pushed. The buffeting, they were taking, made their task difficult, but somehow they dragged the stretcher to the relative safety of the wheelhouse.

Tarja removed the cushions from the bench seat, and they pushed the stretcher on to it.

Pat was feeling weak and tired, and he would like to sleep but there was no time for that. The storm was still battering them. It was now time to turn on the bilge pump that he was trying to keep in reserve. He started crawling towards the switches but Tarja anticipated what he was doing.

'Leave that to me and get some rest.'

He needed sleep. His eyes wandered to the blue statue of the Virgin Mary attached to the dash. A neighbour, back from the Knock shrine, had given it to the skipper. It might be a lucky omen and, now, they needed all the luck they could get. Exhausted from pain and effort, he lay down on the floor, and Tarja pushed a cushion under his head.

Without steerage and running skewed before the weather, the trawler threatened to broach and roll over with disastrous results. They were in real danger, but he was so exhausted that he was past caring about controlling the trawler. Nobody leaves this world alive; he wouldn't mind being dead, but dying was the problem. The sea had taken them on and the sea was winning.

'I can't keep Coleman awake any longer,' she said. He was lying on the bench across from the skipper, and had fallen asleep, snoring.

'Let him sleep and hope for the best.'

With her back to the swaying bulkhead, she was crying,

'What a way to end it all. I made a mistake letting the Skipper take the trawler out in this weather. You should never have been on-board, the risk was too great. It'll be a miracle if we don't drown in the Atlantic.'

Tarja didn't say anything. She probably knew the risks, as well as he did. She lay down close to him and held his hand. It must feel cold and lifeless like the rest of him. She was talking to him; well, he thought she was.

'If only I'd met you in the past, I'd have had less suffering and a more fulfilled life.'

He was thinking about her parents - they didn't deserve this. How would they hear of the tragedy? Her passport in the holdall in the hotel would have her home address and telephone number. The Garda would telephone her parents. She was still talking,

'You're the driving force, you must keep going.'

A spent force! He had not much left in the tank, but he would give his all to save them. They were on their own out here and the emergency services wouldn't start a search until the storm was over and the fog had cleared.

Right now, so many things on the trawler needed his attention, but he was so tired.

'If we're to survive at all, we'll need to repair the steering.'

It wasn't going to be an easy job getting the steerage linkage working again. He eased his hand from her grasp and managed to sit up.

'We better do it now,' she said, getting to her feet and helping him to stand upright. With his shoulder paining him, and with the see-saw motion of the trawler, he was finding it difficult to stay balanced without her holding on to him. Coleman had to cope with the difficulty of handicap all his life, but he must have learned to compensate. One way or another, he never complained about having only one hand.

The noise was horrendous and the trawler was ploughing forward while rising and falling with the moving waves. It was like a sound from hell, lost souls in despair, battering away on their anvils, although he hadn't heard of anvils getting battered down there before – had only heard the expression. His Franciscan teachers had talked a lot about the fires of hell, the blaze, the white heat and stench of burning souls, but there was never a mention about anvils.

20

The trawler swayed, and Pat groaned in agony when he hit his injured shoulder against the hull.

'Pain is the worst - it saps your energy,' she said as she supported him. She helped him to sit down. For awhile, the pain was agonising, and then it settled back to a dull ache. He took a few minutes to regain his composure.

'Let's head for the engine room.' While the pain didn't look like it was going to ease any time soon he needed to try to get the steering working again.

'I can't take your full weight, but I will try to balance you as best I can.'

She held on to him as he took the first few faltering steps. He didn't say anything - the effort to speak would take too much out of him. Tarja let go of him when he could balance himself against the plunging of the trawler. They would probably end up to their necks in water and sump oil. She crawled along the floor to get the first aid kit from the drawer.

'Take this morphine tablet it'll help with the pain.' He looked at the tablet, thinking that an overdose was a preferable death to drowning. He couldn't give in to defeatist thinking and he had better not dwell on it.

He swallowed the tablet without a word, but he knew she was keeping a check on the dosage he was taking.

Once again with Tarja supporting him, they staggered down the companionway and stepped up to their waist in oily water. It filled the passageway from end to end, and with the trawler ducking and diving, it sloshed all over them. He hadn't bargained for the smell and the fumes.

'It's hard to breath,' she shouted, coughing and spluttering.

'We need masks.' That would be a luxury in their situation. They half stumbled and half swam to the engine room. The gunge stuck to their weather gear and left a high water mark around their chests. He imagined them as sea birds caught in a tanker's oil spill and flapping around helplessly. In the engine room, with Tarja's help, he climbed on to the bench, near the broken steering cable. When it shattered, it had cut a groove along the wooden hull. A reminder that they could suffer injury or death, if the cable snapped again while they were repairing it. It was a risk they had to take. For this job, they needed a few strong hands, but all they had were three and one badly compromised operator - himself.

'I'm not going to be much help to you. You are going to have to do most of the work.' He was trying to wedge his feet against the hull to stop moving about with every roll of the trawler.

'What do you want me to do?'

'Bolt the ends of the cable together.'

He pointed to a box of U-bolts stacked on the corner shelf. After they spliced the cable, they would have to tension it using the only suitable tool they had, the wire fence stretcher. It was lying around somewhere on one of the shelves. He never had considered that they would have use for a fence stretcher on the trawler and wondered that someone had the foresight to bring it on board for this purpose. It certainly was not the skipper; he was a rough-and-ready individual with no thought for his own or anyone else's safety. Well, that's the way he was.

'I hope it's strong enough for the job.'

As she searched the shelves for the fence stretcher, the heaving mix of sump oil and water threatened to suffocate her. Pat's eardrums were bursting from the noise of the storm, and if he ever went to sea again he would bring earplugs. That's if they lived through this hell, and at this point he wouldn't take any bets on it.

Tarja found the fence stretcher, attached it to both ends of the cable and pulled them together. He felt she was dexterous enough to be a brain surgeon. One handed, he tightened the nuts on the U-bolts with the ratchet spanner and that was it.

'I'm going to tension the cable, go as far away as you can in case it snaps. There's no sense in putting both of us at risk.'

'Be careful.'

This showed concern for him, but it was irrelevant, he was being as careful as he possibly could be.

With the ratchet spanner, he turned the nut on the fence stretcher and gradually pulled the rudder into a straight-ahead position. With each turn of the spanner, the tension on the cable increased with a pinging sound. The taut cable, out of its protective sleeve was rubbing along the side of the hull, and tearing into the wood like a rasp. In their circumstances it didn't matter, so he tightened the cable fully.

'It's holding. Let's get out of here, and bring some water buckets with us. I might manage to take one.'

To let Coleman know that they had repaired the cable, he hit it with a spanner. That was a funny thing about trawlers - even in a storm, sound carried. The cable started to move. They had steering again.

They could use the buckets as sea anchors if they got them back to the wheelhouse. Slung from the stern of the trawler they would have a similar effect as the parachute deployed on a military jet to slow it down on landing. They floated the buckets before them. One tipped over, filled up with sludge, and with a gulping sound, disappeared to the bottom.

They made it back to the wheelhouse without losing any more buckets and Pat took over steering the trawler from Coleman, who was barely conscious. The straight-ahead mark on the top of the wheel was no longer accurate; they were travelling sideways. By trial and error, he found the steering wheel position that held them on a straight line course. With Tarja's help they tied the wheel to the floor. Each wave was a falling curve of tonnes of seawater as it crashed down on the trawler, blotting out the curtain of fog that surrounded them as it landed on the deck. Pat knew that it wasn't if, but when, they would go under.

Something was different and it took Pat a few seconds to realise what it was. The slurp, slurp of the pumps had stopped. The batteries, out of charge, were dead and there was nothing to power the pumps. From this point on the trawler was sinking. Out of the corner of his eye, he saw Tarja staring at him. He would have to call it, something he hoped he would never have to do.

'We'll need to abandon ship, the pumps are gone, and we're going down,' he said quietly. It didn't register with her for a minute.

'What will we do now?' She caught hold of his arm.

Coleman was only half awake and couldn't focus on what was happening. What to do next was a good question. Pat had been thinking about it since the trawler started taking water and there wasn't an easy solution. The big challenge was how to get everyone into the life-raft after launching it. The best way was to push the life-raft overboard and keep it tied to the trawler to stop it floating away, but the next step was tricky. The crew would need to jump overboard and swim to the life-raft. In their present condition, neither the skipper nor Coleman was fit to swim. In that sea and with his injuries, it was debatable if he himself could swim.

'I don't know how we're going to get to the life-raft when it's in the sea,' he said.

'In my wetsuit, I can help everyone out of the water and into the life-raft.'

'Maybe in a calmer sea but out there we could lose everyone.'

He looked out over the mountainous waves; that was understating it. Tarja seemed relieved, although she was doing a good job of trying to hide her fear. There must be some other way. It was strange but of all the books he had read on sea rescue, none of them addressed this predicament.

Bleary-eyed; his head was still pounding, and he hadn't been able to clear it. Right enough when he had seizures in the past he had gone to bed and slept off the effects. Chance would be a fine thing. The morphine, helping with the pain, was contributing to his fuzziness. While Tarja was supportive, and encouraging, all he wanted was sleep. A miracle wouldn't go amiss just about now.

Maybe the right way forward was to send her off on her own in the life-raft and leave him and the others behind to meet their fate. She wouldn't agree to that one, although in many respects it was the logical way to go about it, save one rather than lose all. The army types would applaud that approach and before leaving, they would probably shoot those left behind - collateral damage. It would provide a neat solution. None of them - the skipper, Coleman or himself - valued their lives much. He had thought of a risky solution to their difficulty, and one he wouldn't have considered if their circumstances weren't desperate. It might work. He would run it past Tarja.

'What if we put everyone into the life-raft on the forward deck, and wait for the trawler to sink low enough in the water so that we can float off?'

'I have never heard of that tried before,' she said.

'I know it's chancy. The trawler could pull us down with it,' he said, but there was no other option he could think of.

'When we get the lifeboat into the water, we'll have to paddle like crazy to get as far away from the trawler as soon as possible before it sinks,' she said.

'I'm in no great shape for paddling with my shoulder injury,' He tried to move his damaged shoulder and wincing with pain.

'We can't just give up. Let's try it,' said Tarja.

He had come to trust her judgement a lot, and if she was saying 'yes' they might have a chance. There was one serious weakness to his plan that he hadn't mentioned. He was expecting the bow of the trawler to sink first to allow the life-raft to float off the forward deck. If that didn't happen and the stern went down first they would be thirty feet in the air and sliding backwards into the ocean and to certain death. If she weren't under such strain, she would have probably spotted the flaw herself. Well, he assumed she hadn't spotted it. It was, without exaggeration, a life or death decision for him to make, and it wasn't only about his own life.

'The bows might not sink first.' He waited for her reaction.

'I know, but it's the only chance we have.'

She had second-guessed him. She reminded him of someone else, his beloved Hazel. He thought about Hazel, and the positive way she looked on life. She would have said something similar - 'Go for it, Pat.' It was her way of showing approval, and if it failed, she wouldn't criticise him. He thought he felt her presence close to him and that was all he needed to keep him going.

'Let's take the skipper down first.'

Moving the skipper down to the life-raft on the forward deck wouldn't be easy. Tarja was the only able-bodied person, and she would have to do most of the hauling.

'OK, but I think we should give him morphine in case he's in pain. I hope it doesn't do him harm.' She opened the morphine bottle, shook two tablets out into her palm, and waited for Pat to reply.

'Go ahead; it's the humane thing to do. We'll use the makeshift stretcher again.'

'Ok.' She set about rolling the skipper from the wheelhouse bunk onto the plywood stretcher. Manhandling the skipper in this fashion was not doing him any good, but they had to get him to the life-raft. They hauled him tied to the stretcher, down to the life-raft. Coleman followed instructions like a robot, without answering back.

'I think Coleman is suffering from concussion,' she whispered.

'Is there anything we can do?'

'Don't think so, he needs medical attention.'

'Like the rest of us.'

The inflatable rubber life-raft was the best piece of equipment on board the trawler. It was a former Royal Navy eight-man life-raft. The skipper's ex-wife had found it at a marine auction in the UK. She was over there on a trip to visit her family. She had the skipper's safety in mind, considering the age of the trawler, when she bought it.

The tent canopy over the top of the life-raft would act like an umbrella and protect them from the bucketing rain. On the downside, the life-raft's navy camouflage, olive green with black daubs would make it difficult for rescuers to spot them. Their best chance was to make it to shore somewhere, but with their luck, it would probably be on a deserted island at the back of beyond. The skipper remained motionless where they laid him on the life-raft and his shallow breathing was the only sign of life. It was terrible looking at him and feeling so powerless. Pat decided to talk to him on the off-chance he could hear.

'Hang on in there, skipper, we'll soon have you home.' He didn't expect a response and none came, but somehow he felt it was his duty as a nephew to make some gesture. He felt relief.

'They're the worst seas I have ever seen, skipper, worse than anything in Finland.' Tarja gave Pat a knowing look; the skipper liked to think of himself as macho man.

'Give me a minute to catch my breath. We have a bit more work to do.' Pat was sitting on the side of the life-raft and supporting himself with his good hand. He was feeling faint; he had used up his energy moving the skipper from the wheelhouse to the life-raft.

'You poor man, you're exhausted.' She was sitting on her hunkers before him, holding his head in her hands. He sighed and felt like just letting go. To hell with it, maybe it was all over for them.

'Get on with it, Pat; you know I'm here with you.'

It was Hazel's voice in his head and the joy of hearing her energized him. He was ready for the next step. He wouldn't tell Tarja about the voice, or she would think he had lost it. He gently pushed her hands away from his face.

'We need to slow down the trawler before launching the life-raft. If we drop the anchor it might help a bit.' He started crawling along the deck towards the anchor winch.

Normally, they used the engine to let out the anchor, and it was a familiar sound on the trawler, the clank of heavy chains moving across the deck. This time they would have to do it by hand, cranking the winch handle until the anchor finally reached the ocean floor. The pain in his injured shoulder was almost unbearable even before he started to turn the winch handle. The only thing keeping him going was Hazel's voice, encouraging him,

'You can do it, Pat.'

They took it in turns and Tarja was giving her all, winding the handle for twice as long as he did and only stopping when she was on the point of collapse. It took a long time, an hour or more of effort, until the anchor finally hit the ocean floor.

'You did a good job.' He lay down on the deck to rest. He had overdone it, his breath was coming in gasps, his heart was racing and its beats were pounding away in his ears.

'So did you.' She lay down beside him and gave him a peck on the cheek. Tarja was first to move, she went over to check on the skipper and Coleman. Pats system had quietened down, there was no pulsing in his ears; but the ache in his shoulder was still there.

'There's no great change, about the same as before.' She checked their pulses and started to feed them water from a spoon.

'I think it's time for you to take more morphine.'

'Thank God for morphine. I don't know how I'd manage without it.'

Fully awake, he realised that things were not going as he had envisaged. The trawler was lower in the water all right, but it was going down stern first. This was a catastrophe if it continued. They would find themselves in the life-raft looking down at the waves thirty feet beneath them and sliding backwards into a watery grave.

21

Under the blanket of clouds, lightning lit up the trawler and highlighted the crest of the wave breaking over the stern.

Pat was sitting on the deck with his back to the life-raft and up to his stomach in seawater. Tarja was sitting close to him and above the howl of the storm; he heard an angry clap of thunder. A few feet more of water on the deck and they were in danger of getting washed overboard.

'That didn't work well.'

He moved awkwardly to look at the deck tilting backwards towards the stern.

'The bows should have filled up first,' said Tarja

'Well that didn't happen, now we're in a right fix.'

Good Lord, what could he do now? He was searching for a solution and whatever he came up with this time, would have to work. He was running out of second chances. There might be something. If they opened the seacock in the forward hold, the trawler would sink nose first, and they could float the life-raft off the deck. It was worth a try. He would have to call on all his reserve to remove the tonnes of pig-iron ballast to get to the seacock.

'If we take out the seacock the bows should flood first.'

He didn't tell her about the pig-iron - that would come later.

'You are so jaded.'

She was looking at him with concern, and then she got down on all fours and crawled to the ladder leading to the hold. He followed more slowly, sliding on his rear along the deck, in pain from his shoulder. Nauseated, he felt a weakness in his stomach; maybe the eastern types were right that all strength comes from the lower gut. She climbed down the ladder, and he followed holding on with his good hand. It gave him some idea of the difficulties the one-handed Coleman must have in doing even simple jobs onboard the trawler.

Without the gale trying to blow them over, it was easier to move around inside the hold than on deck, although the trawler was yawing and rolling as before. When he opened the door to the forward compartment, it was, as he expected, stacked with pig-iron ballast.

'Oh, I didn't know that was there.' She sounded surprised.

'We'll have to move these lumps to get to the seacock,' he said.

Tarja got down on her knees and started to carry the pig-iron, one lump at a time into the main hold.

'Fling them, there's no need to haul.'

Pat used his good hand to lift and toss the smaller lumps of pig-iron into a pile behind him, and he had to leave the bigger lumps for Tarja to heave out of the way. He would have needed both hands to shift them. The hold was stifling and before long, they had to take off their weather gear, Tarja easing his oilskins over his shoulder. Past the point of exhaustion and pain, he was barely aware of his actions.

Eventually they uncovered the seacock, screwed into the trawler floor and coated with grease to keep it from rusting.

'Let's turn it together.'

With Pat pushing and Tarja pulling on either side of the T-shaped handle the seacock opened slowly and water trickled in. With the seacock fully opened, the flow didn't improve much, and it was far from the deluge he expected.

'It's not filling fast enough.'

'We couldn't have known that beforehand, we had to give it a try.'

Scuttling the trawler wasn't an everyday event, and the designers had probably put in filters to slow the flow of water, in case there was a change of mind and that, for whatever reason, the crew decided to halt sinking the trawler.

He thought he could see disappointment and weariness in her eyes and a 'what next' question. He needed divine inspiration to get them off the trawler alive.

'Let's get back on deck.' He grabbed his weather gear in his good hand and tried to make his way to the ladder. He had to leave the oilskins behind. It didn't matter - they had a spare set in the wheelhouse.

Safely out of the hold, Tarja crawled to the wheelhouse to get the spare oilskins, leaving Pat to consider their next move. The oilskins didn't matter much - he was wet to the skin anyway. It would be suicide to try to launch the life-raft from the bows. On the crest of a wave, they were as high as a two storied house above the sea. There was one more throw of the dice: move the life-raft to the stern of the trawler, but they probably didn't have enough manpower to budge it. He was still thinking about how to shift the life-raft when Tarja returned. He groaned when she raised his arm to push it into the oilskin sleeve and the pain in getting the oilskins over his injured shoulder was almost unbearable. He dropped his head on his chest for a few minutes to recover.

'We'll have to move the life-raft to the stern and launch it from there. Coleman might manage to help,' He tried to sound casual. He could see Tarja staring at him, taken aback by what he said. He couldn't blame her. What he was asking was nearly impossible.

They sat on the deck with their backs against the side of the life-raft and the water cascaded over them from the lifeboat cover. There was no point in going back inside the life-raft for shelter; the action they needed to take was out here, on the deck. He was aware of the added danger when they tried to move the life-raft, it might blow over and crush them to death. Their heads under their oilskins were close together, as they tried to make themselves heard above the howl of the storm. He was too tired and uncomfortable to cover all the angles. It crossed his mind that he should cover his mouth and nose and jump into the sea, it might be better than waiting for the inevitable, a slowly lingering drowning. That kind of death was never his preference, and now he had to consider the lives of the other people on the trawler.

'We need rollers from the engine room.'

'What do they look like?' Tarja's hair was hanging down in a dirty wet mat over her face.

'Round poles of wood.'

'I'll go and get them.' She crawled away from him along the deck to the hatch cover. Pat didn't argue. He knew that he couldn't manage to swim the length of the hold to the engine room and bring back the wooden poles. To swim that length in pitch-blackness and in water covered with a film of oil was a terrible task to give to her. In the past, he never had to hand over a difficult job to anyone; his strength and determination had always carried him through. The poles had lain unused in the engine room from the shark fishing days, when the fishermen had used them to roll the carcasses up the pier for processing.

Tarja's swim to the engine room and back would test her to the limit of her endurance. Swimming underwater, there was a danger that she would snag on a piece of equipment, and be unable to free herself before she drowned. That was unthinkable. Good Lord, he had no right to send her on this mission. How long should it take? He counted away the minutes in his head - there was no point in looking at his waterlogged watch, which had probably stopped by now. He kept pushing the seawater out of his eyes and staring at the open hatch, hoping to see Tarja appear. Ten minutes elapsed, and there was no sign of her. What should he do? What could he do?

If he had tied a rope around her waist before she went into the hold, he might have been able to pull her out. It was too late for that. Why did he let her go down there in the first place, her death would be on his conscience? Anyway, it probably didn't matter; they would all soon be dead. Without her help, there was no hope of their survival. An agonising fifteen minute passed, before Tarja's head popped out of the hold. She climbed on to the deck pulling the poles behind her and made the mistake of standing upright. An avalanche of water hit her and knocked her off her feet. She crawled over near him, covered in black slippery oil. She seemed unaffected by her adventure.

'Well done.' He hoped she could hear him above the noise that was all around them. They would need Coleman's help, if he was still conscious, to get the life-raft on to the rollers and shift it to the stern. This was their last chance.

Black clouds hung like drapes over the trawler as it ploughed through the waves driven by gale force winds. With water gushing from the scupper holes, the deck looked like the top of a submarine breaking the surface from the deep. He would have to be vigilant to keep a dazed Coleman safe while they moved the life-raft aft for launching. He could easily fall over the side and drown in that raging sea.

Regardless of the personal sacrifice, Pat felt it was his duty to get everyone safely back to port, especially Tarja. It was going to take every ounce of their collective strength to move the life-raft, although the water on deck might help as a lubricant under the twin keels. The storm blew Coleman over when he climbed out of the life-raft, and he rolled around on the deck. In a confused state, he was unaware of where he was, or what was happening to him. Pat tied one end of a rope around his waist and the other end around Coleman to keep him safe.

Tarja placed the rollers in front of the life-raft and Pat and Coleman pushed from the rear while she pulled on the rope attached to the bows. The life-raft refused to budge. He saw Tarja stumble and fall to her knees. She looked like she was crying, probably from frustration. He roared 'Pull' at the top of his voice. Although he couldn't be sure that she had heard him, she started to pull. He motioned to Coleman to continue pushing again.

Pat closed his eyes, his shoulder hurt. It didn't help that the gale force wind raging around them was threatening to blow them overboard. The water churned from the bottom of the sea was lashing across his face, it tasted and smelt like raw sewage, and the relentless noise was like the wails of a thousand demons from Hades after his eternal soul. A sound, even if he lived to the age of Methuselah, he wouldn't ever forget. It terrified him.

He couldn't be sure that it wasn't his imagination but the life-raft moved a few inches, and then shot forward on the rollers. It caught Tarja unawares; she slipped and fell into the path of the moving life-raft. He looked on in horror as it passed over her body and left her prone on the deck; she was either dead or badly injured. If alive, she would drown if he didn't get to her quickly. He should have anticipated the danger of having her out there, in front, pulling the life-raft from the front. Stupid, stupid! He untied Coleman and scrambled across the deck, and lifted her head out of the water, and on to his knee. After what seemed like an age, she coughed and struggling for breath she gasped,

'Oh my God! I nearly smothered. I'm trembling so much.'

'You're in shock.' It was all he could say, and he didn't know if it was right or wrong.

'Have you broken anything?'

She didn't answer, but it didn't seem so. She was a dead weight lying against him, and it took a few minutes before she shouted, 'I'm fine. I'm fine!'

She must have fallen between the keels of the life-raft, and it passed over her body without making contact. That was their first good luck. She sat up.

'Can you make it to the life-raft?'

'I think so.' She started to crawl on all fours towards the life-raft, now at the stern of the trawler. Pat went back for Coleman and led him like a child on hands and knees to the life-raft. Immersed in cold water for so long, Pat felt frozen, and his exposed skin, caked with salt was beginning to crack and bleed.

Coleman was more vacant than before, and he looked just about conscious. He wouldn't be able to give them much further help and that's what they needed most, apart from divine intervention. They half carried and half dragged Coleman across the deck towards the life-raft, with Tarja doing most of the work. They had to stop and rest every few feet and when they got to the life-raft, Pat's good shoulder had gone numb from the effort. They stretched Coleman down in the life-raft close to the unmoving skipper. The water was just about deep enough to float the life-raft off the deck and into the sea.

'You get in and I'll push it off.' It would be one hell of a scramble for him to jump into the moving life-raft, but he couldn't ask her to do it. She'd had enough traumas since joining them to last a lifetime.

'Not in your state, I'll do it,' she said, not waiting for an answer. She crawled around to the rear of the life-raft and tied a rope to its stern. He could see what she was trying to do. If she didn't manage to climb into the life-raft before it hit the sea, she could grab on to the trailing rope and haul herself aboard when they were afloat. It wasn't without risk, and she would need luck to survive. To make sure there were enough ropes out there to catch on to, she tied a second trailing rope to the lifeboat's sternpost and flung it overboard. Caught by the gale it blew under the trawler where it wouldn't be of much further use to her.

He had to be sensible and accept that with his injuries, he was unlikely to climb into the moving life-raft. He was finding it hard enough to climb into it while it was stationary. It was time to go and with Tarja's help, he boarded the life-raft and watched as she pushed to get it moving off the deck. He hoped the life-raft, designed to self-right would land right way up in the sea. It probably would, although they never tested its self-righting qualities. He dreaded the thought of a death, trapped upside-down in that sea. Hit by a wave, the bows of the life-raft hanging out over the deck, shot forward. Tarja, caught off-balance, lost her footing and landed face down on the deck. When she got to her knees, the life-raft and trailing ropes were away from her grasp. The only course left to her was to jump into the sea. With his good hand, he grabbed a rope tied to the trawler as the life-raft dropped into the water.

He was hoping to keep the life-raft close to the trawler until she managed to haul herself aboard. Even using all his strength, he wouldn't manage to hold on to the trailing rope for long, and she would have to drag herself aboard quickly before he had to let go. He was shouting 'Jump!' at the top of his voice, but she couldn't hear him. Struggling to hold on to the rope, it twisted around his little finger and snapped it off at the joint. Followed by a stream of blood, he saw the rope blowing out to sea and taking his finger with it. He felt nothing for a few moments and then came the searing pain in his hand and, not for the first time on this trip, he felt faint, but he would have to hold on.

Tarja jumped from the trawler. Caught by the wind she somersaulted before disappearing under the waves. Only half aware of what was happening, he would have to stay conscious and hold on to the rope.

'Don't faint, don't faint,' he repeated over and over again like a mantra. Tarja head bobbed up on top of a wave, near the life-raft, and then vanished. When next he saw her, she was trying to swim towards them. She would have to get to the life-raft soon, he couldn't hold for much longer. On the crest of a wave, she managed to grab a trailing rope next time she appeared. He couldn't do anything to help her fight against the sea. Hand over hand; she pulled herself along the rope until she climbed into the life-raft. He was fainting from pain and exhaustion, and he was powerless to resist unconsciousness.

22

Pat opened his eyes and for a few seconds, he couldn't work out where he was. Then it came back to him. The life-raft was rocking from side to side.

'Is it painful?'

Tarja was lying across him to keep him steady while she untied the tourniquet from his arm. A bandage covered his hand where his little finger should have been and a red bloodstain was showing through the dressing. She had attended to the wound while he was unconscious, and he was grateful for that. He couldn't have looked at the stump where his finger had been and the thought of the naked bone made him feel sick. He was never good with blood and gore. The pain kicked in.

'It's bad, thanks for bandaging it up.'

'Take those.' She placed two morphine tablets on his tongue.

'Try to gulp them down without water, I can't get to it.'

He tried to swallow the tablets, but his mouth was dry, and they stuck in his throat and almost choked him. In panic, he coughed up the tablets, and they dropped into the bilge where rubbish collected.

'Can you find them?'

With a look of disgust on her face, she searched around with her hands, in the mucky water for the tablets. She couldn't find them; they were water-soluble and had melted away.

He filled his mouth with spittle before she gave him the next two tablets, and he managed to swallow them. He kept his eyes tightly shut and waited for the pain to lessen, and tried to keep the reality that he had lost a finger out of his mind, he could deal with that later.

'We're going to die,' she said, resigned and tearful.

'No, we have every chance.' If only he could believe it. They were in a water filled coffin, and it was only a matter of time before they rolled over and stayed upside down. The skipper and Coleman were lying motionless in the bottom of the life-raft. Occasionally they coughed and sighed, the only indication that they were still alive.

'Tie everyone to the life-raft, Tarja.'

It took her a few minutes to respond, and without enthusiasm say, 'OK.'

The straps attached to the sides of the life-raft would hold everyone in place when, and if they rolled over. Part of the canopy cover had shredded from the terrible battering it was taking and water was pouring in on top of them. Pat could hear the self-bailer gurgling away, but it was no match for the inflow of water. They would have to start bailing with buckets before long, and he might not manage, with his damaged hand and shoulder, to help. Bailing, although it was undoubtedly a two-man job, he might have to leave to her.

His head was light and there was that taste of salt in his mouth, it would be such a blessing if he could drink something to take it away. Buried in the sea up to the gunwales, the life-raft didn't feel safe, and he could stretch out his hand and touch the water. Then there was the never ending noise of the storm, like a jet engine screaming on an airport runaway. He missed the sense of security of the trawler, with its diesel engine throbbing away day and night, ready anytime to take them back to the safety of their home port. Tarja was right - they were coming near the end. Each time the life-raft rocked violently from side to side, gallons of water poured in over the gunwales. The raft seemed doomed, and that was that. The life-raft was filling up more quickly than he expected, and they would have to take action or sink.

'Will I start bailing?' Before he could answer, a heavy squall hit and the life-raft danced on top of the waves before gradually tipping over on its side.

'Watch out!' Pat shouted as they turned upside down. Anything not tied down floated to the surface, and was taken away on the waves. Tarja was sobbing, loud heart wrenching sobs, and then she screamed, 'We're drowning!' In the darkness, her arms were flailing around in panic until she grabbed on to him. They were breathing normally, in a pocket of air trapped in the bottom of the life-raft. The sea, churning up inside the upturned life-raft, was making a slapping sound. It was cold and dark, and they would surely die of hypothermia. The life-raft seemed so flimsy. Would the wooden sides hold out?

'It's self-righting - we'll come back up!' shouted Pat.

Yes, they would, that was the theory. This was not a great time to have regrets, but it would have been simple, in the shallow waters of the harbour, to turn the life-raft upside down to see if it righted itself.

The pocket of air inside the upturned life-raft wouldn't last forever. It wasn't the worst death, they would drift off to sleep from lack of oxygen, and never wake up. The morphine was doing its work, and he was getting a little detached from it all. He probably would have fallen asleep if Tarja hadn't kept talking to him.

'Will it be long before it rights itself?' She tightened her grip on his arm. That was a good question, how long is a piece of string.

'Any time now, try to relax.' It was so stupid to tell her to relax in this situation.

'I'm so frightened.' Pat could feel her body trembling beside him. He couldn't say how long they had been upside down before the life-raft started to turn in the water and come right side up. Amazed; he hadn't expected that. The life-raft was full of water, and the buoyancy tanks were keeping them afloat.

'I'll start bailing.' She loosened the straps holding her to the life-raft.

'I'll give you a hand.'

She untied him and, kneeling, they started bailing. Each bucketful he threw overboard was sheer agony. His shoulder hurt and the salt water cut into his hand and started it bleeding again. Blood dripping from the bandage was forming little pools in the water around them. How many pints of blood did he have in his body, and if he didn't stop bleeding soon, would it all flow away leaving him dead. He didn't know the answer to these questions, and he wouldn't bother Tarja by asking her. Their progress was slow, maybe they had thrown enough water overboard, and it was time to stop bailing. Pat reasoned that even with a boat full of water, the buoyancy would keep them afloat. An empty boat, on the other hand, sitting high in the water was more likely to blow over. It would be uncomfortable sitting up to their necks in water, although the storm would eventually blow itself out. Would any of them live to see it?

Pat stopped bailing and shouted to Tarja, 'We've done enough.'

'We should empty it out completely.' She continued to bail. He was too tired to shout above the noise of the storm, and he started bailing again. She might be right - there was no guarantee the buoyancy tanks wouldn't fail and the life-raft would sink to the bottom of the Atlantic. Bailing was an impossible job, with half of the water in their buckets blowing back on top of them. The bailing went on forever and Pat's body and mind had gone numb. He had lost all sense of place and time when Tarja took the bucket out of his hand.

'Rest, Pat.'

'I'm done out.' The torture of bailing was over for now. She held a bottle of water to his lips, and he drank as much as he could. With the shaking of the life-raft, some of the water splashed into his face irritating his cracked lips. None of it mattered, he was so parched and the only cure was to drink water. He had heard tales of sailors going mad from drinking saltwater, although he didn't know if it was true. They should be OK for fresh drinking water; they had stacked more than enough for the trip. The life raft was the only space big enough on the trawler to store it, and barring a disaster through either losing it in capsizing, or getting it contaminated by saltwater, they should be ok.

'I'm going to give the skipper and Coleman a drink.'

'OK.'

He didn't doubt but that they needed water, and he watched as she fed them from a spoon. It needed patience - with the motion of the life-raft the water tended to spill. Each time it happened, she started again. The job completed, she tied them back to the side of the life-raft.

'Will we turn over again?' She was shaking beside him; and he had noticed that she seemed less terrified when she had something to do. Should he tell her the truth that they could turn over anytime or should he try to lessen the blow?

'It will take a big wave to swamp us completely.'

That was a good one, considering that all the waves raining down on top of them were massive, and it was a miracle that they were still afloat.

'Please Lord don't let us capsize again.' She was clutching on to him with both hands.

'The storm has to blow itself out soon.' It was a hopeful guess. He was looking up at the translucent plastic canopy, and he could see the torrents of water raining down on them as the waves passed over. It was doing a reasonable job in keeping the waves from filling up the life-raft each time one passed over the top of them. Tarja had started praying in Finnish. They needed all the prayers they could get if they were to survive this onslaught. Pat guessed it was a Lutheran prayer; it was in his head that she had told him she belonged to that Church. He couldn't pray himself from the feeling of numbness building up in his head. It felt squeezed in a vice and everything around him seemed a great distance away.

The next big wave hit with a bang and a rush of water descended on the canopy, the life-raft started to roll over on one side until the gunnels were level with the sea.

Tarja screamed. The life-raft having righted itself once was no guarantee that it would do the same again. Pat was beyond caring at this stage. He hadn't bothered to brace himself for capsizing. Tarja's strong grip was hurting his injured hand, but she probably didn't hear him shouting,

'Let go, let go.'

Incredibly, before capsizing, the life-raft righted itself.

Tarja was staring at him with a vacant look in her eyes, as if she wasn't inside her head. It was scary as if her brain had shut down to save her from the horror of what was happening. He squeezed her arm to reassure her, although she probably wasn't aware of it. What was he supposed to do now? Many times on this trip he had asked himself this same question. Eventually, like switching on a light, she was back in her head. She tried, but was unable for a few seconds to form words, and then spluttered, 'Thank God.'

'Are you all right?'

'Sorry, I was out of it for a while.'

'You're back now. Are the skipper and Coleman OK?'

He couldn't see their faces from where he was lying. She turned her head to look over at their slumped bodies.

'There's no change, I think. Will I start bailing?'

'Leave it to the self-bailer.'

He hadn't the energy or the will to bail and the life-raft would only fill up again the next tumble they took. He wasn't going to fight it any more, let the sea take him. He'd keep his eyes closed and try not to think.

The waves kept crashing down on top of the plastic canopy, and it was a miracle that it hadn't collapsed. Not designed to take this much of a battering, it wouldn't last much longer. He was almost looking forward to the end, the blessed peace of death, where he couldn't hurt anymore. To go to a place where Hazel and Mark were waiting for him, and they'd give him a royal welcome. It had been a long time, since he'd seen them, and baby Mark might not even recognise his dad. Would he have grown bigger in heaven or would he still be a baby?

His mind was slipping a bit, and at times he couldn't distinguish between past and present. Some of the time, he was with Hazel and Mark, and it was so joyful, and then he was back in the grim reality of the life-raft. He wasn't sure how long they were in the life-raft. Was it hours, days or weeks?

23

The change came when he was least expecting it. The wind dropped in ferocity and swung around to starboard. The sea took longer to settle, but gradually the rocking of the life-raft lessened.

'I can see a patch of clear sky,' said Tarja pointing directly above them. He looked up and saw a piece of blue peeping through the clouds. That was like their manna from heaven. It signalled the storm was over.

'We've made it this far,' he said.

'My prayers…my prayers – the Lord has answered my prayers.' She was getting hysterical, a nervous release from their terrifying ordeal.

'Thank you, Lord for saving us.' She was praying quietly and then suddenly dropped to her knees in the sump water and started screaming like a deranged person.

'It's OK Tarja. It's OK.' He put his hand on her shoulder to reassure her, but she pushed him away. Her shrieking was terrifying and he didn't know how to stop her. He was near that stage himself with a sledgehammer banging away in his head. They had been through too much. After what seemed like an age, she collapsed, whimpering.

He helped her out of the water and on to the seat, she lay there, and he put a pillow under her head. He gave her two sleeping tablets. They were lucky the skipper had a supply of them onboard and although contaminated by seawater, they were still effective. The sobbing stopped and she fell asleep. What else could he do, he had always heard of the healing power of sleep. Over the next few hours, the wind dropped to a whisper and the black clouds moved on. The sea calmed and a weak current propelled them along at a few knots. He felt they were still going northwards although he couldn't be sure. Their compass had gone to the bottom of the ocean when they capsized. With the soothing movement of the life-raft as it slid over the surface of the water, he dozed, and drifted into a fitful sleep. Her voice woke him,

145

'I'm so sorry about the hysterics. I couldn't keep it together any longer. I just lost it.'

'It's over and we're OK.'

Here the sleep had a positive effect, and she was back to herself. He wouldn't want her to have another outburst like that; there was enough distress onboard without it. He helped her to her feet.

The 'OK now' might be premature - they weren't safe yet. Adrift and alone, somewhere in the North Atlantic, was nothing to feel excited about, though in fairness their circumstance had improved a bit, or had it? He shut everything out and, in his imagination; they were in a punt, floating along on the still waters of a lake, with a picnic in the offing. Tarja went to check on the skipper, and Coleman, her voice brought Pat back to the present.

'The skipper doesn't look well.'

'Neither does Coleman,' he said. They needed rescuing, or to make land soon, for everyone to receive medical attention. He wasn't feeling that well himself with pains radiating up his arm and across his shoulders from the stump of his little finger. Tarja was already busy, folding down the canopy to let the sun in and dry everything onboard.

'I'll search around to see what we've got.' In the calm after the storm, she could stand up and walk around the life-raft without getting blown into the sea.

'Good idea.'

Pat, with his back propped up against the bulkhead for support, was also taking stock of the life-raft. Half decked, with both bow and stern pointed; it looked bigger than when it was sitting on the trawler deck. It was a clever design that protected the bunks in the bows and stern from the elements.

Tarja emerged from under the forward half deck where she had been rummaging for anything that might be useful.

'I've found this.' She handed him a small transistor radio.

'It'll be a miracle if it works. I don't know how long it's been there.'

He fiddled with the controls and through the rustle of static he heard a voice, faint and crackly of a Radio Eireann newsreader.

'The worst storm to hit the Atlantic North-West Coast in a decade is over, and a search started at first light for the fishing trawler 'The Annie

L.' There hasn't been any contact with the trawler since it left port, and there are fears for the safety of the three man crew, and their female passenger. The NLI life boats, and the search, and rescue helicopters stationed along the West Coast have joined the search. We will broadcast further bulletins as we receive them.'

'They're searching for us,' said Tarja, giving the skipper and Coleman more sips of water. If those two were to have any chance of recovery, they couldn't allow them to become dehydrated.

'Yes, they are.'

They were out there all right, looking for bodies if the broadcast was anything to go by, and when they didn't find any, they would extend the search area a bit. That didn't offer much hope, finding their small life-raft in the Atlantic Ocean was like finding the proverbial needle in a haystack.

Their main hope was that one of the coastal helicopters would spot them, although they probably had drifted outside helicopter range.

'We'll only listen to the news every hour to save the battery.' He turned off the radio and set it down near him.

'It's great we have it.' She moved over next to him to change the bandage on his hand. He could see a greenish tinge on the bandage and that wasn't a good sign. The bandage stuck to the wound, and it hurt like hell when she pulled it away and pus was oozing from the finger stump, a sure sign of infection.

'I'm going to clean it up a bit.' She lit the primus stove to boil water.

'I could lose my arm if it turns gangrenous.' He was examining the finger stump, and he was feeling a bit nauseated looking at it. Gangrene was the only condition he could think of although there were hundreds of illnesses that could develop from an untreated amputation.

'We're a long way from gangrene yet,' She boiled the bandage before using it to clean away the puss from his finger stump. He knew that she was being as gentle as she could; but when the hot bandage touched his finger stump, he screamed with pain. She stopped for a second and then continued to clean the wound until it started to bleed.

'That's good, we must keep it clean,' she said, as she carefully bandaged the stump and secured the end of the dressing with a safety pin.

'Thanks, I couldn't have faced that myself.' The pain in his finger was almost unbearable.

'Try to sleep, you need rest.'

He couldn't sleep from the throbbing pain in his finger stump, and he checked the RTE news every hour on the hour. The search concentrated on the porcupine shelf where the islanders normally fished. Eventually, they broadcast the news he was expecting. A helicopter had spotted debris floating on the surface of the sea, and the rescue ships, with divers, were congregating in the area. Oil, presumed to be diesel oil, was floating on the sea in the vicinity and diving conditions were good.

The islanders had scheduled an interdenominational service for that evening, in the Franciscan Monastery Chapel, to pray for the safe return of the Annie L and its three-man crew and female passenger.

'The divers will take a while to look around down there,' he said, placing the radio down beside him with care - it was more valuable to them than gold.

'It's a dangerous job.' She was looking behind her as she said it, as if half expecting the rescuers to come suddenly over the horizon. That was unlikely to happen. He was thinking of the Monastery Chapel. The parishioners gathering for the service with the sun streaming through the stained-glass window above the marble alter, and into their eyes. From the cloisters, the monks walking in single file into the Chapel, dressed in brown habits, and cowls covering their bowed heads. Praying would go on for a long time, as did all solemn chapel services on the island. He hated long chapel services and somewhere in his mind, he was glad not to be there, although he couldn't get away from the fact that the parishioners would feel they were attending a funeral Mass. It wouldn't be the first time for such an event, as the recovery of bodies of islanders drowned at sea was rare.

'I think I can see a ship,' she said excitedly, grabbing a yellow waterproof, and waving it up and down to attract attention. Pat stood up and almost fell over. He was weaker than he thought, but sure enough there was a ship barely visible on the horizon, probably a tanker. He watched it for some time but there was no mistaking that it was sailing away from them. They obviously hadn't seen the life-raft.

Tarja was still trying to get their attention, screaming and jumping up and down, waving her hands about in desperation. She finally collapsed from the effort on to the seat beside him. He guessed that whatever she was saying in Finnish weren't prayerful. She became silent and listless, and had lost the will to go on. He put his arm around her.

'I think we've crossed a shipping lane.' He sat down heavily; he'd have collapsed if he had remained standing for much longer.

'Lord forgive me,' she said quietly.

Pat decided to say nothing. What could he say? There'll be another ship along, and it will surely pick us up? That wouldn't happen as these big ships would never manage to spot their little life-raft among the Atlantic waves.

'Should we stay in the shipping lane for the next boat to come along?' she asked.

'We're drifting away from it with the current.'

They could have dropped anchor, but he didn't want to do that, in the dark there was a chance of getting run over by one of these ships. They were drifting out of the area, and that was a relief. It made no sense to worry her about it. By nightfall, they would be well out of danger. To add to their misery, they heard the drone of an aircraft overhead, and they scanned the sky looking for it. It was likely a passenger plane on its way to the USA, and not a helicopter searching for them.

Pat turned on the radio and, through the crackle of static; they could hear the voice of the RTE newsreader clearly. Her first item of news concerned their trawler.

'Divers have located the missing trawler 'The Annie L' on the sea bed about one hundred miles out in the Atlantic. It's lying on its port side at a depth of two hundred and fifty feet with a jagged hole near the stern, there's no news on the three-man crew and the female passenger. The life-raft is missing and they may have escaped from the sinking trawler in it. The search will continue for the life-raft, and the advice to shipping is to keep a look out. Experts say that it is unlikely that such a small boat could have survived the storm.'

The radio died and there were no replacement batteries.

'It's good, they are widening the search,' said Tarja, scanning the horizon behind them.

'Yes,' he said. It confirmed his thinking that the emergency services were now looking for bodies. Nothing had changed for them; they were on their own again, at the mercy of the currents. Heaven only knew where they were going to end.

'I'm shivering cold,' His teeth were chattering and his limbs felt icy.

'Lie down; Pat and I'll cover you with sleeping bags.' She helped him to get into one of the bunks under the front half deck, and she piled sleeping bags on top of him. Half an hour later he felt so different.

'Tarja, I'm roasting now.'

She removed the sleeping bags and put a wet towel on his forehead.

'You're running a temperature.'

For hours, he fluctuated between shivering and sweating until he started talking rubbish. He knew he was rambling, but he couldn't stop it, and from faraway he heard Tarja say,

'Pat, you're feverish, your temperature must be high.'

Everything went grey before he lapsed into unconsciousness.

24

He heard Tarja calling him as he came round, and he felt confused and unsure of where he was. Then, it came rushing back to him: they were adrift in the life-raft, and he had passed out. The pain had gone out of his finger, he didn't feel hot and cold anymore, and he was more like his normal self. Tarja was bending over him, rubbing his cheeks as if willing him back to consciousness. Her face looked drawn, and anxious, and her voice sounded mumbled and indistinct.

'Are you OK, Pat?'

'There's no pain in my finger.'

'I put a bread poultice on it made from stale crusts, let me take a look.' She removed the bandage from the stump and the wound was clear with puss stuck to the residue of bread on the bandage.

'It's a well-known home remedy.' To sterilise a fresh bandage, she dropped it into the kettle and boiled it. They had no other way to make sure it was clean.

'It has drawn out the infection, I think,' he said still looking down at the stump of his little finger. Thirsty, he took a drink of water.

'You were out for a long time, and I felt so lonely here on my own.' She started to cry and her shoulders shook with each sob. He stretched out his hand to comfort her.

'How are the skipper and Coleman?'

'I think the skipper is a bit worse.'

With his finger re-bandaged, he went to look at them. They were both still unconscious, but the skipper's breathing was rasping and shallower than before. There was nothing more they could do for him, except make him as comfortable as possible in the bunk.

Except for the wide expanse of sea, there were no landmarks out there, and he couldn't be sure if they were on the same sailing track as before or not.

'Did we change course?'

'I don't know, it was so quiet here without you, no sound except the water lapping against the boat.'

The surface of the sea was like a duck pond - they'd be standing still if they weren't drifting with the current.

She started to tidy up his bunk and fold up the spare sleeping bags, and then she went over to check on the skipper and Coleman.

'I don't like his colour.' She searched for a pulse in the skipper's neck.

'Is he breathing OK?'

'It's shallow.'

Pat knelt down, and put his ear near the skipper's face. There was a harsh sound as he took each breath.

'His pulse is irregular.' She had her fingers on the big vein in his neck, and it was throbbing faintly.

They took turns throughout the night to stay awake and sit beside the skipper. He knew he was a sick man but Pat couldn't bring himself to ask Tarja if she thought he was dying. With all his faults, the skipper was his last living relative, and without him, he would have no one. He had given too many people up to death already and this looked like another one. Sitting there in the boat under a starry sky, he thought about the skipper. He was a man's man, but he seemed happiest when married to his English wife. She had been good for him for as long as it lasted. Heavy drinking plagued the skipper for most of his life and in the end; she couldn't cope with it anymore, and left. In her defence, she put up with a lot from him and stayed longer than most. She often said the skipper was gentle, and kind when he was sober, and if a neighbour needed anything he was the first to help. He always wanted children, but they hadn't been lucky that way. Perhaps if they had children his life might have been different.

The sea was so calm, and the sounds so rhythmic that it had a hypnotic effect on him. The cruel way it had tried to batter them to death didn't seem part of the same sea. People were like that, so much good or so much bad just under the surface.

Tarja woke and came over to check on the skipper's pulse.

'I think he's worse,' she said, tucking the sleeping bag more tightly around him.

'Is he dying?' Pat's voice sounded strange to him. He had a lump in his throat, and he felt tearful. The skipper was family although he could be the devil to deal with. Pat couldn't let her see him like that, and he rubbed his sleeve across his eyes to dry them.

'I don't know for sure.'

The skipper's left-hand slipped out from under the sleeping bag, and she went down on her knees to tuck it back in.

'He's wearing his wedding ring.' She sounded surprised and she held up the skipper's left-hand to admire the gold band on his ring finger.

'He never takes it off. It's the only thing left in his life that he values.' Pat was looking anew at the gold band.

'He must have thought well of his wife.'

'Yes, she was his soul mate and when she left, it was the biggest loss of his life'

'He doesn't strike me as the sensitive kind.'

'He only shows his tough side.'

'I can still feel his living presence even though he's unconscious,' she said, getting up off her knees to come to Pat.

'Not a man you could ignore when he walked into a pub.'

'That's for sure.'

'Where did he meet her?' she asked.

'London, he drove a bus for London Transport and was doing well in the job until he started drinking heavily.'

The skipper's mouth fell open and the pattern of his breathing changed from rasping to a quieter intake of air.

'Loneliness was part of it.' Pat was leaning over the side of the life-raft looking into the still water, and he could see the outline of a large fish keeping pace with them. It was probably something harmless like a porpoise.

'Far from family can be lonely,' she said as if talking to herself.

'London Transport sent him to AA meetings, and he was dry for awhile. He met his wife Millie on the bus and they got talking. She was the barmaid in her father's pub, and it wasn't long before he was the best customer in the Fox and Hound.'

'Was he drinking, and going to the AA at the same time?'

'No, I don't think so.'

'They married, bought a house, and he settled into domesticity, although he always had a hankering to return to Ireland. He made rapid progress in the job, and they promoted him to an inspector. He had many problems to contend with. Drivers came from all over the world to London Transport and their lack of English was a difficulty, especially when they had to detour because of road works. They couldn't understand the fleet controller directions on the radio. It wasn't unusual for a bus to go missing for anything up to half a day before the driver managed to make his way back to the garage.

'The skipper would take out another bus and cover the route, saving them from getting fired.

'A humane side to him,' she said, getting up and moving over to sit on the centre seat of the life-raft.

'Strange as it may seem, when he was sober he avoided conflict like the plague.'

'I'm amazed to hear that,' she said.

'Spot checks on the drivers was part of his job. One of their favourite tricks was to drive past people waiting at bus stops and carry on to the terminus with an empty bus. The skipper felt that boredom was the problem, the never ending tedium of the stop and go of London's traffic. Others he caught driving under the influence. Stress of the job possibly, but he started drinking heavily again.'

'That was terrible. Did he go back to the AA?'

'No, as you know, he is headstrong with a short fuse. Millie came with him to Ireland and when he couldn't control his drinking, she left and went back home for awhile to give him a wake up call. He didn't change or he couldn't change, so she finally divorced him. It was the last thing on earth he wanted.'

'It's such a sad story,' Tarja said, looking up at the sky. Silent and lost in thought, she put her arms around Pat.

The gentle movement of the sea barely disturbed the life-raft.

There was little change in the skipper - his mouth was hanging open, and his breath coming in short almost soundless gasps. Coleman was in better shape and his breathing was strong and regular, he moved a little in the bunk and then settled down again. The skipper remained motionless. Pat looked out over the rippling sea as the life-raft continued to drift in the direction that he thought was northwards. It was twelve noon and the sun was directly overhead on another long day at sea. In an instant, the skipper's breathing stopped, and Pat heard a gurgling sound coming from his throat. Tarja rushed over to him and got there first.

'O my God he's dying.'

Bending down, Pat whispered the Act of Contrition into the skipper's ear and followed with a rosary, counting each decade of the sorrowful mysteries on his fingers. That's what they did on the island when someone was dying – like a reflex, he did the same. He jumped up when the loud croak of death came from his throat. In shock, he stared at the skipper; his heart was beating so fast that he thought it would jump out of his chest.

'He's gone,' he said. The skipper's eyes were staring and glassy, and his skin had gone pasty with a translucent hue. Pat never realised that death could change a person's features so quickly. He knew that he should close the skipper's eyes and mouth; but he looked so grotesque that he couldn't bring himself to do it.

'I'm so sorry, Pat.' Tarja closed the skipper's eyes and mouth. Then he looked at peace with the stress lines that had rutted his forehead gone forever. The skipper's body lying there brought back all the emotions, the sorrow and loss at the death of Mark and Helen and Pat couldn't hold it in any longer, it all came out in a rush of words.

'I carried the small white coffin out of the house and put it into the back of the hearse. He was just a tiny baby and so vulnerable. It was like a barrier coming down between Mark and I when they closed down the tailgate of the hearse. Mark…Mark…don't take him away.'

Tarja cradled his head to her shoulder gently rocking him back and forth in time with the motion of the life-raft.

'Sh, sh,' she comforted him.

'A year passed before the undertakers took the next coffin out of our house. It was Hazel's. The sun reflected on the brass nameplate as they pushed the coffin into the back of the hearse and closed the tailgate. The skipper and Hazel's father held me back, and all I was trying to do was to stop the undertakers taking her away from me. I couldn't afford to lose her, then or anytime. My legs weren't working, and I couldn't rush over and stop them. Hazel never wanted to be in a coffin; she felt haunted by the tales of those unfortunate people buried alive, in the Middle Ages. When they woke out of their coma, they tried to scratch their way through the coffin and in their struggle, they left blood and broken fingernails stuck to the coffin lids.

'I was shouting at them; don't bury Hazel alive.

Please leave her with me.' Pat was sobbing loudly on to Tarja's shoulder.

'I was standing there looking into Hazel's grave in Mount Jerome Cemetery; it looked deep with straight cut sides and square corners. Alive, she couldn't ever look into a grave. 'The black hole of Calcutta', she called them. She must have felt that I had deserted them. The pall-bearers lifted Mark's little coffin out first, when I took it in my arms it was lighter than I remembered it, and the white paint had blackened from earth staining. I wanted to keep holding it forever. I talked to Mark inside that little coffin, telling him not to be afraid, that his mother was coming to look after him. If only I could have gone myself, we would have been a family again, all together in one place and the world couldn't hurt us anymore. The hard man, the skipper, was howling into the open grave.

'Pat you're so upset,' Tarja said, as she stroked his face.

'I couldn't save them,' he said. He felt her bony shoulder against his face.

'Not from cot death and cancer,' said Tarja brushing away his tears.

'Mark had slept in his cot beside our bed. The night he died was no different from any other night. Hazel had got up to feed him during the night, and she tucked him back into his cot. The clock radio woke us as usual and Hazel went over to the cot, stared into it for a few seconds, and started screaming. He was laying there like a porcelain statue with his little hand out over the blankets. He used to curl his hand around my fingers and pull them towards his mouth. Everything he could get hold of went into his mouth. In death, he had a little smile on his face as if to say; I'm going home. I can't help myself; I'm sobbing as loudly today and shaking as much with grief, as the day it happened. Although with Hazel at my side I managed to cope somehow. She was my rock and she blamed herself for Mark's death. Hazel's dying, so soon after Mark's took all the will to live out of me. There was no point to it anymore. An aggressive ovarian cancer they told me. Even with that diagnosis, I expected her to live and who wouldn't, a young woman with all her life ahead of her? I'm so lonely,' he said into Tarja's shoulder.

'Time heals, Pat,' said Tarja using a bandage to dry his eyes.

'I'll never heal. The pain is the same as the day they died. Hazel suffered so much.'

'My grandmother did as well,' said Tarja.

'Hazel had chemotherapy and radiotherapy, and it had drained her, most days she could only get out of the bed for a short time. Her hair fell out and she felt annoyed at being bald. She suffered for nine months, getting progressively worse. It was terrible. I had to push her around in a wheelchair and near the end; she had to go into respite care. Her weight had dropped to six stone before her death. Skin and bone was the only way I could describe her. It's such a terrible way to go. It was so difficult being without her.'

'I know. It's something you don't forget.' Tarja was holding him tightly in her arms.

'I was with my grandmother at the end,' she said.

'I heard people on the island say that when somebody died after a long, painful illness that it was a happy release for them. That wasn't the way I felt about Hazel, I wanted her cured. I took her to the shrines at Knock and Lourdes and to all kinds of healers. It wasn't to be. I'm sorry for dumping all that on to you. I don't normally do that.'

'Don't apologise, Pat. It shows how much you loved Hazel and Mark.'

'Yes, I did.'

'It's late, Pat; we should go to our bunks.'

'I won't sleep much.'

'You need rest.' She went over to the skipper and placed a towel over his face,

'That will keep the flies away.'

'Flies,' he said.

He had read something disturbing about flies and corpses, and he wished he hadn't. What a time to remember it with flies already buzzing around the skipper's corpse.

The common housefly lays its eggs in the mouths and noses of corpses. They hatch into flesh-eating maggots that eventually consume all the rotting flesh of the corpse. When they have devoured all the flesh, they eat one another until there is one massive maggot, the coffin bug. It was terrible to think that this had already started on the skipper's corpse.

'You're shivering, Pat,' she said, placing her hand on his shoulder.

'Upsetting thoughts, I have plenty of them.' That was true enough, but he couldn't tell her about the flies and corpses, it was horrific.

'We can't do anything else until morning,' she said, turning around and balancing her way to the bunks in the bow of the life-raft.

'Goodnight,' he said, what a silly remark, lost in the middle of the ocean in a life-raft with a corpse on board. He couldn't even get that right.

'Goodnight and get some rest,' she replied.

He would give her time to settle and maybe sleep before he turned in himself. The night was calm and warm; he climbed into the sleeping bag. The loss of Hazel and Mark and all that happened during the day and the awful maggots kept beating about in his head. He was glad no one could see him, he was crying into his pillow again. It was going to be a long night.

25

His torment continued until the noise of Tarja unzipping his sleeping bag distracted him.

'Move over.' She squeezed in next to him. He couldn't see her in the dark, but he felt the warmth of her naked body pushing against him. She turned him on to his back, treating his injured shoulder with care, and kissed him on the lips. Their lovemaking was as gentle as the rocking of the life-raft. When it was over, lying beside him, she tucked her head into his shoulder. He fell asleep.

The sun shining on their bunk woke him. Tarja was still asleep and he had his arm around her. He could hardly believe that they had made love so near the skipper's corpse. It was easy for it to happen with their emotions running high. She woke and smiled as he was getting out of the bunk, it was good to see her happy again. He didn't want to spoil the moment and remind her that they hadn't used any form of birth control last night, or indeed back in the hotel. She may be aware of it.

'We'll have to bury the skipper at sea.' She pulled on her clothes and went over to Coleman's bunk to see how he was doing.

'Any change?' He was thinking about the awfulness of dumping the skipper's body overboard. It didn't seem right and there was another way to deal with it.

'He's no worse, I think.' She was spoon feeding him with water, and he didn't respond when it gurgled down his throat.

'I don't want to bury the skipper at sea. We'll tow him behind the life-raft until we reach land.'

Tarja stared at him looking puzzled.

'OK, if that's what you want to do.'

'I know it sounds strange, but I want to give him a proper burial in a coffin in a graveyard. He deserves that.'

She was silent for awhile considering what to do next.

'We'll sew him into the canvas sailcloth - there's enough for that - and tow him behind us,' he said.

He started to haul out the sheet of sailcloth. Tarja lifted out a tin box from under the rear deck and opened it.

'We have a sail makers' needle and yarn here,' she said, holding up the needle for him to see.

'That's what we need and we can cover the seams with duct tape.'

'That's a good idea; it will make them waterproof and odour proof.'

She started searching around for the duct tape. They rolled the sailcloth around the skipper and tucked in both ends. Pat couldn't look at the skipper's face, what would he think of the way they were treating him? Wrapped up, the bundle looked like something between a shroud and a body bag.

'It's time to start sewing,' said Tarja, looking around for a box to sit on.

'I can't help much with my injuries.' Pat placed a wooden crate on the floor for her to sit on.

'I know, and I wasn't expecting any. You've done well to cope.'

Even though the motion of the life-raft was gentle, threading the needle became a major task. Repeatedly, she failed to get the thread through the eye. With perseverance, she succeeded and started to sew the skipper into the sailcloth, starting at his head. Her hands weren't strong enough to push the needle through the sailcloth and Pat handed her the pliers.

'That'll do it.'

She hesitated, 'I'm afraid of spiking the skipper's eyes.'

'We have to be tough, he won't feel it.'

Handling the skipper's corpse was emotional for him, and he understood what was going through her mind, but they had to do it. The task was a slow one, and they had not finished as night started to fall.

'Tarja, you're tired. Leave the rest until morning.'

'There isn't much to do. I'll finish,' she said, putting in the final stitches and reaching for the duct tape.

'This is tough on you, Pat, but it will be over soon.' She covered the lines of stitching with duct tape, beginning at the skippers head.

'I'll get the rope ready.' Pat set about gathering all the pieces of rope together.

'Do you need a hand?' asked Tarja putting the finishing stitches to the skipper's body bag.

'I'll manage.'

With all the pieces tied together the rope was about ten metres long. Pat tied one end around the skipper's legs and the other on the sternpost of the life-raft. As they prepared to lower the corpse into the sea, Tarja said, 'We should say a prayer.'

'Let's pray silently,' said Pat.

'OK,' Tarja nodded her head. They prayed in silence for a few minutes and then lowered the skipper's corpse into the water. It didn't make a splash, and Pat felt relieved. It floated on top of the water. It would be horrible if it sank to the bottom. The current took it slowly away from them until the rope went taught, and they were towing it behind them.

Pat felt saddened at losing his last relative, but he was also angry with him for dying. Although he rarely displayed it, the skipper was always there for him in the bad times. He showed he cared when Mark and Hazel died, by grieving nearly as much for them as Pat did. There was a chance that instead of burying the skipper at sea, they could lay him to rest beside his other relatives in the island cemetery. Truth to tell, none of the islanders would give a damn about where he buried the skipper, and probably the skipper wouldn't care either. Perhaps he would have seen his burial at sea a fitting end to his life.

Pat was now alone, with no one caring if he lived or died. He was free to go wherever he wanted. It was a lonely freedom that he didn't particularly want. He woke to an azure sky and a sea as flat as mirror glass. They were drifting northwards at roughly three knots. At that rate, it was going to take a long time to reach anywhere. He felt alone in the vast Atlantic. Coleman's condition hadn't changed, although with an injury like that it was hard to say what was going on inside his skull.

Pat was looking over the stern of the life-raft, as the skipper's body, still attached, rotated in their wake. He hoped the spinning movement would stop the seagulls from landing on the sailcloth, and pecking at the skipper's corpse. It might also keep that terrible hagfish away, said to wait around to bore up the anuses of dead bodies. He didn't want to think about that now, and he wished Tarja hadn't told him about it.

'How is Coleman?' Tarja was sitting up in the bunk, resting on one elbow.

'His breathing seems strong enough.'

She got up to give Coleman some of his daily allowance of water, or what they thought was the intake of water he needed each day to stay alive.

'I wish we could do something more for him,' she said between spoonfuls.

'Not until we hit land.' At the rate they were going, that was going to be a long haul. They would get there a hell of a lot faster if they were walking.

'Pat - set up the hose, I need a shower.'

Tarja came out of the bunk naked and stood in the middle of the life-raft. He turned on the hose to a low pressure and sprayed her from head to toe with seawater.

'No shampoo on this voyage,' she said, using carbolic soap on her hair. She sponged off the saltwater with fresh water from a basin and sat out on the forward half deck to dry in the sun. With the light glistening off her skin, she looked like one of the female marble statues holding up that famous building in Athens. He had gone on holiday there once.

Then it was his turn for a shower. Tarja washed him down with the hose, and he sponged himself with the same water she had used. They had to be careful not to waste any of it, or they wouldn't survive long without drinking water. Still full of Catholic inhibitions, he didn't feel like walking around naked and dried himself with a towel.

'We should have kept a track on the number of days we're out here,' he said.

'I don't know how long we've been out here,' she said, vigorously drying her hair with a towel.

Early on, they had kept a log of the number of sunrises and sunsets, but it had all fallen by the wayside. Another passing day or night didn't make that much difference, since each was more or less like the previous ones. The skipper's corpse whirling like a spinning top, on the end of the rope behind them, fascinated him, for some reason.

Suddenly, a wave lifted the life-raft, and tilted it to starboard, knocking Pat to the floor, and into the dirty bilge water.

'We're going over!' shouted Tarja. Thrown out of the bunk, she landed in a heap on the floor.

'No, no...We're not.'

The boat righted, and danced on top of the wave for a few minutes before it stabilised.

Thankfully, Coleman strapped to his bunk, didn't move. Without the ties, he would have landed on the floor as well.

In view, on the port side was the basking shark that nearly capsized them.

'That's a magnificent specimen,' said Tarja, changing from fear to admiration of the huge basking shark.

'The first one I've seen alive.' Pat could feel his wet trousers rubbing against his legs, but they would soon dry in the sun. The self-bailer was working continuously, although a few inches of water always remained in the bottom of the life-raft.

'They are not a threat, unless you're in a small boat like ours.' He was watching for the shark to slap down its tail and create another wave before diving. They were ready for it this time.

'Their main enemy is man,' said Tarja, as she combed out her hair with her fingers. The basking shark wasn't showing the slightest interest in them. There probably were more of them about, as they weren't solitary creatures, but travelled in shoals. It would be the height of bad luck if one of them surfaced under the life-raft and smashed it to smithereens.

'Hold on.' Pat saw the massive tail strike the water and the wave it made rushed towards them. They held on to the sides of the lifeboat, while it rocked from side to side. They didn't let go until the water settled. It didn't affect them as much as before, the element of surprise wasn't there and anyway, it would take a much bigger wave than that to sink them.

'I hear a plane - there it is above us.' She was pointing to a line of silver vapour running across the sky.

'They won't see our life-raft from up there.'

With the cloud cover and the height they were flying at, they probably wouldn't even see something as big as a cruise liner on the sea below them.

'It's galling to think there are people so near and yet so far,' she said, sounding despondent.

'At a guess, with planes overhead, I would say, we're near the North Atlantic flight paths. That would put us somewhere between the Donegal coast and Iceland. It's not pinpoint accuracy, but it's there or thereabout.'

That gave him a lot of latitude for error. Silently, they watched the plane until it went out of sight.

'I suppose, we must be tiny on this sea,' she said, thoughtfully. He wondered if she had realised that it would take a miracle for search planes to find them out here.

26

'What's that noise?' Tarja was standing up in the life-raft trying to locate the source of the sound.

'Don't know.' It was coming from straight ahead; he hadn't heard anything like it before at sea. It reminded him of the roar of a waterfall and that couldn't exist in the middle of the Atlantic.

'It's scary not knowing what it is,' she said.

'It's probably a big rock.' It sounded believable, although he was sure that whatever was causing the noise wasn't a big rock. It would have to be the size of Everest to stick up its head in the middle of the Atlantic Ocean, and have a waterfall running down its side. The sound grew louder as they drifted towards it and yet there was nothing to see. The surface of the sea and the weak current they were travelling in hadn't changed. Whatever was ahead wasn't affecting their progress, although it was making them nervous. The sound was all around them, and it was difficult to tell which direction it was coming from.

Then he saw it, straight ahead.

'It's a whirlpool.'

The sheer volume of water disappearing into the swirling hole in the sea was astonishing. They would have to stay well away from it; nothing could survive the crushing power at the centre of that vortex. It would pull them in and smash them to matchwood if, in passing, they touched the edge of it. On their present course, they should just about skirt it safely.

'It's an awesome sight.' Tarja was holding on to him tightly.

'I think we'll clear it.' Well that was the plan, but he didn't know if its pull went further out than the circle of eddies at its edge. What they needed was a working diesel engine to take them miles away from this place. Unfortunately, the skipper had taken the engine out of the life-raft and put it into an old truck, and he hadn't bothered to replace it.

The whirlpool was sending a fine mist into the air, and they were soaking wet.

'I'm freezing.' Tarja was trying to get her oilskins back on.

'Get under the half deck, there's shelter there.'

He had heard tales in the pub of Atlantic whirlpools. Once caught in the rotating water, there was no escape and the whirlpools could destroy a vessel as large as a cruise liner. Up to now, he hadn't met anyone who had encountered one and, at the time, it sounded like another seafarers' yarn. It was horrible to imagine that they could end spinning around inside the whirlpool until it crushed them to smithereens.

Thank God, it hadn't started to draw them in, although they were passing close to it. If it did, there was nothing they could do but pray.

They edged past the whirlpool. He could feel his heart pounding inside his chest.

'I'll stay close to you,' said Tarja, not daring to look into the whirlpool. The swirling water captured all the surrounding flotsam and jetsam and continued to spin it until it disappeared into the abyss. It reminded him of what he had read about black holes in space. They hauled in everything in their gravitational range and crushed it down to such a dense level that even light couldn't penetrate it. They were past the whirlpool, and he turned around to look back. Tarja still had her eyes closed.

'I'm afraid to look, are we safe yet?' she whispered.

'Open your eyes, we're OK.'

Then he saw it, the skipper's corpse on the end of the towing rope, caught in the outer eddies of the whirlpool. The spin at the edge was strong enough to pull in the corpse, but not strong enough to bother the life-raft. The rope pulled taught, as the corpse went further and further into the whirlpool. He expected the rope to snap, but it didn't, and the whirlpool was gradually hauling the lifeboat back to destruction.

'We'll have to cut the rope!' Pat shouted, getting his Swiss Army knife from his pocket.

'Open it up, Tarja,' he said, handing it to her.

'That's the largest blade.' She handed him the opened penknife.

It was difficult to hold in his bandaged hand, and before he could make any impression on the rope, it slipped from his grasp into the sea.

'Quickly Tarja get me the axe!' With his injuries, he wouldn't be fast enough to get it himself. She would have to search under the forward deck, and they were sliding backwards into the abyss all the time.

'Here take it.' She handed him the short handled axe, and he started chopping at the rope. It finally parted. Broken free, the skipper's corpse was rotating as though it were on the wall of death, before it plunged into the centre of the whirlpool. Pat wasn't going to have a chance to bury him in a graveyard on the island.

'That was a close call.' Pat was trembling and, covered in sweat, was struggling to breathe. They weren't clear of the whirlpool yet and a random current could take them back into danger again. The noise of the whirlpool was still in his ears, and he didn't want to move in case it might affect their getaway somehow.

'I'm afraid to talk out loud.' Tarja was trembling. They remained motionless and silent until the whirlpool was out of sight, behind them.

It was the skipper's place of rest and Pat would never see it again. It would be impossible to find in this vast ocean. Not marked on any marine charts, even experienced sailors denied the existence of Atlantic whirlpools.

'I feel bad about leaving him there.' Pat wiped his eyes with the back of his hand.

'You had no choice.' Tarja put her arms around him. She was right; they didn't have a choice, although it would be good to have had the skipper's grave on the Island where people could visit it, that's if anyone would want to.

'People cremated in other countries have graves on the island without remains in them. Maybe I should do that for the skipper.'

'Yes, you might feel better about it.' She hesitantly asked, 'Are there more whirlpools out there?' From the fear in her voice, she was dreading the answer.

'They're rare, even sailors seldom, if ever, see them.' He was hoping against hope that they wouldn't come across another whirlpool on this trip, although you never could tell with the luck they were having. They watched the evening sun going down like a red ball into the horizon, as though it were slipping into the sea.

'That's where the west is,' he said as they sat side by side on the gunnels of the lifeboat.

'We must be going north then.' She stood up in the life-raft and, with outstretched arms, pointed to where the cardinal points of the compass were.

'I think we've been going north since we got into the lifeboat.'

'I'm tired, Pat, and I'm going to lie down, are you coming?' She started moving towards the forward bunk.

'I'll join you later. I want to wake the skipper properly. That's the island way, stay up all night keeping the corpse company.'

'Don't worry about waking me up.' Tarja looked tired and drawn.

He didn't have a corpse, but he knew where it was and there was no one else to mourn. He wondered if he should let the skipper's ex-wife know that he had died. She cared about him and it was the decent thing to tell her. Even if she had married again, the skipper had been a part of her life for a time, and she never ceased to be part of his. She was always in his head. How would he find her address in London? That might be difficult. He would send a letter to her last known address and someone might forward it to her. He would make the effort; it wasn't her fault that they had split up. Aha, the skipper was a foolish man; talk about cutting off your nose to spite your face.

Pat felt determined to stay awake for the whole night out of respect for the dead. With the gentle rocking of the lifeboat, and the sound of water, he nodded off. His sitting position on a hard seat with his back against the side of the boat was so uncomfortable that he woke up again after a few minutes. Finally, overcome with tiredness and with his head hanging forward on to his chest, he fell asleep.

When Pat woke, he couldn't work out how long he had been asleep. He tried to lift his head, but he had a severe crick in his neck; and he couldn't look left or right without turning his whole body around. Some 'Deep Heat' rub would be a luxury, to free up his neck and take away the pain. His condition guaranteed one thing – he wouldn't drop off to sleep again in that position. It was a bright night with hardly a ripple on the surface of the sea, and it sparkled with dashes of silver, where the moon shone on it. He checked on Tarja, asleep and snoring gently. He should pray a rosary or two - that's the way the islanders kept a vigil - but he didn't feel like it. Anyway, he was alone and there was always a crowd praying together during those vigils. He tried to lose himself in the sounds and rhythms of the prayers. His mind was rarely blank nowadays - his wife was always in his head and tonight was no exception. Her memory gave him comfort and his thoughts drifted back to the first time they met.

27

It was springtime and the college notice-board displayed the usual club notices of forthcoming pub crawls and gigs. One particular item from the Ramblers caught his eye. The following Saturday they were having a leader led walk in the Dublin Mountains from Kilternan to Carrickgollogan. He hadn't tried this activity, and he felt he might like it. The essentials were walking boots and wet weather gear and the final instruction was to bring a packed lunch. That wouldn't happen; he would buy a roll or something along the way. The starting point for the walk was Kilternan.

On Saturday, he took the No 44 bus from Hawkins Street and passed through the Dublin suburbs of Ranelagh, Dundrum, and Stepaside. He arrived in good time at the starting point for the walk, Kilternan. Agnes, the motherly looking leader, introduced herself as he was the only new walker in the group.

'It's hard to believe there are woods and hills so near the centre of Dublin,' she said, adjusting the straps of her rucksack to a more comfortable position.

'I'm from the country,' said Pat as he picked up his own rucksack by the shoulder strap and followed her towards the Sports Hotel.

'Most Dubliners don't know about these walks either,' she said with a smile. She turned around to ensure the others were following: a troupe of about seventy walkers, dressed in colourful outdoor gear, with walking poles in their hands like skiers. They were an all age group with slightly more females and the sport attracted outgoing people. There was a buzz of non-stop talking from the group.

'It's traditional to have a cup of tea or coffee before we start out,' said Agnes, talking over her shoulder to him as they walked up the long driveway to the hotel.

Tea and coffee break over, 'Right let's go,' said Agnes as she hoisted her rucksack on to her shoulders and led the way along the footpath.

'Single file, we don't want anyone getting killed,' she shouted, walking backwards to ensure that they carried out her instructions.

Long before she fell into his arms, Pat's attention focused on the girl with the red rucksack walking ahead of him. It wasn't exactly the rucksack he was looking at, but her shapely legs covered in skinny jeans. He couldn't see her face, but he did see her long blond hair, flowing back from the baseball cap perched on top of her head. Almost hypnotised, he watched her move, his feelings of sexual lust unbridled.

His next visit to the confessional would take care of that, and he was willing to say the usual few Hail Mary's as a penance. It was worth it, although it would be difficult not to commit that same sin again of harbouring "impure" thoughts. She turned her head to look behind her. With that open smile and classical high cheekbones, she was beautiful. Even without knowing her, she was everything he wished for in a girl.

They entered the Scalp wood through a stile in the wall and started on the long climb on the forestry path to the summit. The slippery tree roots had grown through the topsoil across the wet pathway and, if you felt like it, you could slide for Ireland on them.

He was keeping an eye on the girl with the red rucksack and when she slipped on a tree root and fell backwards with flailing arms he rushed forward to catch her. With both arms around her waist, he lifted her high into the air. That took the momentum out of her fall and stopped her from rolling down the hill. He held her for a little while longer than was necessary. She was light in his arms, and he liked the feel of her.

'Put me down, I don't want to stay up here forever.' He set her down on a tree trunk. His weight training had paid off, although she wasn't that heavy. An awkward silence developed between them, finally she spoke.

'Thanks for catching me,' she said, perched on a tree trunk, and sipping tea from a plastic cup.

'These roots are dicey.' Pat was rubbing his boot back and forth on a root to show how slippery they were.

'Cuts and bruises are part of hill walking,' said Agnes as she helped the girl to her feet for the next part of the climb. She walked alongside him.

'I'm Hazel.' She stretched out her hand in a polite and formal manner. He wondered where she had learned such manners.

'I'm Pat O'Malley.' He shook her outstretched hand. Her fingers were thin and bony with little flesh on them. They walked silently, exaggerating the need to avoid the roots growing across the path. The higher up the mountain they climbed the more infrequent were the roots, until there was nothing to avoid on the pathway.

She was the first to speak, 'Where are you from?' She turned around as they reached the top of the mountain, and looked into his face. It seemed as if she was examining every pimple and blemish between his beard and forehead. She smiled and the unease between them vanished.

'I'm from the islands, I'm doing accountancy.'

Her gaze made him uncomfortable, and he looked away. Had she guessed already that he fancied her? However, it was more than that, it felt like she was looking into his soul, uncovering his innermost secrets. No one had ever looked at him like that before.

'You're the first I've met from an island.' She bent down to pick up one of her walking poles.

'What about the island of Ireland then?' Pat quipped, smiling and lifted his leg on to a tree trunk to tie his shoelace.

'You know what I mean.' She tightened the strap of the walking poles around her wrists. She was laughing and there was so much joy in her laughter, it was infectious. He laughed. Agnes had stopped at the summit of the Scalp.

'We'll let everyone catch up,' she said, taking notes from her rucksack and leafing through them.

When the rest of the group had caught up, she started to fill them in on the flora and fauna of Barnasligan Wood, which they were about to walk through. It was the educational part of hill walking.

With the talk over, they took the forestry path from the summit of the Scalp into Barnasligan Wood.

'Accountants are dull and boring,' said Hazel.

'I'm the exception - young, bright and vibrant.' He was smiling as he sat down on a forestry seat for a few minutes. She was mischievously running her hands over the smooth surface of a wood sculpture.

'An Australian carved that with a chain saw. What do you think it is?'

'A Madonna and child or just a hole in the wood, and as you know a cigar is sometimes just a cigar, but islanders wouldn't know anything about that.'

He knew she was winding him up.

'Islanders know everything. Anyway what do you do for a living?'

'Not a living - more of an existence. I'm a trainee Nurse in Tallaght Hospital; and I live with my parents and younger sister in Terenure.' She ran her hands over every wood sculpture.

'Be careful on the loose rock,' said Agnes as the group reached the base of Carrickgollogan, and she selected a zigzag path to the summit. The walking poles used by most in the group seemed a great help in climbing. If he were going to continue hill walking, he would need to buy some.

'It's awesome the first time you see it. We climbed here with Dad when we were children.' Hazel got to her feet and pointed out the landmarks from their vantage point on top of the hill.

'I think I have a blister, it's these new boots' grumbled Pat as he sat down, untied the laces and took off his sock.

'Let me have a look, you have a trainee nurse here, you know.' Hazel was smiling and she bent down to have a look.

'It's a beauty of a blister,' she said, taking a lump of gauze and sticking plaster from her backpack.

She worked away for a few minutes.

'Right we're done here and we're even.' She straightened up, and repacked her rucksack.

'Thanks, as long as you don't fall again,' laughed Pat, getting to his feet and gingerly testing his dressed heel.

'Yea, as long as that heel doesn't go again. We have a fair bit of walking to do yet,' she said, looking down to see if he was still limping. Hazel's nursing skills were in demand again when an older walker's big toe started to chafe against the side of his boot.

'Sock is too rough,' she said.

'Our resident nurse is a ministering angel,' said the older walker, as he carefully put his sock back on, tied up his walking boot and tucked in the legs of his trousers, army style.

'Less of the angel,' she said with a smile.

On the return journey, Agnes took the group past a farmhouse, into a field and over a barbed wire fence to see a three-thousand-year-old dolmen.

'It's called a wedge tomb. Look at the two upright stones holding up a stone roof that's estimated to be a ton weight. How did they ever manage to set them in place?' Agnes rubbed her hands up and down the huge stones.

'That's impressive,' said Pat as he put his hands up to touch the stone roof. He could feel where flints had roughly chipped the surface to a rectangular shape. Grey lichen was growing all over the dolmen.

'I hope you've impressed with all of it. Will you walk with us again?' asked Hazel, rubbing her hands over the stones.

'I'm converted to hill walking,' he said. He toyed with the idea of asking to meet her during the week, but he didn't know how she would take it and in truth, he was afraid of her saying, 'no.' Better to wait for a while, until he knew more about her. Perhaps she had a boyfriend in the background. It wouldn't surprise him, if she had. Being impulsive at this stage could ruin everything.

Pat continued walking with the group every weekend in order to be with Hazel. They talked a lot and in time had started to fall behind the group, engrossed in their own world. He had thought about it for ages, and now he was about to do it. He hoped that whoever had said, 'faint heart doesn't win fair lady' knew what he was talking about.

The others were well out of sight when he asked, 'Can I kiss you?' He didn't wait for a reply but bent down and kissed her. She kissed him back. That was the start of it, and whenever the group couldn't see them - down in a hollow, in the shrubbery or behind oak, alder or even skimpy fir trees - they kissed.

'I want to see more of you.'

'That's a naughty thing to say,' she said, smiling.

'You know what I mean. I want to see you more often, during the week.'

'Don't I see you every weekend?'

'That's not enough?'

She was silent and then she began to cry.

'Hazel what's wrong?'

'We will have to stop seeing each other,' she said between sobs.

His head was running away with him. Was she married or did she already have a boyfriend? He was holding her in his arms.

'Mother warned me not to have anything to do with Catholic boys. As children, we did not mix with them.'

'But I love you.'

'And I love you too, but my family would never agree to it.' She was weeping all over his t-shirt, and he could feel the damp getting through to his skin.

'I'm so sorry; I didn't mean to lead you on. I didn't want our friendship to go as far as it did.'

He dried her eyes with a handkerchief from his pocket, her tears were as important to him as any other part of her. If only he knew what to say and make all this go away.

'I am so sad and depressed.'

'So am I,' he said.

'Please let me go, Pat.' He did as she asked, and he watched her hurry away to catch up with the group ahead.

Pat stopped hill walking - he couldn't face thinking about Hazel each step he took. She left numerous messages on his answering machine,

'Hazel here, call me, we need to talk.'

He couldn't call her, to say goodbye to her again would have broken his heart for a second time.

28

Since parting from Hazel, he spent his time with long sessions in the college gym and study marathons in his attic flat in Rathmines. The attic was hot and stuffy, and he kept the roof windows open day and night. With its sloping walls, the attic resembled a tent and except for the centre of the room, he couldn't stand up straight without hitting his head on the roof.

He would never forget the night his doorbell rang late. He thought it was fellow students looking for course notes or a textbook. He stuck his head out the window and, in the light of the street lamp; he saw Hazel standing on the pavement, carrying a hold all. A taxi was driving away.

She looked up, cupped her hands around her mouth and shouted,

'Let me in!'

'Stand back, I'll throw down the keys.'

She moved well away and he watched the door keys as they fell down four storeys to the pavement. The flat was a mess. With the state, his mind was in; he hadn't bothered to tidy it. He rushed around gathering dirty laundry and empty cans and hid them behind the sofa. The empty pizza boxes went under the bed. He could hear the click, click of her high heels on the bare treads of the stairs. He opened the flat door for her. She looked beautiful with her face flushed from the effort of climbing the stairs. He wanted to take her in his arms and kiss her. He dare not do that, her visit might be to reaffirm that their relationship was over, as if he didn't know that already.

'I left messages all over the place for you, but you didn't ring me.'

'I couldn't.'

'Why?'

'It would have killed me to have to part from you again.'

'Come here, you won't have to.'

They kissed passionately. She gently pulled away from him.

'I had a terrible row with my mother. She now knows how we feel about each other.'

'She might change her mind about us eventually,' he said.

'You don't know my mother.' Hazel was silent for a while and Pat would have liked to hear more, but she had already moved on. She was looking around the room with a critical eye and was playfully scolding him.

'A typical bachelor flat, it needs a good tidy up.'

'I didn't know that I was going to have a visitor.'

'I should have made an appointment then.'

He didn't mind what she said as long as she was back with him.

'There's a week's waiting list to get in here. You were right to chance it.'

They sat down on the sofa. He took her in his arms.

'Are you on night shift?'

'No but my mother thinks so.'

'Will you stay tonight?'

'We'll see.'

He kissed her again. They talked well into the night. Now was the time to ask her the question he had wanted to ask her for so long.

'Can I make love to you?'

He was trembling so much that it was, as if as if he developed a shaking illness. Her face reddened and she looked down at the floor.

Had he said too much?

'I don't know?'

'What's wrong?'

'I'm scared, it's my first time.'

'You're a virgin?'

'Yes.'

'It'll be all right.'

He wanted her to think that he had experience in these matters, and in control of everything; but in truth, it was also his first time.

The day he went into the pharmacy in Rathmines to buy condoms and lubricant, he was giving in to every young man's fantasy of readiness in case he got lucky. He felt embarrassed when a young woman about his own age came to serve him. He couldn't ask for condoms or lubricant, and he bought a bottle of cough mixture that he never used. It took a few more trips before he managed to get them from a male pharmacist.

Since it was his first time he didn't know what to expect. He was keen to get it right. What would she think of him if he couldn't perform what they were about to do?

'Would you prefer not to?'

That was rich, his whole body was screaming out to make love to her. He hoped he hadn't wrecked their friendship by asking her.

'I'm not sure but I want you to be the first. Have you anything to drink?'

'Yes but you don't drink.'

'I do tonight.'

'Would wine do?'

It was his only bottle of wine, half full, and it had been there for ages.

'Yes, it's fine.'

They drank the wine slowly. A teetotaller, it was a measure of how fearful she was, that she was sipping wine with him. They were both getting a bit tipsy and his head was in such a spin, like being on a rollercoaster and one he didn't want to get off anytime soon.

Hazel was so direct about everything; that was her way and he liked it.

'Can I use your toilet?'

He hoped he had left it reasonably presentable.

'Yes, go ahead.'

She gently extracted herself from his embrace, went to her hold all, and took out a toilet bag and nightdress. He got a quick glimpse at it before she tucked it under her arm. He wasn't a connoisseur of nightdresses, but even though it wasn't exactly see-through, there was a lot to like about it. His dream was to see Hazel's curves in the flesh, although covered in this flimsy nightdress would be next-best. His hormones were running wild.

Hazel went to the bathroom, taking the toilet bag and nightdress with her. She returned wearing the nightdress and Pat's heart was racing with excitement. He could see, as if behind a veil, the lovely curves of her body.

'I need to cover up, nobody has ever seen me like this before,' she said, avoiding his eyes.

'You're beautiful.'

He got up off the sofa to take her in his arms, but she evaded his grasp, jumped into bed, and pulled the sheet up to her neck. Pat took off his clothes and quickly got into bed beside her and covered himself up with the sheet. He wasn't too keen on anyone seeing him naked either. The wine had taken effect, and she started to giggle,

'It's your first time too?'

'Yes.'

'We'll learn together.'

They kissed, laughed and giggled for ages. He hadn't used a condom before, and he had difficulty getting it out of its wrapper. It fell from his trembling hands into the bed. They started a playful search for it, pulling the sheets off each other and rolling around in the bed. They found it eventually and, bashfulness gone, he was no longer afraid of not knowing what to do.

They were in each other's arms kissing and fondling. He kissed her lips, ears, nose, and breasts before gently making love. She sighed and relaxed. They were somewhere in time, and space, euphoric, and lost to the rational world. He rolled over on his side and held her in a tight embrace.

'Was it all right?' she whispered anxiously.

'It was great.' He kissed her gently on the forehead.

'Did you enjoy it?'

'It was lovely. I felt so close to you.'

She kissed him a long lingering kiss on the lips.

They slept in each other's arms for the rest of the night. He didn't know then that she was going to die so soon.

A fish surfaced yards from the life-raft. It was gone again in a second, leaving behind a few eddies to show that it had been there. The ocean continued to rock the life-raft in a leisurely fashion.

His life, or what remained of it, had to go on.

29

'I'm sleeping on the outside tonight,' said Tarja, pushing Pat to the back of the bunk and up against the side of the life-raft.

'Okay.' But it wasn't okay. He wasn't sleeping well. If he was on the outside of the bunk, rather than lying there awake, he could get up without disturbing her. He often sat during the night in the main part of the life-raft, keeping an eye on Coleman and checking their course. He was powerless to change the direction they were going in; observing was all the action he could take.

'It's colder tonight,' she said, getting a second duvet from the spare bunk.

She was soon asleep and snoring. He never mentioned to her that she snored. He couldn't sleep. Hour after hour he listened to the ocean and the noise of the creaking timbers of the life-raft. He was dozing when he heard a thump against the hull. It startled him, but he decided it was a plank of wood bumping against the side of the raft. That wasn't unusual - balks of wood and all kinds of containers were floating around out there on the ocean, washed overboard from ships caught in a storm. From the light tapping sound it made, it wouldn't do any damage.

He woke again when Tarja thumped him,

'Wake up sleepy head,' she said, getting up, and starting to dress.

'I'm wide awake and ready to go.' It was great to see her in such an upbeat mood. It helped a lot to lift the terrible burden he felt at having her out here in the first place.

'I'll make tea.'

Seconds later, she shouted,

'Come quickly!'

'Coming!' He jumped out of the bunk and stubbed his toe against the bottom of the life-raft. Damn it, he should have looked at what was hitting them last night. They might be taking water.

'He's drowned,' she said tearfully. She was on her knees in the bottom of the life-raft, holding Coleman's head out of the water.

'Keep his head like that!' Pat shouted as he struggled to turn Coleman over on to his back.

That was the thump he had heard last night – Coleman falling out of the bunk and landing face down in the water. There were only a few inches of it, but it was enough. He was cold to the touch.

'Lift him back into the bunk,' said Pat, gripping Coleman by the arms. He was heavy and it was a struggle for them to move him, but somehow they managed to manhandle him out of the water and on to the bunk. Pat was shaking and Tarja was crying. They clung to each other. Lord, this was a terrible way to lose Coleman. If he had been up during the night, as he always was, he might have been in time to save Coleman.

'What in heaven's name are we going to tell people when we get back?' said Pat.

He had visions of the coroner's court on the island trying to establish the cause of death for the two missing crewmen. A misadventure, buried at sea would be the verdict. Tongues would wag on the island, as they always did. There was nothing like a juicy gossip to get them going. He and Tarja would be the prime suspects for having murdered them. His imagination was torturing him, it was a long way back and there was a big question mark on whether they would make it or not.

'It's so sad, but it was an accident,' said Tarja with tears running down her cheeks. She closed Coleman's eyes and mouth taking that awful gaping look off his face.

'It was Coleman's dream, to have a prosthetic arm fitted in the US and to be like everyone else even for one day,' said Pat, looking down at the corpse.

'None of it matters now,' she said, tidying Coleman's hair.

They sat quietly for a long time, drained and deep in thought. Jinxed from the start, or so it seemed, he wondered what would happen next. Had fate decided that they die one at a time or go together? Tarja spoke first,

'You're not going to tow the corps same as before, are you?' she asked, looking at him.

'No, we've had enough of that.' Although it would be good to bring Coleman's body home, since they had given the skipper up to the sea. Forget that.

We'll bury him at sea, but I think we should wait for a while and have a wake for him.'

'I'll prepare the shroud.' Tarja was on her feet, and going to the stern of the life-raft where the stored sailcloth and needles were. Coleman was getting a beautiful day for his funeral - sunshine, light winds and a sea as calm as a paddling pool.

'We'll wait until nightfall before we bury him,' he said. It wouldn't feel so terrible pushing the corpse overboard in the dark.

'Okay.' Tarja was shaking out the sailcloth and measuring the amount needed for the shroud. Pat helped her wrap Coleman from head to toe and then sew up the seams. He didn't say anything, but it was a relief to have the corpse packaged up in sailcloth. It was more anonymous than having a lifeless person lying there. Even death couldn't take away his human presence.

They held their wake for Coleman during the day and Pat said rosaries, counting the decades on his fingers.

'Other Churches are suspicious of rosary beads, it's mysterious and a bit suspect,' she said, having patiently listened to him reciting the prayers.

'It's a Catholic ritual,' he said, moving back a bit from the shrouded corpse.

'And the Russian and Greek Orthodox as well,' she said, moving to sit near him.

'They're for counting prayers,' said Pat who hadn't thought much about it. As far as he could see, there was no mystery about it - he had been doing it since childhood.

'That doesn't tell me much,' she said, looking out over the calm sea.

'Bible based mysteries; that's what the rosary is about, and then there's the "Our Father".'

'What do you mean by all that?'

'I'm making it up as I go along. The truth is that I haven't looked up the origins of the rosary, and its beads.'

'I think you need a refresher course on your church,' said Tarja, smiling.

'My main priority when we get back,' he said, as if getting back was a given.

'I'll keep you to it.' The banter kept him away from the gruesome task that lay ahead, of pushing Coleman's body into the sea.

'What can we use to weight down the corpse?' asked Pat. If they didn't weight it down with something it would float on the surface and probably keep pace with them.

'I don't know, there isn't much,' said Tarja, looking around the raft.

The anchor hidden in the stern of the boat would be ideal for the purpose. He was reluctant to use it, as it was an important piece of equipment if they had to prevent the life-raft from crashing on to rocks. Unfortunately, there was nothing else onboard heavy enough to weigh down the corpse.

Pat couldn't get the corpse out of his line of vision. It was disturbing him.

'Let's get the anchor,' he said, making for the stern.

'Hope it's not too heavy,' she said, joining him at the rear of the life-raft. They started to search for the anchor.

'It's covered with rust.' She had found the anchor and was trying to move it.

'Let me help you shift it.' He gave the anchor a heave, but it didn't budge.

'We'll drag it. No sense in putting our backs out.' He knew the anchor was heavy, but before his injuries, he could have carried it without help. His shoulder had set itself crooked and although Tarja didn't notice, he could feel bones sticking through the skin. It would need resetting if, and when they got back to port. He'd never had surgery and he didn't know what to expect. That was another joy awaiting him. He'd be in agony without morphine. They finally hauled the anchor up near the corpse.

'I'm hot,' she said, gulping down water.

'Aye, from the sun and the effort,' he said with a sigh. Pat felt exhausted, although there was one other job he would have to do before he rested. He tied a rope around the corpse where he thought Coleman's belt should be and the other end he passed through the eye of the anchor. Everything secured, they were ready to bury Coleman when darkness fell and since it was summer, that wouldn't be much before ten o'clock.

They dozed for the rest of the day.

'It's such a lovely night,' said Tarja as the moon lit up the life-raft. Pat felt nature was being spiteful, such brightness on the only night of his life, he wanted darkness. There might be a solution.

'Let's bury Coleman when that cloud covers the moon.' He was pointing to a fast moving cloud destined to cross in front of the moon, and cut off the light.

'We need to be quick,' said Tarja as she stood at Coleman's feet. Pat took his head.

'We can't just throw the corpse into the sea, we need something religious.' Pat lifted Coleman's shoulders to get some idea of his weight.

Tarja started to pray,

'The Lord is my shepherd, I shall not want...'

As if on cue, the cloud crossed in front of the moon as Tarja finished the psalm.

'Now,' said Pat and they heaved the corpse over the side. The anchor hit the water and slowly sank under the surface, pulling the corpse down with it. The sea was so clear that they could see it sinking for a long way before it went out of sight. Pat was sad; they had started out with four now they were down to two.

Tarja was silent, and had gone into herself.

'Tarja, talk to me.' He put his arms around her.

She started to cry uncontrollably. He shouldn't have said anything, if he had kept his mouth shut, whatever was bothering her might have gone by morning. She was finding it difficult to say anything.

'Tarja, what's wrong?'

'I'm pregnant.'

'Are you sure you're pregnant?' He knew as soon as he said it that was the wrong thing to say. Her anger showed in the heightening colour of her face.

'You don't seem pleased about it?'

'Yes I'm pleased. I'll be happy to have another son.' He didn't sound convincing.

'It might not be a son,' she said icily, not looking at him.

'Either would be fine.' Even that, somehow, didn't come out right. Good Lord he was tense and the sweat was running down his back.

'I can raise the child myself. You don't need to feel responsible.'

'No I want to be a father again.' He was trying to persuade her of his sincerity.

'I'm going to bed,' she said, ending the conversation. She ignored him and headed for the forward bunk.

He had lost the argument and, in truth, he didn't know how he felt about her pregnancy. How could she be pregnant so soon? On balance, it would be better if it hadn't happened. They should have training courses for men, on how to deal with this. He wasn't ready for this complication in his life so soon after losing his family, although he was willing to support her, and their child in every way possible. He would not walk away from any child he had fathered. The problem was, he didn't express his feelings well - that he wanted to do right by her, and their child. If he alienated her at this stage, she might take their child to Finland, and he might never see them again. Regardless of what she said, he was sure it was a son to replace Mark. He hadn't wanted this type of a relationship with her when they first met, and he wasn't sure that he wanted it now. He should have used a condom, but he didn't have any; and she should have known about these things herself. It was her fault as much as his.

That wasn't good, he was responsible, and he should take the hit for it. Blaming her was as low as he could go. The problem was, did he care enough for her to ask for her hand in marriage? Then there was the other difficulty - she might not want to marry him. Anyway he would leave that topic for a while until they were on better terms. He wouldn't get into the bunk next to her tonight. That was a no-no. He'd let enough time pass for her to fall sleep, and then he'd peep, in order to see if she was OK. When he checked, she was sleeping, although her face was wet from crying. He gently wiped her tears without waking her.

He would have to give her that; she was a great sleeper and she would be out cold until morning. He wanted to wake her up and tell her everything was alright, but was it alright? He sighed; he should have been more careful.

If Hazel was here he could tell her the problem, and she would have a solution. That was rich. Tell her what - that he had got a girl pregnant? He remembered the last time he had to tell her about something like that, but less contentious, and all hell broke loose. It happened before they married. After his mother's death, he went to the Island one weekend, to prepare the family home for sale. Hazel was working and she couldn't go with him. He was happy enough to go by himself, but her sister Joy insisted that she go along for the trip. They needn't have bothered, the neighbours had cleaned the house, and it was ready for sale. They spent a pleasant weekend on the island apart from both getting legless drunk, and finishing in bed together. He remembered her skin, so smooth and soft.

His conscience wouldn't let him live a lie with Hazel, someone so close; he had to tell her. When he tried to explain, she went ballistic and made a terrible scene right in the middle of Grafton Street.

'You pig, get away from me! How could you do that with my sister of all people?' She stormed away from him. He shouted after her, 'It was a mistake, and it meant nothing!'

A passer-by roared with laughter. Hazel didn't look back. She broke off the engagement saying she wouldn't speak to him or her sister, Joy ever again. All his phone calls and letters went unanswered but he wasn't going to give up on his first, and only love that easily. He went the whole nine yards, flowers and cards for every occasion from birthdays to Valentine's Day. He thought he had lost her because of a night of madness. The standoff went on for a year. Finally, his persistence paid off, and they tentatively got back together again. However Hazel made him suffer by dating other lads, to show him that their relationship was no longer exclusive. He hated seeing her with other fellows. She kept him on probation for months. Up to his recent dalliance with Tarja, that was the only time he was unfaithful, to her or to her memory. He should have learned by now.

A gull with a large fish in its mouth crash-landed and slid along the forward deck. Two other gulls followed and a squawking fight ensued on the deck for the fish, a prized meal. One of them managed to grab it and tried to fly away, in the melee it fell from its mouth and dropped with a splash into the sea. Was there some message in that? If there was, he couldn't fathom it out. He would need to shake himself out of this nonsense, being a superstitious islander, looking for psychic messages in a simple act of nature. Sleep was impossible, and he would have lots of thinking time from now until morning.

30

Pat came out of his musing. Something about their situation had changed; the life-raft was going faster, and swaying from side to side. The speed of the current had increased tenfold and there was no sign of what was causing it. The rest of the sea was like a millpond. He stood up and looked out over the ocean to try to figure out what was going on. Tarja jumped out of the bunk, rushed to the side of the life-raft, and vomited into the sea.

'This shouldn't come for some time yet.' She was talking more to herself than to him, and from her manner, she didn't want a reply. Morning sickness was proof that she was pregnant. The juddering of the life-raft was the likely cause of its appearance so soon into her pregnancy. It would be horrendous if she had a miscarriage. How would she cope with that? She looked unwell. Her face looked putty coloured, and her tangled hair was hanging in strands around her face. His own beard, brittle from sea salt and growing half way down to his chest must be some mess. There might be something nasty nesting in it and one of his first jobs, if they made it back to shore, was to cut it off.

'What is happening?' she asked, wiping away the residue of spew from her mouth with a head scarf she was clutching in her hand. She didn't look at him.

'Don't know for sure.' Ahead the waves were getting larger in the speeding current.

'You know or you don't know?' She had an aggressive edge to her voice. There was no place to hide on such a small boat, and it was going to be a long trip with her in this a mood.

'Look, what I said last night was wrong, but I will always be there for you and our child.' She looked at him for a while considering what he said.

'You were far from sure last night.'

'I'm sure now.'

He was getting a bit concerned about the speed of the current. It seemed ridiculous that there might be another whirlpool up ahead, although he couldn't rule it out.

'We'll see,' she said, and without another word returned to her bunk. That was telling him where he stood. She fell asleep again.

The fast drift continued with no letup. It occurred to him that this variation in currents could be all over the Atlantic, and in the trawler with its powerful engine, they went unnoticed. It was a different story in a small life-raft, buffeted around by any slight roughness in the sea. That wasn't a convincing line of argument. There was something else up ahead, drawing them closer and there was nothing he could do about it. His unborn son could be at risk, and to lose him now was unthinkable.

By midday, Tarja was awake in the bunk.

'Would you like to eat?' He had to be careful what he said.

'No, I'm nauseous,' she said, sitting up.

It was an improvement having her speaking to him, and you never knew, they might manage to be civil to each other again. Maybe he was being too harsh with her. All she had done was to show irritation when he didn't seem to care about her pregnancy.

'OK,' he said. Their food came mostly from tins, and he hoped they'd strike land soon, to get her the variety of nourishment she needed for herself and their child. He didn't have any control over that; and they had long since eaten all the bread and fresh fruit on board. Tarja didn't protest when he sat down beside her.

'I'm terrified; we're going to capsize again.' Even with her best efforts to hold back, tears started to roll down her cheeks.

'That won't happen, currents are always speeding up and slowing down,' he said, putting his arms around her and holding her close to comfort her. She didn't pull away. What he had said was vaguely true, although it wasn't the whole truth. There was something else out there reeling them in.

'I think I'll get up.' She pulled away from him and sat up, but she had second thoughts, and lay down again. That was how she survived the days at sea, staying up for a while and then going back to her bunk to rest. Although he had limited experience of expectant mothers, Pat felt this was going to be a difficult pregnancy. Anyway, a life-raft adrift on the high seas wasn't the best place to be pregnant.

She dozed for a while, and then he heard her call, 'I'm hungry again, I'll have to get up now.' She opened the flap of her sleeping bag and got out of the bunk. With the pace they were travelling, it took her a few seconds to get her sea legs, and he put out his hands to steady her.

'I'll get something to eat for both of us,' he said, starting to clean the rusted cutter of the tin opener. Mixing the tastes of tinned fish with tinned meat or, even worse, with mixed fruit did nothing for their appetites. It might be the right time to open the medicinal brandy, and offer her a glass to celebrate her pregnancy, although he didn't necessarily see it as a blessing.

'To us and our new baby,' he said handing her a glass of brandy.

'I'll only take a sip. It's not recommended,' she said as they touched glasses. Pat emptied her glass as well as his own. Shortly after Tarja had eaten, she felt tired, and he helped her back to the bunk. She fell asleep almost as soon as her head hit the pillow. He hoped and prayed she was going to be OK.

He continued drinking brandy long after Tarja went to sleep and by dusk, he felt drunk. There was half an idea forming in his head, it was time to ask her to marry him, and that would ensure that his son would always be with him. Right, no time like the present, and he went forward to Tarja's bunk, and woke her up.

'Have we slowed down at all?' she asked, hauling herself up to a sitting position.

'No but everything is OK.' He sat on the edge of the bunk beside her.

'You're drunk!' She must have smelt the alcohol of his breath; he didn't think it showed in any other way.

He put his arm around her shoulder; he thought that was romantic.

'Tarja, will you marry me?' He moved closer to her.

She looked outraged and removed his arm from around her shoulder.

'No, you're drunk. Anyway I won't be yours or anyone else's slave. That's what marriage is.' She lay back down in the bunk and turned her face to the hull.

'I want you as my wife and not as my slave, equal partners in everything.'

She didn't respond and he felt he should try again.

'What about us living together then.'

'I don't want anything to do with you.'

Even in his drunken state, he knew that was a refusal. He returned to the living area. He didn't have much practice in making marriage proposals and this was his first refusal. So what, he probably wouldn't live to tell the tale. Nothing mattered at this stage. He dozed for a while and when he woke the effects of the alcohol had worn off, and he had a terrible headache. What was he thinking of? Another apology would be needed in the morning for asking her to marry him. At least until they got off the life-raft, he wanted peace and not war. He was having another night without much sleep, as they rushed towards something unknown ahead. Based on their experiences on this trip, it was unlikely to be anything good.

The dawn light woke Pat as the sun, an orange disc tipped with gold, was rising above the sea on the eastern horizon. They were still moving fast in the current and the rest of the ocean was as calm as it had been for days. The scene was almost spiritual. The poets would call it romantic; but after yesterday evening's debacle, the life-raft wasn't the place for that. It had all spun out of control, and was still spinning. The drinking excess of last night was the cause of his woes and his splitting headache. After all the hassle, Tarja had put him through, who could blame him for drinking too much? This was only the second woman to whom he had proposed marriage and she had refused him.

Well, better to be positive, his record was a fifty per cent success in that area, or was it fifty per cent failure? Somehow that didn't help. His first child had died, and his second unborn child could be living away from him, in Finland. Apart from dozing now and again, he had been awake for most of the night, agonising over his life and the mess he had made of it. He was thinking badly and he knew it. He was being so self-obsessed, self-pitying, and thoughtless. It was his fault as much as hers that she was pregnant. She was the one burdened most by his cavalier and reckless behaviour.

Tarja came swiftly out of her bunk in the forward hold and just made it in time to the rail, before puking over the side. It was becoming a morning ritual. He was now able to clean her vomit without feeling sick.

'I'm sorry, the stench is terrible,' she said as she moved away from the side of the life-raft.

'It's not your fault. Would you like something to drink?' He filled the kettle from one of the plastic water bottles.

'Weak tea,' she said, examining her clothes to see if she had splashed herself.

With a limited choice, he could give her either tea or water. He knew she wouldn't take brandy. There was nothing else onboard for drinking. Doubtless pregnant women needed loads of pills, vitamins and other things that they didn't have onboard. She didn't seem aware of it, and he wouldn't mention it.

He waited for the life-raft to rock to one side, and before it rolled the other way he handed her a cup of tea. He felt pleased; he didn't spill any of it. She sipped it slowly, afraid that she would vomit again.

'I was rough on you last night,' she said, looking up at him.

What should he say about that? He hadn't changed his mind about wanting to marry her, or even to live with her outside marriage, but he had chosen a most unfortunate time to ask her - when drunk.

'It was my own fault,'

'You drank a lot of brandy last night. Do you still mean what you said?' She was holding the cup in both hands to cushion it against the rocking of the life-raft.

'Yes, I meant every word of it.' He shifted his gaze on to the roughening sea. It would cause them no difficulty except to shake them around a bit, although the cause of all that turbulence ahead was a mystery.

'I'm flattered that you asked, but I'm against marriage. It's slavery for women.' She was looking to him for a reaction.

'Some people think that,' he said. He felt her recent past had coloured her view on marriage, but there was nothing to gain from starting an argument. He didn't fully agree with her. Happily married to Hazel, he had wanted nothing more than their marriage to continue forever. Unfortunately, life or should he say death, intervened. As far as he knew, Hazel was happy in their marriage as well; and it hurt him to think that she might not have been as contented in the marriage as he was. He just assumed that because she was the right woman for him, that automatically, he was the right man for her. Tarja's story had brought this doubt into his head.

Tarja cut in on his thoughts. 'I want to live with you without marriage getting in the way,' she said hesitantly.

'I would like that,' he said.

That might be putting his wish to have his unborn son close to him before his other needs. He didn't have feelings as deep for Tarja as he had for his dead wife and was it fair to her? He should accept that his bond with Hazel was special, and he might never again find anyone else as compatible. Comparing their relationship with the way he felt about Tarja was confusing him and holding him back. There was no doubt that he had feelings for Tarja and maybe in time these would develop into love. It was time to move on from the past.

'We will live in Finland,' she said, planning it all in her head and looking excited at the scenario she was creating.

'What about a job for me, and the language?'

'They all speak English and there's a shortage of accountants.'

She stood up shakily and managed to hug him. He hadn't considered having to move to Finland. Up to now, he had planned to spend the rest of his life on the island. It didn't appeal to him to become another Irish wanderer on the 'four winds and the seven seas'. How would he ever manage to live in Finland, a foreign country with a different language and a freezing climate? If it came to it, he might have to. It was a mess and largely of his own making. Better say nothing or he would only dig himself in deeper.

Of course, after the death of the skipper he didn't have anyone else on the island to worry about, and he was free to go wherever his fancy took him. He would have to think about it all, and they were a long way from the stage when he would have to decide about it. Meantime there was the immediate problem of trying to keep them alive long enough to get to shore.

'Their first grandchild! My parents will be so thrilled,' she said, freeing him from her embrace. The rocking of the life-raft caused her to sit down heavily rather than tumble over. She was happier than he had seen her for a long time, probably building castles in the air about their future life in Finland.

'We'll stay in the ice hotel and see lots of reindeer,' she said enthusiastically.

'Can't wait,' said Pat, immediately sorry he said it like that. It wasn't like him to be cynical, but he felt her planning was getting out of hand. Tarja didn't pick up on it and, on this occasion, he was glad she didn't understand all the nuances of the English language.

'My parents will be so pleased to meet you.'

'Wait until they see the state their daughter is in, they might feel different, and have second thoughts about me living in Finland.' He had to say something and didn't want to increase her expectation that they would move to Finland.

'They'll be so pleased. They have been waiting a long time for a grandchild.

It was beginning to look as if his son was not going to be his but owned by some foreign family. He'd need to stop thinking like this. His head was all mixed up, and what he needed was some movement. He had seen binoculars in the life-raft about a year ago, and they might still be there in the rubbish collection under the stern deck. They were worth searching for, and they might let him see what was up ahead. He got up, and like a tightrope walker staggered to the stern. With the increase in pace, they must be getting near whatever was causing them to speed up.

'What are you searching for?' Tarja stood up to test the sway of the life-raft, and sat down again abruptly.

'A pair of binoculars.' He was digging down through the rubbish and throwing it left and right out of his way. Maybe he should dump all this waste overboard, but he wouldn't do that. He was against polluting the ocean and his principles had not yet deserted him. Now that he had another son coming into the world, he would be even more determined to stamp it out. A pollution free planet was what he wanted for his son.

'I'll help you look for it.' She crawled on all fours to where he was on his knees at the stern.

'I'm no good at this work,' he said, frustrated by junk he was sifting through in the search. They might not even be there.

'I've found them.' Tarja hauled out a set of rusty binoculars from the debris.

'They don't look too good,' said Pat. The lens seemed intact; but because of the rust on the focusing mechanism, it might be difficult to see anything with them. He went forward to the bows, and rested his elbows on the half deck and scanned the sea. The lens focus did not suit his eyesight; it was like wearing somebody else's glasses, but it would have to do. Everything was a bit foggy, but suddenly he saw something on the surface and almost out of vision. What the heck was it?

31

'Can you see anything?' Tarja asked as she peered ahead over the ocean.

'Not much. These binoculars are hopeless.'

Pat crouched over the forward deck with the binoculars held hard against his eyes; he was not getting any clearer view of what was ahead.

'Give them to me and I'll wipe them.'

She opened a bottle of water and got a cloth to clean the lens.

'OK, but the centre screw looks rusted up.'

He couldn't focus them: so he handing her the binoculars and climbed down off the forward deck. Perched up there with the boat swaying, he could fall into the sea. If that happened, Tarja wouldn't manage to haul him back onboard. She was going to have his child, and he cared enough for both of them, not to put them into any more danger. If he did this right, he wouldn't have to involve her at all.

She got up stiffly and held her hand to her back for a few seconds before moving. At times the boat rocked so much that she couldn't find her balance. The longer they remained cooped up like this, the more laborious their movements were getting. Before long they would resemble ninety-year-olds. She in particular needed exercise, but in her pregnant state it was difficult for her to do anything like that on the life-raft.

'We could grease the screw if we had oil,' she said, cleaning away the grime from the lens.

'There's penetrating oil somewhere under the rear deck and that would free it up.'

It was a blessing the lenses were safe from cracking or scoring, but they were useless if he couldn't free the screw and focus them.

He stood up and spread out his hands ready for a circus tightrope walk to the other end of the life-raft. He took the first step and started to wave his arms about to get his balance, like a duck flapping its wings taking off from the surface of a lake. He waited for the life-raft to settle before taking the next step. His performance was silly, he would do better to get down on his hands and knees and crawl along the floor to the stern, even if he made slower progress. Cop yourself on man, how could he be so daft trying to walk upright in these conditions? He got to the rear of the boat and the aerosol container of penetrating oil was sitting on the top of the pile of debris. He hoped that it was not empty.

'I've found it,' he shouted to Tarja. He picked up the container and pointing the nozzle away from him, pressed the plunger. A fine spray of oil plumed into the air. Still kneeling, he sprayed the binoculars adjusting screw. The spray went everywhere even on to his clothes. He waited a few minutes to give it time to work. Tarja seemed relieved. Time up, he tried the focussing screw and it turned easily. On his hands and knees he crawled back to Tarja.

'Can you focus them?' she asked when he came in range.

'I think so.'

Focusing the binoculars was going to be a tricky job with the way the life-raft was jumping about. If only it would stay still for a few minutes. He would see farther out to sea if he stood upright on the forward half deck, although the movement of the boat made it a dangerous manoeuvre. Not worth taking the risk of toppling into the sea, and anyway in such a precarious position it would be difficult to hold the binoculars steady. Staying on his knees was the best alternative.

Expectantly, he scanned the horizon for the cause of their increased speed and sea turbulence. He was about to give up when he saw it against the edge of the horizon: a bubbling caldron of seawater where three currents met. It seemed like they were fighting for dominance until the strongest current won the battle, forcing the others to go with it in a south easterly direction.

'It's Atlantic currents meeting.' He handed the binoculars to her. She had difficulty focusing them and eventually she saw what was causing their problem. With shaking hands she gave them back to him.

'Are we going to capsize again?' she asked through tears.

'It'll be a bit bumpy, that's all.'

'I can't cope with the thought of it.'

He wished he could take her and their child out of here to a safe place, but that wasn't possible.

'We're through the worst of it.'

That might not be true. He didn't know how the turbulent currents ahead were going to affect them; although it didn't look too bad, but there were few certainties at sea.

'It might be better if you stayed in your bunk until we are over this rough patch.'

'OK.' The jerking motion of the life-raft caused her to stumble, and he held out his hand to steady her. He helped her into the bunk.

'I don't want to be a burden.'

'You're anything but.'

He had taken a lifejacket with him and gave it to her.

'Put this on just in case.'

She draped the life jacket over her head, pulled it down over her shoulders and wrapped the ties around her tummy. She jammed her knees against the bulkhead, to stop her from toppling out of the bunk, as she fastened the cord around her back.

The level of water on the floor was rising as it splashed in over the sides. He wasn't too worried about that yet; the self-bailer could cope with it.

'Strap me to the side, Pat.' She lay down on the bunk and pulled the cover up over her head. She was sobbing silently.

'Tarja, don't be so afraid. We're going to get through this,'

For the umpteenth time, he was giving her lame assurances. By now, they probably weren't helping her deal with the disaster thoughts that must be in her head.

'I think we are all going to die,' she said in a muffled voice from under the bed covers. He tied the safety straps holding her in the bunk.

'I love you and I'm going to make sure we don't die,' he whispered, laying his hand gently on her stomach. Her sobbing stopped and she put her hand over his.

'I love you, too,' she said, sticking her head out. He hadn't meant to say that for a while yet, but perhaps now was the time to let her know how he felt. He waited until she fell asleep and crawled back to the living space. The life-raft was swivelling faster in the increasing speed of the current. It hadn't been in water for years and the boards had shrunk leaving gaps between them. The choppier sea was forcing water in through these spaces in the hull, and he started bailing before they became water logged and sank. His predictions that they would get through this new obstacle might be premature.

Lathered in sweat, and with most of the water gone, he stopped scooping it out. It was hard work and he sat down to catch his breath and take stock. The motions of the life-raft were different now to when they were in the storm. Then, the bows were digging into the waves and threatening to capsize them; now the life-raft was surfing along on top of the water like a jet ski. The noise from the hull was just as loud as in the storm, but it was a different sound. The pounding had gone and a screeching hum had replaced it.

He went to check on Tarja. She was still sleeping and he tried not to disturb her. It was possible that nature looked after pregnant women, by giving them the capacity to sleep whenever they had the opportunity. Some of his ideas were bordering on the bizarre and that one wouldn't make the medical journals.

The sea ahead was boiling and a damp mist was rising from it and spreading out over the ocean. They were within its range and the binoculars were fogging up. He was wet to the skin. The night was warm and he didn't mind the dampness, although he would like to keep Tarja dry in the bunk. Raising the canopy would ensure that, and it was just about manageable by one person, if the sea conditions were right, although it was safer as a two-man job. Their situation was far from safe; and if he were unfortunate enough to fall into the sea, the speeding life-raft would leave him behind in seconds. He must take all precautions, using a lifejacket and attaching himself to the raft with a safety line. He was unlikely to fare much better, hauled behind the life-raft attached by a line, than if he went overboard in freefall. Either way, he would be unable to get back onboard again.

He climbed on top of the life-raft's half deck, and kneeling, he attempted to raise the canopy. He reckoned he would have to use force to hoist it into place. He heaved as hard as he could on the canopy, and it shot into place. He had miscalculated the effort needed, and the momentum propelled him backwards from the half deck on to the floor. He landed on his bad shoulder, and roared with pain. He lay there in the wet bottom of the boat with seawater showering in on top of him. Had he dislocated his shoulder again? He didn't dare move for what seemed an age; then he cautiously tried to raise his arm. He was in luck - there was movement in his shoulder. It was about the same as before the fall. Possibly luck wasn't the right way to think about it; he didn't have much of that recently. He painfully raised himself off the floor and turned over on to his knees. He would have to stay like that for a while until the pain lessened a bit.

They were heading into the middle of the currents and the boat was tossing from side to side on its keel. Beaten into frenzy, the sea was pouring down on the canopy. He felt relieved that it was giving them some protection from a deluge. It was remarkable that Tarja could sleep through it all. With such currents, there was a good chance of capsizing, or ending stuck in the middle of the flow unable to break free. They were in real danger; he hadn't experienced this type of sea before and even if he had, there was nothing he could do about it, in such a small boat.

He tied himself to the side of the hull, and prepared for the worst. The life-raft reached the centre of the currents, and started to spin like a top. It was making him dizzy. He closed his eyes, and tried to stop his head spinning. That didn't work and he threw up. This torture would have to end soon, one way or another. He could do it quickly, loosen the straps holding him to the side of the life-raft and take his chance with the ocean. Not much of a choice, but it was better than getting his brain jellied by the whirling of the life-raft. It wouldn't stop; it was like when he was a child swinging around on the playground rides. He didn't like it then; and he didn't like it now. He started to roar.

The life-raft turned faster, and faster, in the current until the momentum flung them into open sea. His head spun for a long time before settling down. He guessed they were now travelling in a south-easterly direction.

'Are you all right?' shouted Tarja from her bunk.

'Yes, we are out of it.'

He loosened the straps holding him to the side of the life-raft.

'There's a lot of water in here. Are we sinking?'

'I'll get rid of that water in a minute.' He was going to have to start bailing again and this time his shoulder was even worse than before. The vomit would be first to go over the side, it made him nauseous looking at it sitting there on top of the water.

'I'll come out and help,' said Tarja. He could hear her trying to untie the holding belts.

'No, no, stay where you are.' He didn't want her to see his floating vomit.

Pat started the painful work of bailing again. He could throw half-full buckets of water overboard at a time, and that was about it. When the vomit disappeared over the side, he felt relieved. Somebody told him that fish eat it, and it's a delicacy for them. That's if fish have delicacies.

'Help me with these straps.' Pat went forward to untie them. Her bunk was dry. Water hadn't risen high enough from the floor to reach it and the canopy had prevented water blowing in. He helped her out of the bunk, her movements were getting more rigid, and it concerned him a lot.

'Have you any pain?'

'Just stiff all over,' she said, stepping into the water on the floor in her bare feet. Gone was the lithesome girl he had seen on the pub forecourt with her ponytail bobbing up and down. He hoped all that would come back after she got away from the confines of the life-raft. He helped her along to the main living space, and she sat down awkwardly with her back rigid. He wondered if her stiffness would affect her pregnancy. He was agonizing about her health and there was no one else to talk to. He didn't want to make Tarja more anxious by discussing his concerns with her.

'Was it rough while I was asleep?' She was splashing her feet in the water on the floor of the boat.

'We took in water, but we were safe enough.' He started bailing again.

'Let me help you.' Tarja, holding on to the side, was trying to stand up.

'No need, I'll finish in no time at all.'

That's if he didn't collapse from pain and exhaustion. She sat down heavily. Their pace slowed in the calm sea, and he felt relieved that they were travelling away from the violent currents.

'How did you get the canopy up?' She seemed to be enjoying splashing her feet in the water, and it helped him to see her so playful. At another time and place, the temperature of the water would be ideal for swimming.

'OK, but I fell on my shoulder.' He looked up from bailing. His strength was going, and he would have to stop soon although the sump had some water left in. That amount shouldn't cause any problems.

More worrying was the way the planks were bending when he moved about on them. Made from oak, they shouldn't be flexing like that, although he knew they had worn thin. The life-raft would sink in minutes if one of the floor planks sprung a leak. It always came down to the same problem - their past carelessness in maintaining the trawler and its safety equipment.

There was no sense in telling her about another possible calamity. He didn't know what effect her fear would have on their baby, but he felt determined not to increase it. Keeping secrets wasn't the best way to develop a relationship though his motives were to protect her.

'Last night, you said, 'I love you', who were you talking about?' Tarja was looking down at her bare feet and wriggling her toes as she asked.

He had meant what he said last night that he loved her. It was as much as he could love anyone except his wife; and he hoped he wasn't being unfair to Tarja. Many relationships were like that, and he wouldn't have known the difference if he had never met his dead wife Hazel.

'You and our child,' he said, careful not to say son.

She looked at him for a long time and then got up with difficulty and came over to sit beside him. She kissed him on the cheek,

'I think you mean it.' She rested her head on his good shoulder.

'It's not something I take lightly, and I wouldn't say it if I didn't mean it.'

They were silent for a time before Tarja asked, 'Where are we heading?'

'My guess is the west coast of Scotland.' He looked around him for some clue to back up his assertion. There was nothing ahead except the slow current rippling over the tranquil sea. He had given her the best outcome, although he didn't know how far north they had gone before the currents redirected them south-easterly. Their worst situation would be to drift into the icepacks on Russia's northern coast where their chance of getting rescued was virtually non-existent. Except for an occasional icebreaker, that sea was almost empty of shipping. They would remain stuck in the ice until they froze to death.

32

With a light wind behind them, he guessed they were travelling towards Scotland or Russia. He had no immediate concerns about the sea, although it could change quickly, and they could find themselves in another storm. Would he have the reserves to cope with it and, even if he had, how would Tarja manage?

'Can you see anything?' she asked, sitting on the bench next to him. For the umpteenth time, he held the binoculars to his eyes, and did a three hundred and sixty degree scan of the horizon.

'No change but we're getting there.' He was trying to be optimistic. He had his own demons to contend with. The implication of not seeing land was keeping him awake at night, and leaving him tired from lack of sleep. If they were unlucky enough to hit the ice fields on the north east coast of Russia, a terrible death was awaiting them.

'I look a mess in these.' Tarja, dressed in Pat's trousers, and jacket, and Coleman's peaked cap to shade her eyes from the sun was leaning over the side, and gazing at her mirrored image in the water. Her matted hair was a dirty brown colour, and it reminded him of the coconut twine used on sailing ships in the old days.

'You look fine.'

For however long, thinking about her appearance would take her mind away from the impossibility of their circumstances.

'I think I smell.' She was sniffing her armpits.

Pat laughed. 'I'll keep downwind of you, although I'd say I'm not all that sweet smelling myself.'

'Then I must stay downwind of you.'

'It'll be like musical chairs with each of us trying to get downwind of the other.'

With dusk falling, he watched the sun set below the horizon, and without doubt that was the west.

'Time for our beds,' she said, stretching out her hand and leaning on him for support, as they went to the bunks in the bows. He was sleeping on the outside tonight.

'Are we going to be OK?' She was holding him tightly.

'Yes, it's only a matter of time until we hit land.' He turned over on to his bad shoulder and put his arms around her. Her grip relaxed and in a short time, she was asleep.

Their nightly routine was to go to bed with the darkness and get up with sunrise. Seemingly it was the way some African tribes lived. That's what a missionary priest told the congregation, one Sunday, during the mass sermon in the monastery chapel. Pat couldn't remember the other observations the priest made about Africa.

Apart from bouts of dozing, he would remain awake for the rest of the night as he always did. It was a mistake on his part not to have kept track of the number of days and weeks they were at sea but it hadn't been a priority when they were trying to stay alive in the storm.

Sometime during the night, dark thoughts started to torment him. He had lost everything when Mark and Hazel died, and he didn't have much to live for. He could end it now and not wait around to try to deliver a baby in an unstable boat. For God sake, what did he know about birthing? They couldn't be sure when Tarja would give birth as they didn't know how long she was pregnant.

Without waking her, why would he not slide out of the bunk, put a plastic bag over his head and wait a few minutes before going overboard? They had plenty of plastic bags, and it would be a painless death. According to his Catholic faith, it could mean hellfire for eternity, if he was in his right mind when he took his own life. It was debatable what state his mind was in. However, eternally damned, he wouldn't see Hazel and Mark again. They were in heaven; he was sure of that. If he took the choice of going over the side, he would leave Tarja and their unborn child to survive the sea voyage alone. Pat wouldn't do that. He dozed.

The sun woke him from his slumber, to the familiar creaking of the timbers, as the life-raft rolled from one side to the other. This morning, there was a salty smell coming off the sea, whatever that meant weather wise. He guessed that they were still going in a south-easterly direction.

Tarja, lying behind him, was the first to get up. She clambered across and playfully rested her full weight on top of him. He heard her laugh and there was joy in her laughter.

'I liked that,' she said.

'I hope it doesn't catch on, or we will have a country full of squashed men.'

'Room service, do you want tea or tinned juice,' she shouted in his direction.

'Tea and a fry up.' That was some joke, they had no milk for their tea, since they capsized and, even if the ingredients were available, they didn't have the facilities to cook them. Tinned food was the best they could do. In the wet conditions, the labels had come off the cans, and each time they opened one it was a gamble what they got. Often it was the opposite of what they were expecting, like finding fruit when they wanted soup. There was silence for a while apart from the gentle splash of the keel as it cut through the water.

Suddenly Tarja shouted, 'I can see hills!'

Without haste, he rolled out of the bunk. They might be phantom hill, after being adrift for a while; people often saw things at sea that were not real. He would bet it was happening to Tarja - they had been out here on their own for a long time. When he emerged from under the forward deck, what he saw took him aback - mist covered hills ahead on the skyline.

'We've made it. I think it's the Scottish coast.' Pat, not exuberant under normal circumstances, was shouting and jumping up and down.

'Thank you God. I shouldn't have doubted; you have brought us safely to land,' said a tearful Tarja, trying to hug Pat as he leaped about.

'We'll celebrate.' He took out the medicinal bottle of brandy and poured half a cupful for himself. Tarja took a teaspoonful. They started to tidy up the boat in preparation for a landing. Throughout the day, the hill crept nearer and by midday, through the binoculars, he could see some buildings on the shoreline.

'Where there're houses there's people.' She sounded ecstatic that their ordeal was ending.

'They look like some holiday chalets.' He was trying to get a clearer view of them. The current curved around and, all being well, it would deposit them on to the white sandy beach.

'It looks like a good place for sunbathing.' He was confident that they were about to make land after so long. He wouldn't have believed it twenty-four hours ago.

'I'm overjoyed that we are safe.'

'Amen to that,' he said, hardly taking his eyes off the approaching shoreline. It was an island off the west coast of Scotland, and that was a lot better than the Russian ice fields. Soon medical attention would be available to them.

'I think they are timber chalets.' He grimaced with pain when he tried to give her the binoculars with his injured hand.

'Is it still sore?' she said, taking the binoculars from him, and looking at his arm held stiffly by his side. She waited for a reply before raising the glasses to her eyes.

'Yes, and stiff when I try to move it.'

She focused the binoculars.

'The buildings look new, but there's nobody about.' She took her time surveying the scene. Maybe their jubilation was premature - it would be just their luck to have landed on a deserted island.

Pat counted four well-maintained chalets. Two of the buildings had windows and looked like living quarters while the others looked like stores. They had almost reached the shore when he saw the land at the back of the chalets fenced with rusted barbed wire. What was that all about? Probably, a landowner making his presence felt. Because of the damage it did to animals barbed wire hadn't been in use for years. The bow of the life-raft rammed into the sand. They had landed. Pat went into the water and tried to push the boat further into the sand without much success. It was a pity they'd had to use the anchor to hold Coleman's corpse down – they needed it now. The life-raft, wedged into the beach gravel, should stay there securely while they explored the chalets.

'Help me out of here.' She was laboriously trying to climb out of the life-raft.

'I've got you,' said Pat, holding up his hands to lift her out of the boat. His injured shoulder gave out under her weight, and they tumbled into the water. Stretched on their backs in the water, they laughed like kids and splashed each other before making their way ashore.

'The sand's so lovely on my feet.' She bent down and picked up fistfuls and played with it. Pat looked around and saw the faded sign attached to the barbed wire. It was bright red when painted there during the Second World War: "Ministry of War. Warning to visitors, this island is unfit for human occupation."

33

Tarja saw the warning plaque as she walked up the beach towards the chalets.

'What's that about?'

Pat remembered reading somewhere about this island, and he wished he hadn't. A good memory wasn't always a blessing. There was no way he could soften the blow.

'I'm a bit vague about it, but I think they spread anthrax here during the last war. They wanted to develop it as a weapon.'

'O' no, Anthrax! We didn't hear about that in Finland.'

'They lost control of it, and the island has been in quarantine since then, although it didn't spread to anywhere else.'

'Are we safe here?'

'I don't know.'

It was anyone's guess, how long the island would remain infected. Other countries considered a live experiment with anthrax too dangerous. As far as he could remember the anthrax spores had killed all the sheep, birds and rabbits on the island and probably all other living creatures as well. He wasn't going to give Tarja this information. If anthrax was still alive here, they had been exposed to it, as had their unborn child. He heard her gasp.

'O good Lord that's terrible.' She covered her face with her hands. 'Will this ever end?'

'That was long ago, I'm sure there's nothing here now,' He didn't fully believe that; but he said it to give her some hope.

'We didn't study anthrax in my training, but I think it can remain dormant in the ground for a long time. I want to believe we're going to be OK.'

Without expert knowledge, it was difficult to judge the danger of the situation. It was unlikely the authorities would have built new chalets on the site, if there was no need for concern.

He ushered Tarja towards the chalets. Whatever hazard they were facing, they would be safer inside the buildings rather than outside in the open.

He thought he might have to break a window to get inside, but when he tried the door it opened, and they stepped into the hallway. A glass partition separated them from the rest of the chalet. High visibility suits, resembling space attire hung on pegs in the hallway. They were ready for use, complete with domed helmets and pipes for attaching oxygen cylinders. The observers evidently suited up when they ventured out of doors on the island.

'This equipment is new.' She was looking at him for a response.

'A precaution only, they probably never used them.'

'It's like a luxurious hotel,' she said as they explored inside the chalet. The lounge and kitchen were in the front with a view of the beach; and the bedrooms with en-suite toilets were at the rear of the building. The chalet, heavily insulated for the cold and damp of the Scottish winters, had prints of Monet and Goya hung on the walls. Worn Axminster carpets covered the living room floor; and the furniture was reproduction antique with the settee and chairs finished in leather.

'I bet this stuff came from a hotel,' he said, running his hand along the chair backs.

'It's worn and formal, but I like it. It's a change from the boat,' she said.

Although they didn't open, the plate glass windows and skylights provided light, and the ventilation system supplied fresh air. The storerooms had stocks of frozen foods, spare parts for ancillary equipment such as ventilation, and batteries ready for charging by the wind turbine.

'After what we've been through, it's like heaven. We could live here forever. I'm going to have a shower.' She discarded her trousers, and jacket.

'Be my guest.' After their ordeal, he could see how she might think it was like paradise, but he felt troubled by their predicament. What were the symptoms of anthrax and how long would it be before they started to feel ill? He didn't know, and he wasn't going to ask Tarja. He had an idea that the skin of infected people turned black before they died. Leave it - he should go and have the shower he had been looking forward to for so long.

He looked out the window, the wind had increased and the life-raft was drifting southwards in the current. It was at least two hundred yards from shore, and there was no way of getting it back. He should have made it more secure but how could he have done that? He would have needed more manpower to push it further up on the shore.

He rushed around to the shower.

'Tarja, the life-raft's gone,'

'We're stranded here now.'

Wrapping in a towel, she looked out the window. The life-raft was travelling fast in the current, and it would soon be out of sight.

'There's nothing on it we need.'

Although, it was difficult to know, would they have been better to have stayed on the life-raft?

'With the setup we have here, we'll soon have plenty visitors.'

'The shower was so refreshing, now it's your turn.' She gave him a hug and a peck on the cheek.

'I'm ready for it,' he said, responding to her advances. He had seen her in many guises, socially and in life and death situations; but none of that mattered. What was important were his feelings for her. He was now sure that he loved her, and he wanted to be with her for the rest of his life. She, of course, might not feel the same and might want to get away from him when their ordeal ended.

The showers invigorated them and they dressed in new tracksuits from the stores.

'It's so good to feel clean and washed.' She stretched out next to him on the sofa with her head on a cushion. Strange, they had no television or telephone in this place, but there were loads of books in the small library, although none of them were recent publications. Just now a telephone would be a welcome sight.

'You think someone will come soon?' she asked and, with her eyes closed, she seemed relaxed

'They wouldn't have built a place like this if they weren't going to use it.' He was hardly aware of what he was saying. He had realised that, when fishing boats found the life-raft from the Annie L. empty and drifting, it would be sufficient proof that the crew of the Annie L. had perished at sea. Case closed. Who knows, it could be anything up to a year, or longer, before the next monitoring crew came along? That's if they returned at all.

'Will I get us something to eat?' She sat up on the sofa.

'That would be great.' He took her hand, and helped her to stand.

'I need exercise. I'll walk on the beach every day.' Her knee joints looked stiff as she shuffled to the freezer. She took out two oven-ready meals, and placed them in the microwave.

'Help me get this going.' She was fiddling with the controls. 'I wish they'd put the same type of switches on everything in the kitchen.' It took them a frustrating ten minutes to get the microwave going. Pat finished his food.

'That's the best turkey and ham ever.'

'It tastes so good after all we have been through.' She handed her empty plate to him. There was something on his mind, and he was waiting for the right time to ask her - how would they know if they had contracted anthrax? It might cause her distress; but he needed to know the symptoms and if there was anything they could do to save their lives. He decided to ask.

'Is there any cure for anthrax?'

'There's probably a book about it in that lot.' She looked towards the library.

'I thought you felt we are OK?'

'I do, but I would like to know more about it.' That was a lie. The authorities did not put these costly precautions in place just for the fun of it. He might stay up after Tarja went to bed, and search the shelves for a book on anthrax. He didn't have long to wait.

'Pat, I'm going to turn in. Are you coming?'

'I'll stay up for a little while longer.'

With Tarja away he started searching the library. Its stock was mostly novels, and old copies of Time and Newsweek. This was a field research station, and they would have the relevant information back at base. He found one dog-eared pamphlet on anthrax which had bits marked with a yellow high lighter. It wasn't uplifting reading. The only known use for anthrax was germ warfare. Most people who contracted anthrax died, and it appeared that those who survived, had taken appropriate antibiotics before the symptoms developed. The spores remained in the ground indefinitely and reactivated when a host, either animal or human became available. It wasn't looking good in their circumstances. Flu-like symptoms and breathing difficulties would herald the start of the attack. In their situation, death was inevitable after the symptoms developed. He had read enough and he hid the pamphlet behind a row of books, where Tarja was unlikely to find it. He turned in but couldn't sleep. He tossed and turned for the rest of the night.

34

Pat woke, and felt he was still on the life-raft, though the smell of the sea, and the sound of waves thumping against the hull had gone. This far north, the grey light filtering through the skylight was no different to that on the life-raft. He swung his legs out of bed, stood up, stumbled and fell in a heap on the floor. Standing on solid ground again would take some getting used to. Tarja woke.

'I have always slept on my back, but now I have to lie on my side.'

'Your condition?'

'That's the way some of us pregnant women have to sleep. I suppose I'm getting used to it.' She stretched, raising her hands above her head.

'Better than the life-raft.' That was debatable, considering the threat that was out there waiting for them. It may already have contaminated them. Better not to think about it. Cautiously, he stood up and walked into the living room. Yesterday was a blur when so much, had happened; but now he had time to take stock of their surroundings. Their accommodation was equal to a four-star hotel, minus the staff, and of course there was the anthrax threat.

With the wind increasing, the sea was getting rougher but in comparison to what they had come through, it was as calm as a duck pond. He wondered if the life-raft had sunk or reached land.

'I'm getting up,' she said from the bedroom.

'Be careful, we are still on sea legs.' He went to help and caught her before she tumbled to the floor.

'I see what you mean.'

He held her until she found her balance.

'Getting used to solid footing is something else.' She let go and stumbled around on her own.

'We were a long time at sea,' he said. He was looking at her bump to see if it was bigger than yesterday. That was bizarre; nature didn't work that quickly when it came to pregnancy. The thought of having to deliver a baby brought him out in a cold sweat. He said a silent prayer - please God let someone rescued us before that happens.

'We have choices for breakfast,' he said.

'I'd like porridge with loads of milk and berries.'

'Thank heavens we have a supply of them. I wouldn't like to have to go out there, and pick them off the hillside.'

'Pregnant women often develop a craze for unusual food like ice cream in the middle of the night,' he said.

He was searching the shelves for a packet of porridge.

'I like a banana as well for breakfast, but not this morning.' She was looking out the window at the weather. He thought he knew how she felt. Regardless of how comfortable they were, the feeling of being shut in, after the open sea and skies, was claustrophobic.

He found a packet of 'Scotch Oats, original blend' still within its sell-by date. The cooking instructions were simple enough, one half cup of oats mixed with water and heated on full power for five minutes in the microwave.

'Prepare for it – my wacky requests may come yet.' She was moving from window to window admiring the views.

'The porridge tastes wonderful,' she said as they sat at the kitchen counter eating it.

'The stock of food in this place is great.' He was hardly aware of what she was saying; there was something else on his mind.

'Two people died out there, was there anything else I could have done?' She put her hand on his shoulder, 'Stop beating yourself up, it was their time to go.'

She was right, though he was still uneasy about it. The warning was in the weather forecast. He should have heeded it and refused to sail out of the harbour. If he had called it off, the skipper wouldn't have sailed without him. He had been so careless that night and many people on the island would wonder why he had made that error. They would gossip saying,

"That one turned his head," suggesting that Tarja was so alluring that she had cast a spell over him. Tarja returning pregnant after their escapade, would fuel the gossip.

'Come on, let's go for a walk. We'll feel better for it,' she said, getting up and testing her balance.

'We'll need to suit up before we go outside.'

It wouldn't be an easy job getting her into one of these space suits. They looked designed for skinny people, although they probably expanded to fit all sizes. They went through the inner glass door into the hallway where the suits were hanging on pegs.

'I think it's like putting on a wet suit, and I wouldn't try that in my condition.' She was looking at the suits hanging in neat rows on the wall. He took down the nearest one.

'Let's give it a try.'

Tarja stripped to her underwear.

'I think I look like a beached whale.' She rubbed her rounded stomach.

'People travel for miles to see a beached whale.'

'Well I don't want them coming to see me.'

'I think I like beached whales, if you look like one.'

'Maybe I look more like a sumo wrestler.'

'Popular in Japan.'

'We are not in Japan now.' Pat put his arms around her and kissed her, 'I love you the way you are.'

She smiled as she stepped into the suit, put her arms into the sleeves, and he helped her pull it up over her shoulders. Next came the tricky bit, as she tried to zip it up the front. She made a few false starts, before the material stretched to cover her tummy.

'There must be some elastic in it,' she said, turning around to help him into his suit. That was a difficult task as he couldn't raise his arms above his head. She strapped on his oxygen tank, and secured his facemask and helmet. Head and face enclosed, he felt he couldn't breathe and was smothering. He started to cough and choke and tried to tear the mask off his face. Tarja was trying to calm him, but he could barely hear her voice through the helmet.

'Pat, leave it alone, breathe normally. In a minute, you won't have a problem with it.'

Gradually, his panic subsided and his breathing slowed. That was a drama, and it was a pity that she hadn't warned him about using the apparatus.

'Sorry Pat, I wasn't thinking, it frightened you.'

'It's okay now. I'm beginning to like it. I'll have to open a café on the island and sell oxygen,' he said as it filled his lungs.

'They sold it in cafés in Finland for a while,'

'It's good; it's no wonder, they use it in hospitals,' he said.

Outside, the beach stretched for miles. It would make an idyllic holiday resort, where people could come and enjoy the beauty of it all, but instead it was a danger to all living creatures. They walked slowly with the sand crunching under their feet. Through his helmet, he could just about hear the sound of the sea.

'It's warm inside this thing.' The small glass visor restricted his vision, and he had to turn his head around to see her.

'I'm hot and uncomfortable myself.'

The flickering light came from an unexpected source overhead; a plane circling the island. It usually needed a flash of some kind to bring on his seizures; and he was hoping it wouldn't happen this time.

'They can see us. It's a search plane!' She was shouting and waving her hands.

'I hope so.' It was more likely a small plane lost and trying to find its bearings. He had seen similar planes circling his home island, trying to work out where they were. It flew around the island a few more times and then turned away southwards, leaving them on their own once more. It felt lonely - people so near but yet so far away. They walked back to the chalet and started to remove their protective suits.

She helped him to take off his suit. His shoulder had seized up and his arms weren't working well either.

'I'm exhausted again,' she said, although the oxygen and walking had improved the colour of her face.

'Why don't you go and lie down?'

'I think I'll do that.'

Pat read while Tarja was asleep, stretched out and snoring on the settee. She woke after a couple of hours.

'Did I sleep for long?'

'Not too long.' He helped her up and supported her while she stiffly took her first few steps.

'What-'. She didn't finish the sentence. The bang overhead shook the chalet. It nearly burst their eardrums, and they covered their ears with their hands. Tarja fell to her knees on the floor.

The helicopter passed over a few feet from the roof of the chalet and set down on the beach. The RAF insignia of concentric circles painted on the fuselage left Pat in no doubt about its origins. He had seen it many times before, on TV and in war films. Tarja, excited, jumped to her feet waving her arms and shouting. Deafened by the noise of the helicopter, he couldn't make out what she was saying. The rotors stopped turning, and the chalet stopped vibrating. Two figures in protective clothing jumped from the helicopter and, bent double, they started running towards the chalet. They looked fit and agile. Communication wires dangled from their helmets. They didn't knock but came directly into the chalet.

'I'm Nick and this is Jean the Nurse. Sorry about the noise, but I had to come in close,' he said in a clipped English accent, he shook hands with both of them.

'Are you OK?' asked Jean in a Scottish accent. She went over to Tarja, and they hugged.

'You've been through so much.'

'How did you find us?' Pat asked.

He looked at Tarja and she was crying, probably relieved that they were safe, provided of course, they were free from anthrax. He noted the rescuers didn't take off their protective suits; there might be a message in that. No good worrying about it now - it would have to wait until later.

'By a spotter plane, after we found your life-raft,' said Nick going into the hallway and returning with protective suits.

'You're lucky to be alive, we were out here searching for bodies,' said Jean, supporting Tarja.

'Thank God you found us.' Tarja's reservoir of tears had dried up, for the moment.

'We had better get going. We'll help you get into these.' Nick was holding a suit for Pat to climb into. Jean was helping Tarja.

'Watch out for the tail rotor, it could take your head off if you walk into it,' said Nick.

'Have you been in a helicopter before?' asked Jean, linking arms with Tarja on the walk to the helicopter.

'I had a half hour, summer trip around Helsinki.'

'I have never been in one,' said Pat. Nick helped him into the rear seat.

He got a wooden crate out of the back of the helicopter for Tarja to step on, and she climbed in next to Pat. Jean strapped them both in and connected the intercom leads hanging from the roof to their helmets. She sat in the forward seat, clipped on her safety belt, and they were ready for takeoff. Pat looked down through the floor beneath his feet and his stomach churned when he realised that there was nothing between him and the ground except a thin sheet of transparent material.

It was awe-inspiring being in the helicopter, a perspex dome lit with daylight, filled with controls and dials. Pat had a panoramic view of land, sea and sky. The rotors started turning and in a few minutes were a whirring sound somewhere, above their heads. He could hear Nick talking to his base through the headphones. They lifted straight into the air before moving forward. He heard a click of a switch and Nick's voice fade out.

'Are you all right back there?' Jean asked.

'Yes, we are fine,' said Tarja, holding Pat's hand tightly in hers.

'We're taking you directly to the Glasgow Royal Infirmary. Don't read too much into that,' she said. It sounded casual, though Pat figured their trip to the hospital was all about their exposure to anthrax.

'The papers and TV are going to make heroes of you,' said Jean, looking back at them with a smile.

'That's the last thing we need,' said Pat, hoping to get away quickly and return home. He would recover faster on the island and try to put it all behind him, but with grief piled on grief, it wouldn't be easy. He was allowing dark thoughts to take over his head and depress him. This foreign girl might be glad to get rid of him and parting with her and his unborn son, would break his heart. Snap out of it, he told himself.

Jean turned around in her seat and her voice cut in on the intercom,

'We're right over Loch Ness, hope we see the monster,' she said with a laugh.

'What's the big mountain called?' asked Tarja, looking down through the transparent floor, and admiring the mist- shrouded hills.

'That's Ben Lomond, it's over nine hundred metres in height,' said Jean. Pat was afraid to look down or move his feet in case the thin sheet of flooring gave way, and he fell into Loch Ness. Then the monster in there would gobble him up. The sooner he got out of this helicopter the better.

'We're about fourteen miles from Glasgow, and we'll be touching down soon,' said Jean. Pat was looking down at the river Clyde with its derelict dry docks and rusting tower cranes. It snaked along for miles before it broadened into the open sea at the river mouth. The shipwrights down there had built the Annie L. to last for a long time; and indeed the old trawler had given good service.

The west facing hospital lit up with the sun, as they flew towards it. A bright yellow building of either brick or sandstone, stained black by the weather. It looked old and might be a period building listed for preservation. Jean cut in again as if reading his mind,

'It looks old, but it has a new wing with modern equipment, and they will look after you well.'

They flew over the hospital and landed with a bump on the concrete helicopter pad at the back of the building. Two teams in masks and theatre gear, pulling stretchers, rushed towards them. Pat had another dark thought. If they were infected with anthrax, their next trip outside this building could be in coffins!

35

Nick switched off the engine, but the rotors kept spinning. Pat figured the momentum would keep them turning for a bit longer and it would be prudent to watch out for the tail rotor. He knew about engines, boats and accountancy. However he was finding out how little he knew about women.

'We're here, leave your helmets on.' Jean jumped from the helicopter, to warn the hospital team to stay away from the tail rotor. Jean and Nick helped them to the ground and with a, 'good luck', and a wave they were gone to their next assignment.

The gowned figures wheeled Tarja and Pat on stretchers to the back of the hospital. As potential anthrax carriers, the health authorities were doing everything they could to keep them away from contact with the public. The doomsday scenario of a city outbreak of the disease was something they didn't want. He had never been on a stretcher before, and each time they hit a bump in the tarmac he could have screamed with pain. The porter pulling him along seemed oblivious to the pain the jarring bumps were causing him. However it didn't last for long and in minutes, they were inside the new wing of the hospital - their destination, the isolation ward.

A nurse stayed behind, as the porters left with the empty stretchers; but she didn't take off her surgical mask or protective suit.

'I'm Vic, nurse and midwife. How are you feeling?'

'A bit better now that we're here,' said Pat, trying to take off his helmet.

'First time pregnant and a little scared,' said Tarja, pulling at her own helmet.

'Let me take those off for you,' said Vic. She removed their helmets and protective clothing and helped them into hospital gowns.

'Crisp white sheets,' said Tarja as she wrapped the bed linen around her.

'A home from home,' said Pat, trying to be funny, but the joke somehow fell flat. If they had anthrax, they would be going home alright, to that mythical palace in the sky - heaven. Another masked and gowned figure entered the ward and Vic introduced him, 'This is Doctor Hudson.'

'Call me John. I hear you've been in the wars. Let me have a look at you. The phlebotomist will take blood later.'

He examined them from head to toe and took notes as he went along.

'Right, after we get the results of the blood work we'll reset that shoulder.'

'Could you fix it now?' He didn't want to make a fuss about his shoulder, but it was so uncomfortable that he couldn't put up with it for much longer.

'Bloods first, followed by an X-ray and then the theatre. We won't be too long.'

The nurse followed him out of the ward. As they walked along, he was reading his notes, and instructing her.

'I hate doctors examining me,' said Tarja. She turned over in the bed on to her other side.

'Not my favourite sport either.'

Pat wondered about the procedure they had in mind for setting his shoulder. Would they break it again, and maybe have him in plaster for months?

The phlebotomist came into the ward pushing a trolley with many empty glass phials for filling with blood. They'd all know he was a right wimp with a terror of syringes, if he fainted when she stuck the needle into his arm,

'I'm Devenia the feared bloodsucker in the hospital.' She laughed and sat down at the side of his bed. She was wearing white protective clothing and blue latex gloves.

'Give me your good arm.' She tied an elastic tourniquet around his biceps.

'I don't like needles,' He knew the jag would hurt, and he tightened his body in anticipation.

'Men are all the same. You'd think I was killing them. We need a distraction,' she said, holding the syringe behind her back.

'I'll distract him,' said Tarja getting out of bed awkwardly and making her way over to his bedside. She held his hands firmly in hers.

'I'll marry you, if that's what you want, and live on your island.' Devenia was so taken aback by the proposal that she forgot to insert the hypodermic needle.

'Of course I do. I never doubted it.' They hugged each other. He was unaware of the needle in his arm and the phials starting to fill up with blood.

'Congratulations, that's the best distraction technique I've ever seen,' laughed Devenia.

'You're next, by the way,' she said to Tarja.

Tarja stretching out her arm to Devenia and held on to Pat with the other hand.

'Women never fuss about giving blood.'

They remained in each other's arms, while Devenia took blood samples from Tarja.

'I'll see you again before you leave.' Devenia turned at the doorway and waved goodbye. Nurse Vic came back into the ward,

'Congratulations and I hope you will be happy,' she said, hugging Tarja.

'It's sleeping tablets time. Doctor Hudson wants you to get some rest. Those ones are OK for pregnant women.'

They washed down the tablets with water.

'By the way, the press is keen to talk to you.' With that she left the ward. An interrogation by journalists was something Pat was not looking forward to.

'Let's push our beds together, I want to be near you,' said Tarja, getting out of the bed and waiting for him to do the same.

'OK, let me do the work.' He shifted the locker out of the way and the beds, on castors, were easy to move side by side.

'That's better,' she said and caught his arm and put it on her tummy. He could feel the roundness of it, and he imagined their child floating around inside.

'The baby knows you're there.' She sounded sleepy as the tablets took hold.

'He'll be kicking soon, letting us all know about it.'

He was getting drowsy and making plans. With Tarja coming back to the island he could realistically think about their future. For the first time in years he had a life to look forward to. Marriage wasn't a big issue for him, as long as they were together. The thought of her going back to Finland without him was almost unbearable, and he was so relieved that it wasn't happening. He was the only beneficiary of the skipper's will, and they could set up house on the island in the bungalow the skipper had built, before his wife left him. With a protective arm around her, he drifted off to sleep.

When Pat woke, Doctor Hudson was standing at the end of the bed, without his mask. Tarja was already awake.

'Good news, you are free from anthrax and congratulations on your engagement.'

'That's the best news,' said Pat, his voice breaking up with emotion. Tarja cried with relief.

'No need to keep you any longer in this isolation ward. We'll get you to the theatre later today and set your arm.' He moved towards the door.

'Thanks,' said Pat, holding Tarja tightly. Afterwards the porters arrived to take them to their new ward.

'No don't get up - we're taking the beds and all. We're like an airport shuttle bus, moving people around,' said the younger porter.

'And up and down in the lifts as well. A bit like the Grand Old Duke of York when he marched his men to the top of the hill and marched them down again,' said the second porter.

'That's us all right. You have a good man looking after you, Dr. Hudson,' said the first porter.

'I hope so,' said Pat as the porters pushed their beds into the lift.

'The best,' said the second porter. They surveyed their new accommodation.

'This ward's better and there's a telephone,' said Tarja, picking up the receiver and listening for the buzzing sound.

'It's connected and ready for a call.' She handed the phone to Pat.

'Who will I call first, your parents in Finland or the Cabin pub?'

'The Cabin pub. My parents may be on the Island.'

He dialled zero for an outside line and then the code for Ireland, followed by the pub number. There was a delay before he heard Kate's voice, 'Cabin pub.'

'Kate this is Pat O'Malley. I'm here with Tarja.'

'Oh Pat,' he could hear her sobbing, 'we heard about you on the news. How are you?' She shouted to the others in the pub that he was on the line.

'I'm OK, a bit of trouble with my shoulder and the good news; Tarja is pregnant.'

Might as well tell them straight out, to stifle any gossip before it started. The news silenced her for a few seconds as she took it in.

'Are Tarja's parents there?'

'The foreign girl's parents are here,' she had stopped sobbing.

That was news he hadn't expected.

'Where are they staying?'

'Sea and Mountain View guest house.'

'We'll give them a ring.'

'I'm so sorry to hear about the Skipper and Coleman.'

She wailed deeply and started weeping again. He could have been wrong, but he had always thought she and the skipper would get it together one day; they had been such close friends. She was the only other person, apart from Pat, who had any influence over him. He sat at the same bar seat every time he was in the pub; and he and Kate would have long conversations across the counter. The other patrons would nod and wink when they saw them engrossed in each other's company.

'I know that but they didn't suffer, they were both in a coma long before they died.'

'When are you coming home?'

'In a few days, after they fix this shoulder.'

'We're all wishing you the best, Pat.' She held the phone away from her ear, so that he could hear the noisy greetings from the pub.

'Goodbye.'

'Thanks and goodbye for now.' He put down the phone and turned to Tarja,

'Your parents are on the island…will I ring them?'

'Do, it'll be great to talk to them.'

Pat had most of the island's phone numbers in his head. He dialled the Mountain and Sea View hotel and asked for the Finnish people. He handed the phone to Tarja.

He liked the guttural sound of the language, although the only words he recognised were 'Daddy' and 'married.'

The phone call went on for a long time. Tarja was in tears and probably her parents were crying as well. It was understandable; it's not often a daughter returns from the dead. Finally, she put down the phone and explained what she had said to her parents,

'I told them I'm pregnant, and we're getting married, and that we will be with them in a few days.'

'That was a lot for them to take in at one go.'

'I'm so happy and they're overjoyed to hear I'm pregnant. They always wanted a grandchild. They are looking forward to meeting you.'

'It shouldn't be too long now until we're back on the island.' He guided her to a chair. Seated, her stomach looked like a big round bump.

Nurse Victoria came into the ward again.

'Back to bed, the press is ready for you.' She helped Tarja climb into bed. She was fussing, straightening the bed covers and placing vases of flowers on the bedside lockers.

'A photo opportunity and in my state,' said Tarja, pulling the bed covers over her head.

'What worries me are the questions they might ask,' said Pat, not pleased with the setup. Why not do the usual - get a member of the hospital staff to read a press release and afterwards distribute it to journalists. They could interview him and Tarja later when they were in better health, but now the press photographers had arrived. With a, "look this way and that way" they were gone.

The TV cameras however, were more invasive and recording for most of the day. The ward looked like a science fiction set, with lights and reflectors all over the place.

'It'll be a short interview. A few questions and answers to fill a thirty seconds slot on the evening news,' said the TV interviewer. She adjusted her blond hair with her hands, looked around at the camera crew and nodded.

'Right let's do it.

36

'How did you become modern-day Robinson Crusoes?' she asked Pat.

'After the trawler sank we drifted to the deserted island.' It was a short answer but it was the truth.

'You buried two of the crew at sea?'

'They died of their injuries after a factory ship almost ran us over,' he said, slipping down a bit in the bed. The pillows propping him up fell away from behind him. The assistants rushed to adjust the pillows as the TV cameras turned to Tarja.

'The skipper was Pat's uncle; and we were so sad and depressed after they died,' said Tarja, gazing into the camera lens. It was one of the many tips given to them by the TV crew,

'Look at the camera and smile when you answer a question.' You don't have to shout, just imagine you are in a friend's sitting room chatting to them. Treat the camera like a person you are friendly with. Slow down your speech.'

The cameras were back on him again.

'With a severe weather forecast, was it not irresponsible to have gone to sea that night?'

'We would have been OK if our engine hadn't blown up,' said Pat, caught a bit off balance by the directness of the question. With hindsight they shouldn't have left port, but it's easy to be wise after the event. Rather than being defensive, he should have said that. In many ways it was the skipper's decision. That wasn't strictly true either, he could have postponed the trip by saying he wasn't going to sea that night; and he wished he had. It wasn't Tarja's fault that she influenced his decision, he must have wanted to impress her. Blame her now and everyone else, instead of taking the blame on himself, where it belonged. Not a good time for reflection with this interviewer asking him awkward question. He would have to keep a cool head, he felt like she was trying to catch him out.

'Were you injured yourself?' she asked.

'I lost a finger and broke my shoulder,' he said, holding up his hand to show the stump where his little finger used to be. She had a satisfied look on her face as the camera panned in to give a close-up.

'Did you know all along that you are the only beneficiary of their wills?'

'Yes, but that had nothing to do with their deaths. That was an accident,' he said. He felt annoyed for getting a bit rattled. He well knew the media thrived on raising controversy.

'We have nothing to hide, we weren't to blame for their deaths,' said Tarja, wiping away her tears with a tissue.

'Why did the Skipper and Coleman die, and not us? We wouldn't be human if we didn't feel some guilt about that,' said Pat. That stopped that line of questioning, and again she turned her attention to Tarja.

'Is this your first child?'

'My first pregnancy, and I'm terrified of the birth.' Tarja put the tissue away and smiled.

'When is the baby due?'

'Not too sure, but the medical people will know by this evening.'

'Are you ready with names?'

'We haven't talked about that yet.' Tarja was looking at Pat for support.

'A combination of a Finnish and Irish name,' he said with a grin. She had moved away from tricky questions and Pat was more open with his answers. It was her way to end the interview on a happy note.

'You have shared an amazing experience, and I wish all three of you a happy future.'

'Thank you.'

With that smile, she was gone and the technicians started packing up the equipment.

'I don't think I did well,' said Pat, getting out of his bed to sit close to Tarja.

'You were great. That was our fifteen minutes of fame.' She put her head on his shoulder. 'People forget quickly and it's history as soon as the TV news is over.'

Pat was more philosophical about it. It didn't mean a whole lot over the course of a lifetime.

It was Pat's first time in a hospital as a patient, and the ward nightlight was keeping him awake. He tossed and turned and couldn't find a comfortable spot in the bed.

'You're not sleeping. Will I give you something to get you over?' The night Nurse whispered at the side his bed.

'Ok, what time is it?'

'Two o'clock.' She gave him a sleeping tablet and a drink of water.

'Goodnight now.' Pat was thinking about how silently she glided around. He hadn't even heard her coming into the ward. Tarja was snoring loudly and that was the last he remembered before dozing off himself.

Through the window, the morning sunlight pouring into the ward woke him. He looked at his watch, and it was just half past six. He knew hospitals got going early, but he hadn't known it was this early. His head felt heavy, the effects of the sleeping tablets, no doubt.

'Morning, you had a heavy sleep,' said Tarja, propped up in the bed with pillows behind her.

'I had to take a sleeping tablet, and I feel rotten after it.'

'Good strong coffee will wake you up.'

'Not for you this morning - you have a theatre date,' said Victoria, coming into the ward.

'We're taking bed and all,' she said. She removed all the pillows except one from behind his head.

Tarja came over to his bed, and kissed him whispering,

'Good luck.'

'I'll see you later. Don't go away,' he said. She smiled and kissed him again. It was their first time apart since fate conspired to have her onboard the doomed trawler. Without the extra pillows, he was lying flat in the bed, and when it started to move, he felt dizzy.

'Are you missing Tarja already?' said Nurse Victoria jokingly.

'Terribly.' He used the same joking tone.

'I thought so. We haven't too far to go.' Lying on his back, his view as they moved along the corridors was the top of the walls and ceiling, dotted with fluorescent lights. The building was old, and he could have counted the cracks in the ceiling. He wondered why the painters did not fill them in. It must be some time since the ceilings had had a coat of paint.

"Paint the walls, the ceilings are ok," might have been the directive from some unknown bureaucrat. With a succession of bumps, they were in the lift.

'You need an advanced driver's licence for this job,' said the porter and everyone laughed. He probably used the same joke every time he manipulated a bed into the lift.

He and Nurse Victoria were at the head of the bed pushing it along. If Pat looked up he could see them behind him or, rather more accurately, he could look up their nostrils. Nurse Victoria's nose was crystal clean on the inside; but the porter's nose was full of gooey green stuff. Imagine what dentists must put up with, looking up people's noses all day. It must be tempting to use their little mouth spray to clean out all that stuff. He was glad he wasn't a dentist.

'Almost there,' said Nurse Victoria.

"Operating Theatres" signs with red arrows painted along the walls indicated their direction.

Pat expected one operating theatre, but to his surprise, there were rows of them, side by side along the corridor.

'Number five is our stop,' said Nurse Victoria as they manoeuvred the bed into a waiting area beside the operating theatre. The porter left, the theatre door opened and a nurse came out clad in a green gown with her facemask pulled down.

'You're Pat, I'm the theatre sister, and we're ready for you.'

'Good luck,' said Nurse Victoria as she gave him a friendly touch on his good shoulder. He felt apprehensive as they pushed him into the theatre. It was similar to what he had seen on TV - stainless steel everywhere and a circular central light over the narrow operating table, where a couple of gowned and masked figures stood. He glimpsed on a trolley an array of instruments ready to cut, break and sew his already tense body. He felt scared as many gloved hands moved him from the bed to the operating table.

'Hi I'm Greg the anaesthetist. You'll feel a small jab; count backwards from ten.' Pat's heart was pounding in his chest, and he felt warm and sweaty. The needle went into the back of his hand, and he started counting, 'ten, nine, eight...' he didn't remember anything else.

'Pat, open your eyes, and talk to me.' It was Tarja's voice calling him. She was sitting on the bed beside him holding his hand.

'Are you OK?'

'Tired and sleepy.'

'That's fine. Your operation was a success. I'm three months pregnant according to the doctors. You're exhausted, go back to sleep.'

He drifted off again.

It took a few days to get over the effects of the anaesthetic. Today they were in a taxi on their way to Glasgow airport and going home!

'I'm looking forward to seeing my parents,' said Tarja as they sped through the city traffic.

'It won't be long now.' He was thinking there was a terrible sameness in the motorways leading to airports, regardless of the country.

'I hate takeoffs - all that noise and everything scares me,' she said, nestling in closer to him.

'That's only for a few minutes.' A disturbing thought entered his head, was she having a premonition of another disaster? Perhaps they should have taken the ferry, although with their history it might not be any safer.

At the Aer Lingus check-in, everyone knew about them. They made a great fuss of Tarja, and the supervisor upgraded them to business class. The news of their adventures must have made the headlines in Ireland. Tarja closed her eyes and buried her head in his shoulder for takeoff. Once in the air, they relaxed and lay back in their seats.

'We're spoilt rotten.' Sipping orange juice, she stretched out in the soft seat. Pat was drinking champagne.

'Because we're worth spoiling,' he said with a laugh.

'This is what we need for the rest of our lives,' she said with a smile. He was thinking about the future. He could get a job in accountancy and Tarja, if she felt like it, could work part-time as a marine biologist in one of the research stations in the west. He would prefer if she stayed at home and looked after their son. He'd better not get too far ahead of himself. It would all need discussing, to see how she felt about his ideas.

'What do you think about raising the Annie L. from the sea bed? We could refurbish it and use it for leisure trips?' He turned to her for a reply, but he would have to wait for an answer. Tarja was asleep and breathing deeply. When she woke the plane was circling over Howth. This was the holding position for Dublin airport, and they were second in the landing queue. She asked in a sleepy voice,

'Where are we?'

'Waiting to land.'

Pat was admiring the view of Dublin bay from the window, as it stretched from Howth to Dun Laoghaire.

'It's lovely. It's great having those mountains as a background to the sea,' she said, leaning across him to take in the view.

'We can see them this morning, but we get dull days when the mist blanks them out.'

'I've found love and have had loads of adventures since the last time I landed here,' she said, squeezing his hand.

'You could say that all right. We might be better off with less adventure.'

The tracks cut into the side of the Sugar Loaf by generations of walkers were clearly visible, and he remembered the many times he and Hazel had been up there. They used to look out over all of Dublin, and pick out the familiar landmarks: the Phoenix Park, the Airport, and the Poolbeg towers. He felt good about those times, and now he felt good about having Tarja by his side. He was sure Hazel would have approved of her, if she had known her. His guilt at being unfaithful to Hazel's memory had gone. Although his love for her, and Mark was as strong as ever it was now built-in to the love he felt for Tarja, and their child. It was his new family coming home.